Badminton C
and Murder at
Basingrove School

*An
Inspector
Roberts
Investigation.*

D B Bell

Forward

To a young person of fifteen or sixteen years old, body image is very very important. Some teenagers are very happy within their own skin, but others are not so content and some, like my main character, develop a negative body image in their very early teens that doesn't change as they mature. A young man in the following story had had that poor body image in his head from quite a young age, and that image had never changed with time. While his body had changed as he grew older, the negative image in his mind had not. In the story this negative image has caused him to become acutely embarrassed if anybody commented upon his appearance, and he was happiest when he was "invisible". It was, however, this major attempt to be "invisible" that helped contribute to his becoming very visible indeed.

This story is purely fictitious but there must be many young men and women in their late teens that find themselves in a similar position. Perhaps bear them in mind as the story unfolds.

Chapter 1. Basingrove.

The tall blonde man was waiting in his usual spot when he felt a tap on his shoulder. He turned.
'Where's the cash?'
'I'm not paying this time.'
'What?'
'You heard. The quality of the last batch wasn't up to scratch. I'll pay you next month, but only if the next batch is better.'
'Those aren't the terms of our agreement Jean-Paul. Pay up or the agreement ends now.
'Then let it end. I'll easily find another supplier.'
'I don't think so.'
'Watch me.'
The blonde man started to walk away. He reached the gate and paused to undo the bolt, but, as he did so, he heard a sound, and he turned to try to see what it could be. He saw nothing, but what the darkness had hidden was the knife, the knife that nuzzled it's way between his ribs, and then up and into his heart. The tall blonde man fell silently, and he would never see anything again, ever.
'I said I would end the agreement. You should have listened.'

(Day minus 21)
   'I wonder what she'll be like?' thought Jeremy Carter, just

after he had tripped over a tree root that was uncaringly sticking out from the dry soil of the woodland path. He stumbled, but managed to keep his balance, and the event was soon gone from his mind, but that careless stumble had happened because it was his badminton day, and in his head he had been playing in his forthcoming match instead of watching where he was going.

It was September twelfth, so really just at the beginning of his school term and, though Jeremy was now sixteen, he still walked along that path to get to and from school. He had done that since primary school, even after a post school badminton match and, though this walk took him about 20 minutes or so, he loved it. He knew every inch of the area and he would take that route to school, whatever the weather. That day it had been fine and, after school, he was to meet Marjorie Jones, his new badminton coach. Marjorie was an ex professional player who now coached young, promising talent, and he felt lucky to have have been recommended to her. He hoped that he would do well, even though the excitement this meeting had caused him might mean that he wouldn't actually reach school in one piece.

With his only thoughts being for his after school coaching, the morning passed very slowly for Jeremy (Jez to his friends), but things improved during the lunch break because he met up with his best friend John. They had known each other since primary school, but now the tall, blue eyed and fair haired John was the heart throb of many girls at Jez's school. He had an angular jaw and his days at the gym had given him a shapely, muscular torso. He was nearly 17 and was proud of the fact that he had bedded quite a few girls already. He had no interest in having a steady girlfriend, not just yet anyway, because his was a conquest to sleep with as many young women as possible. Jez envied him. John, in return, couldn't see why Jez wasn't trying to do exactly the same thing.

'Do you need me to play against you tonight Jez?'

'Not tonight John because it's my first coaching session with Mrs. Jones. She is going to play against me in my first session to see how easy I am to beat.'

'Mrs,' said John. 'So your new coach is a woman. I'll bet she's hot, sporty types usually are.' Jez hadn't previously mentioned that his new coach was a woman because he knew that John would tease him.

'Dunno,' he said. 'Haven't seen her yet.'

'How old is she?' asked John.

'I think she's about 38,' said Jez. Hearing this about Mrs. Jones, John, as Jez had expected, really went to town on him.

'She will be all over you mate,' he said. 'Good looking lad like you, and she's been married a few years so she's experienced, but probably bored with her husband, and likely to be keen for some young hunk. You might get lucky there. Wear your best badminton kit and put on some aftershave, even though you don't shave yet.'

Though he was an easy going sort of lad, this was a dig that Jez didn't like. John had a full beard and he let it grow, just to show it off to the girls, and Jez only had a gentle fur on his chin. Despite that, Jez actually looked very much a young man rather than a teenage boy. He was just 5 feet 5 inches tall but broad shouldered and very narrow at the waist, which gave him a classic V shape. His arms were thin though, and they seemed to dangle from his shoulders. He didn't weigh a lot and his mother would have liked him to have been a bit more solid, so she kept trying to get him to eat more. Jez on the other hand realised that being light on his feet could be handy while playing badminton because he needed to jump to catch the high shots if he wanted to win maximum points from a game, especially since he was only 5 feet 5 tall.

'Get lost,' was his reply to John.

'You must have seen a picture of her though mate,' continued John. 'What's she like, honestly, is she good looking?'

'She is quite fit yes. Big tits,' said Jez, trying to play the macho guy, but in truth he really hadn't actually seen anything of her yet.

'Lucky bastard,' replied John. 'Take some condoms with you just in case you get lucky!'

'Sod off,' said Jez, who was very pleased to hear the bell ring for afternoon school because he could escape from John before his friend noticed just how red faced he was.

Jez was *almost* a typical 16 year old from 1985; he liked music, watched TV, and he didn't mind football, but his life mainly revolved around badminton. This set him aside from most lads in his year because girls, football and music (in that order) occupied most of his friends' lives. He was a July birth too, so he was quite young compared to the rest of his year group. His pals thought it was a bit odd that he hadn't got, a girlfriend because "getting laid", as was the expression then, was all that *they* thought about, and they couldn't understand why Jez wasn't the same. Jez just felt that he wasn't very attractive to girls, and maybe he was just a bit too young at the moment. He always felt awkward when talking to women anyway and he would easily become embarrassed if a girl spoke to him.

At the end of the school day, Jez had set about packing the haversack which he had had since starting secondary school. It was a grey canvas backpack and it had a painted flap with his old lower school mates names and BOWIE painted on it.

'Off to badminton then?' asked his form tutor as she passed him. 'Have fun.' The racquet sticking out from his haversack was probably the clue that lead to his form tutor's question - it was a really nice racquet that had been signed by some eminent players of the time, including Steve Baddeley and David Hunt. Goodness knows how his dad had got those signatures. It was probably valuable but since it was a present from his dad he wouldn't part with it, ever.

'Thanks miss, I will,' is all that his form tutor had got in return for her question.

The university's badminton club was available to non students when it was free and it was almost next door to Jez's school, so his journey there took just a few minutes. As always he had changed before leaving school so he could quickly get on with his game. Students would usually fill the court during their Wednesday sports afternoon and this meant that Jez got to play there every Thursday without exception. On the other weekdays he would always walk past the club on his way home, hoping that if the court was empty he could find a student to play against. It was one of those student opponents that had recommended him to Marjorie Jones, and he was really looking forward to meeting her that night.

Marjorie turned out to be a youthful thirty eight year old who wore a typical sporty outfit that fitted her proportions perfectly. She was indeed very attractive, with startling blue eyes, genuinely blond hair and a classic hour glass figure, but Jez hadn't noticed any of this. John on the other hand would have been impressed and would likely have spent more time chatting her up than playing badminton.

After some very quick introductions, and a few questions from Mrs. Jones, the game was underway with Mrs Jones watching him carefully. Jez couldn't believe how difficult it was to play against a pro; the shuttlecock had flown so fast and so accurately and, though he *thought* he had been watching it carefully, it didn't ever seem to go where he had expected it to. They played 24 sets and Jez felt that overall the game had gone fairly well. He hadn't won any of the sets but he had scored *some* points, which he was pleased with, especially since he had been playing against a professional player. Mrs Jones though wasn't so impressed, she was a bit of a misery really and never smiled once. After the game there was a debrief.

'Have you been playing long?' she asked.

'About 3 years,' said Jez.

'Do you go to a gym?'

'No.'

'You need to because you're short of arm strength. In fact your upper torso doesn't look strong at all. Your arms are just hanging from those shoulders and your free arm isn't able to fully counterbalance your racquet arm. Though the shuttlecock is light you need power to control your shots and make them more accurate. You need to be able to dip the shuttlecock right in front of your opponent, or put some power and spin into the "birdie" so that they don't know where it's going, or they end up hitting it too hard themselves and it ends up out of play. Arrange some gym sessions and I will see you next Thursday.'

Jez didn't know what to make of her comments. Was he any good? Did she think he might have promise? Why did muscular arms matter? He could beat John and John was covered in muscles! These phrases were going through Jez's head while he packed away his racquet. He didn't change out of his kit before going home because there hadn't seemed any point. His school clothes were in his haversack and he'd only change back out of them when he got home anyway. After that dressing down, Jez remembered his conversation with John earlier in the day. 'I can't really imagine ever needing any condoms while with her,' he thought while thinking back to John's comments, and he couldn't help smiling to himself. He would report back to John tomorrow to hopefully shut him up!

He looked very glum as he made his way out of the club but he *did* notice a bonny girl with tight curly hair watching him. She wore glasses and these emphasised her rather lovely dark brown eyes. Jez didn't usually notice these things so he was quite pleased with himself. Despite having felt so dejected by Mrs. Jones comments he managed to smile at her and he was surprised when she called his name and walked up to him.

'Hi Jez,' said the girl.

'Hi,' said Jez 'Did you watch me play? Did you think I was any good? Mrs. Jones says I am a weakling. She didn't talk about anything else. She didn't even say whether I was any good. She's a proper old dragon!' He had suddenly realised that he was babbling so he stopped abruptly, feeling rather embarrassed and he had to endure yet another episode of blushing.

'She is,' replied the girl. 'Very like a dragon I mean. I know her very well and I get her criticisms all the time.'

'Really? Do you play badminton too then?' asked Jez, 'Oh and how do you know my name?' Before he could babble on any further, she smiled and replied.

'Yes, I do play, and your new coach told me about your name on the way here. She doesn't think much of my playing either and moans constantly at me too.'

'Right misery then,' said Jez unusually pessimistically.

'Actually, she's my mother, so I know that she can *really* be a dragon, and you haven't seen anything yet!'

'Whoops, sorry,' said Jez and he blushed yet again, heavily this time.

'Aw, don't worry, she really can be quite severe. I'm Paula by the way.'

'Hi. I'm Jez. But you know that don't you,' he said awkwardly. 'So, do you always come here when your mother coaches?'

'Most times yes. I hope she keeps you on because you seem fairly normal compared to most of her other clients.' She smiled again.

'Thanks,' said Jez. It was the nearest to a compliment he

had ever had from a girl. 'Normal,' he thought. That was good, wasn't it?' He suddenly felt much brighter. 'See you next week then maybe,' he said.

'Perhaps,' she replied, with a now flirty smile. And off she went.

'She was nice,' thought Jez. 'I hope she really does play badminton, and that she will play with me,' and then he laughed at the potential double meaning of that thought.

In fact, he hadn't had to wait until the next week to see Paula again because he spotted her at school the following day, during afternoon break. It turned out that she was in the year below him and as she approached, they struck up a conversation. They found that they got on really well and to his delight, it transpired that she did indeed like to play badminton. 'Do you play often then?'

'Not really,' said Paula. 'Mum is such a grump because she says I'm not very good. She criticises me constantly.'

'Tell me about it. Do you want to play tonight? The court is usually free on a Friday.' This was unusually bold for Jez when talking to a girl, but he had said it before he thought about it. It was just an opportunity to play another game of badminton after all.

'Yes, if mum can collect me afterwards.'

'Will I get some free tuition if she comes along?' asked Jez.

'No chance!' said Paula.

'When you talk your glasses slide down your nose, and you have to keep pushing them back into place. When you play badminton, don't your glasses fall off when you jump about?' This hadn't been much of a chat up line but it was perhaps a start for Jez!

'I can see well enough without them for badminton,' she said and she promptly took them off and smiled at him. Now he could see her eyes more clearly he was struck by their deep brown colour and he was surprised to feel a little flip from his heart.

'Wow!' is all he could think of to say to her.

'I look OK without my glasses then?' she replied with a cheeky smile.

'You are beautiful with or without them.'

'You *definitely* look better when I take them off!' teased Paula.

'Thanks,' he said, 'I think!' Paula was slightly taller than Jez at about 5ft 6 inches and she had a figure very like her mother's, obviously very feminine but honed, as though she had spent a lot of time working out. Jez hadn't noticed that yesterday but he had been struck today by how gorgeous she looked, even in her school uniform, which wasn't the most flattering of styles for young women of the eighties. Girls weren't required to wear ties and some girls had exploited this by wearing a very low cut blouse. Paula hadn't done this, but Jez considered that she hadn't needed to do that, nor to wear makeup, which many girls applied despite it's not really being allowed. Jez had kept the image of her with him for the rest of the day and wondered why he hadn't noticed her before.

They met up at the badminton club that night, and Paula's mum sat and watched them. They played for about 40 minutes and had enjoyed their games very much but, though *they* had had fun, Marjorie had not. She had considered that both were giving each other bad habits and she spoke to both of them sternly when they had finished, being careful not to give any actual critique. That would be coaching and she wasn't getting paid for this little event. After this dressing down Jez had said his goodbyes and he set off happily to walk home. Once in the car Marjorie asked Paula about Jez.

'So just how did you arrange this little match?'

'I saw him play yesterday and then I saw him in the yard at school. He looked a bit sad, so I said hello to him. He remembered me being at the club last night and he asked me if I played. When I said yes, he asked if I would play tonight. That's all.'

'Do you like him then?'

'He's OK mum, but all he thinks about is badminton, so If I did have designs on him, I don't think I'd get anywhere. He's easy to talk to but a bit of a drip and he seems a bit awkward. No fashion sense at all and you are right, there really is no strength in his arms. Makes him look weedy and his game isn't great, I have played against much better. It's a shame because really, all he thinks about, and talks about, is badminton.'

'I don't think he has it in him to be very very good, but he does have some ability, especially in placing the shuttlecock where you don't expect it,' said Marjorie. 'Shame really. Does he have a girlfriend?'

'What do *you* think?' said Paula.

'Would that be a *no* then?' said her mum. They laughed heartily as she started the car to drive Paula home.

Jez on the other hand had really enjoyed the game. He thought he had played well, and he really liked Paula. He had never felt that way about a girl before and he wondered whether they could become girlfriend and boyfriend? He doubted it – she was really pretty so she'd be unlikely to be interested in him. She liked badminton though and he would at least get to see her when they played. Despite the criticism of the game from Marjorie he was feeling happy. Jez's mum noticed this good mood when he got home but said nothing. He had told her that he had been playing badminton with a girl called Paula, and that he had enjoyed the game. His mother put two and two together and smiled to herself.

Chapter 2. New trousers.

(Day minus 19)

Jez and his mum always ate breakfast together on a Saturday and today was no exception. He was a lazy riser, and his morning routine was to get out of bed, shower, and then to don his dressing gown before going downstairs to breakfast. He sometimes didn't even bother to use a towel because, by the time he was ready to dress (usually about 5 minutes before setting off for school) he was nice and dry and putting on his clothes was very easy. His mop of dark hair was longish, with a centre parting, but it was well behaved, and a quick brush of his hair was generally enough for him to look good for the day ahead. Today the routine was just the same, but as they were almost finished eating, his mother announced that his new school trousers had arrived from the catalogue.

'That's good mum. The old ones are getting a bit tatty.'

'Try them on and let me see you in them,' she said. Jez was pleased they had arrived because his old ones were worn and weren't even vaguely fashionable. School trousers hadn't kept up with the really baggy look of fashionable trousers in the eighties, but there was no way a 16-year-old lad was going to parade in front of his mother while she looked him up and down.

'I'm sure they will be fine mum,' is all his mother got as a response from him that morning. Within a few minutes the conversation was forgotten, but it's significance would become really clear a few days later.

(Day minus 17)

The following Monday, just as on every other school morning, Jez had showered and then emerged in his dressing gown for breakfast. He had a very brief chat with his mum about what he would be up to for the rest of the day, and then she got ready for work. Jez, as he always did, waited until the last minute before getting dressed. Today though, things turned out to be a bit different because his mother made an announcement.

'You'll have to put your new trousers on today Jez,' she said as she was leaving. 'Your others are already in the washing machine and your very old ones are in the charity shop.' His mum got a grunt as a reply as he finished his breakfast. Then he noticed the time.

'I'd better get dressed and do it quickly or I will be late for school. That means I'll have to open those new trousers. Damn. Have I got time?' With some excitement he set about opening the package, but he had become increasingly disappointed as the contents were revealed. He had been pleased to see that they were a nice fashionable mid grey but, once out of the plastic bag, he could see that they were that horrible thin, shiny polyester that stretched a lot and clung to the hairs on your legs. He was thoroughly mortified though when he put them on because, to say that they weren't quite big enough, was a massive understatement.

He could get them on his waist, just, but only because the fabric stretched, and when he checked in the mirror, he realised in horror that he looked as though he were about to become the lead dancer in Swan Lake! He set about trying all sorts of things to hide his embarrassment, including squeezing things into the pockets and leaving the top button undone and wearing a loose belt, but he still looked like a ballet dancer, *and* it was clear to the world that he was wearing Y fronts underneath, and nobody still wore those in the 1980s. He couldn't go to school in these, he'd be a laughingstock. The stupid comments he would likely receive began to gather in his head, but he had no choice except to go to school or his mother would kill him, so what could he do? He remembered that he had that pullover that was far too long for him, so he decided that he could wear that, and he could keep his blazer on all day. Not ideal but it would have to do.

'Why didn't I try them on when my mother told me to?' He hoped that nobody would notice them, and he set off to school feeling rather conspicuous and very very embarrassed.

Jez had walked the twenty-minute stroll to school, along the countryside path as usual, before he realised that his new trousers weren't actually as uncomfortable as he had thought, so he began to relax a little. His pullover reached below his crotch, actually halfway to his knees, so he thought he would be fine, but he had decided to keep his blazer on all day otherwise he would look like he had tiny legs.

To say his school day was memorable though is a bit of an

understatement. Everybody seemed to notice the new shiny trousers, and wearing a jumper and blazer was unusual for sixth form lads during breaks. The length of that jumper made Jez an obvious target for foul comments about his gender, but what also didn't help was that some of his classmates had begun to wonder whether he was hiding something under the pullover, which of course he was.

'Jez, what the hell have you come as today?' John stared at the little lad who appeared to be wearing a knitted skirt and a blazer. 'Why are you all buttoned up in your blazer, and why are you wearing that long jumper that makes you look like you are drag act? Are you hiding some booze or are you trying to tell people something?'

'Look,' said Jez. 'Mum got me these new trousers last week, but I didn't try them on, they're too small and now I'm stuck with wearing them, at least for today.' He pulled up his jumper to let John see the top half of his new trousers. 'Look at how embarrassing these are.' He had been expecting sympathy from John but instead he got quite the opposite.

'Wow, very kinky! Are you going cycling tonight or what?' Jez hadn't realised that these could be mistaken for cycling trousers, those stretchy things that men wear when riding a bike, the ones that hide nothing.

'Don't be daft,' said Jez. 'It's just that mum hasn't realised how much I've grown, and she ordered me these from the catalogue.' John deliberately gazed down at the top half of the new trousers.

'You really have grown haven't you, or have you put your socks down there to help you get a girlfriend?'

'Get stuffed,' said Jez as he blushed heavily.

'You have to admit that they aren't hiding much Jez, including those ridiculous Y fronts. Couldn't you have just worn your old ones then?'

'No, they are in the wash.'

'You might look better in your shorts mate,' said John, and added something incredibly rude.

'Sod off,' said Jez. The lack of sympathy from his old mate had made him really angry, so he left John to himself. He couldn't remember ever feeling so embarrassed, but anger had now overtaken that.

Unfortunately for Jez, John hadn't left the teasing there and he let it be known to his friend Jeanette that Jez was wearing some *very* revealing trousers, and that it might be fun for her to find a way to sneak a look under that jumper of his. More unfortunately for Jez was that the girls in his year seemed to have a sort of networking system, and soon a mass plot to tease him seemed to have been arranged. He hadn't found this funny at all because they weren't even slightly subtle, and he had had to fend off quite a few of them, and not just those that knew John.

He got 'Hi Jez, why the long face, and the long pullover? Take the jumper off for me,' and then shouts of "Off, Off, Off". In response, Jez had blushed deeply before simply walking away and the pullover had stayed put, but it had been really embarrassing for him.

'Why are girls so good at planning and organising things?' he thought. 'They all said more or less the same thing, and they will presumably report their "findings" back to each other.' He had just decided that girls must be members of a superior but evil species when a couple of lads arrived and their comments were very very rude, some of which he didn't even understand! He wouldn't repeat those to his mum!

He spent most of the rest of the day trying to hide, especially from Paula, but by the end of the school day the novelty had clearly worn off, and his last two periods had been quiet.

Jez had never been the sort of lad to let anything bother him for long and he would hopefully be able to wear his old trousers tomorrow, and that would be that. Unusually, he had considered a counter tease to play against John, to try to get some revenge, but he decided that it wasn't worth it. He had just wanted the whole affair forgotten. On the way home he had begun to wonder what the girls would have done if he *had* stripped the jumper off for them, but then he blushed again and he tried to forget the whole thing.

In truth, if Jez had spent breaks with his hands in his pockets, it's quite likely that nobody would have noticed how tight they had been, but to the teenage Jez outward appearance had been so important that a molehill had become a mountain.

Later, after she had heard a very heavily edited description of his day, his mum ironed his old trousers for him and said she would send the new ones back.

'I'm sorry, I hadn't realised that you have grown so much,' said his mum. Jez, reminded of what John had said, blushed heavily. Once the red had faded he returned to his mum, and they picked his new ones from the catalogue together. This time he had chosen nice fashionably loose-fitting ones.

'How is sixth form going love?' asked his mum as they studied the catalogue together. 'Any nice girls in your new tutor group?' He decided not to mention that quite a few had spoken to him today and he simply replied with 'I haven't noticed.'

'Better get you some really fashionable trousers then, make you stand out a bit more.' Jez felt that he had had enough "standing out" for one day.

(Day minus 16)

Tuesday had been much more normal for Jez, and he had even spotted Paula in the yard at morning break.

'Hi Paula.'

'Hi.' Paula wasn't her usual bright self, but she did smile when she saw Jez.

'I didn't see you yesterday.'

'No. I was keeping out of people's way yesterday.'

'Even me?'

'No not you, although I would have been very embarrassed if I had seen you.'

'I heard that you were wearing skimpy trousers to impress the girls. Jemma told me that she had been told that there was a lot to see.'

'That would be John's fault,' said Jez as he again blushed a very very deep red.

'You're not wearing them today!'

'Are you surprised?' he replied. Paula felt a bit sorry for him and smiled.

'I'd like to have seen what the fuss was about but never

mind. Mum says that there's a court free tonight. Want a game?'

'Love to,' said Jez. 'See you there after school, usual time?'

'Yes.' That had been the whole conversation. Jez was now so looking forward to the game that he had seemed even more distracted than usual for the rest of the day, and the affair with the trousers no longer seemed important. Paula's comment that she would have *liked* to see him in those stupid trousers kept coming back to Jez for some reason, and he kept smiling to himself.

He had continued to avoid John completely, partly because he wasn't sure what he would say to him, but also because he had considered getting John some Spandex cycling shorts for him to wear all day, but then he had thought better of it. John might actually enjoy parading in them, and this is why the pair of them were so like chalk and cheese. 'It's a wonder we get on at all,' he thought as he headed to his final lesson of the day.

The game turned out to be more enjoyable than their previous game had been. Marjorie had looked a bit more satisfied, and Paula wasn't so hesitant with him, really driving him hard. After the game Marjorie told Paula to wait at the car while she paid the fees.

'Bye then,' said Paula to Jez. 'Actually, do you want a lift? Your house is in the same direction as ours.'

'No,' said Jez. 'I always walk home because I enjoy the chance to think and analyse the game while I walk home.'

'What, even if it's raining?'

'Yes, even if it's raining, or worse. It's a nice path so maybe you could walk back with me one day?'

'Maybe,' said Paula. 'By the way, you need some bigger shorts because those ones are like your tight trousers. *They* don't leave anything to the imagination either!' Jez looked down and realised that Paula was just making that up, but he blushed again anyway. Paula smiled a very mischievous smile and went to find her mother.

'She's teasing me. She's as bad as John.' Feeling a bit put down by Paula, Jez had set off for home in a mood that made him feel awkward, though he did realise on the way that he would have to start taking more care with his appearance. This growing up business had taken a very strange turn and people were suddenly interested in what he was wearing. He would maybe have to get some new kit now as well as new school trousers! 'All too complicated,' is the thought that went through his head as he walked home.

Chapter 3. Getting to know her.

(Day minus 15)

Jez decided to continue to avoid John for the whole of the next day because he felt that he had had enough teasing. He still heard the odd comment about his uniform during the morning, but he had got used to it now. He had also got smiles from some of the girls who had previously been rude to him, two even coming up to him to apologise saying they were only going along with the joke. 'It's one way to be noticed,' he thought to himself. 'I've never had so much attention from girls.' He blushed again.

He had spent a rather dull morning, geography had been OK, but it was about the mountain regions of Upper Mongolia which wasn't really where his interest lay. He was more into map reading and climate studies. Maths was better. He had always liked his maths teacher, Miss von Hofmann, because she was from Germany, and she would often speak to the class in German. She had noticed that this often woke them all up if the topic was getting boring, but she would also do actions to show what the German words meant, which Jez had always found hysterically funny for some reason. Now and again he'd get a fit of the giggles and she would sometimes say 'Oh dear, Carter's in hysterics again,' which would just make him worse. Worse still if she added 'We'll just pause while Carter recovers!' Today he had been in hysterics twice. The rest of the class would always enjoy this spectacle because it broke up the lesson and this time he got an 'Aw' from a group of girls after the second set of giggles, which had made him feel better. He even noticed that one of them was really good looking. He'd tell his mum he'd noticed. That would keep her happy for a while.

He didn't play badminton that night because the court was fully booked and, though he had kept a lookout for her, Paula hadn't been to find him either. 'Getting back to normal,' he thought as he walked home.

(Day minus 14)

Thursday, Jez's favourite day, had come around again and it was his evening for being coached by "the lovely Mrs. Jones", which was now John's name for her. The morning had moved slowly along but he had made up with John and they spent lunch time together. John hadn't mentioned the trouser incident, finally feeling a bit shamefaced about it, but Jez decided that he ought to tell him that his new, fashionable ones, had been ordered. He had also told John that he hadn't minded the attention he had got from *some* of the girls.

'Made a change,' he said. They chatted further about music, the latest from Sade was due out but previews had suggested that it wasn't quite in the same mood as "Diamond Life", her first album. John liked Sade because he had thought her seductive style made it good music to play while "getting to know the ladies" (John's actual words). Jez though had been trying to get into Genesis, or at least Phil Collins, but he was still a Bowie fan and neither of them had managed to get into the "new romantic" groups of the eighties, like Spandau Ballet or ABC. John changed the subject and said that he was off to the gym that night and suggested that Jez go with him.

'Girls like muscles, time you got some,' he said to Jez.

'I've got no chance then,' said Jez. 'Anyway, it's badminton tonight.'

'Ah. The very lovely Mrs. Jones,' teased John.

'Sod off,' were Jez's parting words to John.

At afternoon break he spotted Paula in the yard. They gravitated towards each other, and some general chat ensued.

'Hi Jez.'

'Hi Paula. I am looking forward to badminton tonight. Is your mother in a good mood today?'

'Not really,' said Paula. 'She has to go to see the man who is fitting carpets for us, some bloke called Nige. She doesn't like workman and Nige is only available tonight. She will either have to cancel coaching so that she can take me home before she goes to see him, or I can go straight home with Jemma and the coaching stays on. So, I won't be there tonight because I wouldn't want you to miss being coached. I know mum's a misery, but she is a good coach. So, unless I can arrange a lift home I won't be there. I can't ask Jemma anyway because she's going out tonight with her mother, so I hope you have a good game, but I won't be there to watch you.'

'That's a shame because I will miss you. I like you being

there. Mum doesn't have a car so we can't give you a lift home either. Like I told you the other day, I always walk home along that path that runs next to the woods because the bus takes forever. If you like you could walk home with me after the coaching. You will be safe along there if you are worried about being out in the wild because I will protect you from all the ruffians that we might meet on the way home.' She couldn't imagine ruffians being along his route home, or Jez tackling them.

'What you? You couldn't trouble a tin of beans!' Jez put on a 'hurt' look and Paula smiled at him.

'Tins of beans can be tough!' laughed Jez.

'OK, I'll think about it.' The bell then signalled the end of break and, after they had parted Paula's mate Jemma approached her.

'You getting sweet on him?' she asked.

'Piss off. My mother coaches him so I have to pretend to like him. Boring as hell he is. You couldn't do me a favour though could you? I need to get away from my mother for a while tonight and I wondered whether your mum could give me a lift home?'

'You know we can't,' but she didn't finish the sentence because the look on Paula's face told her everything she needed to know.

'Ah. Like that is it? OK, I'll prime my mother for you but, whatever you are up to, don't do anything I wouldn't do!'

'I won't,' said Paula, laughing at the idea because Jemma had a reputation for being a lot wilder than most.

Jez was surprised and very pleased to see Paula at

coaching. Marjorie was, as Paula had said, in a foul mood and she was pretty evil to Jez at times. She told him he would have no chance with the game until he learned to concentrate on the position of the shuttlecock and control the power of his shot. 'You need muscle control for that,' she had commented yet again.

After practice a dejected Jez had walked over to say hello and goodbye to Paula who, though he didn't know it yet, was on her way to say goodbye to her mother.

'Your mother is talking about my muscles again, or rather my lack of them. Doesn't she know that I can't grow them overnight?' He noticed that Paula was smiling. 'I didn't expect to see you tonight. Did you get that lift home arranged?'

'No. I've decided I want to walk back with you but don't tell mother. I want to watch you tackling those ruffians so that I can tell mum what a strong lad you are, and that she is wrong about you,' and she grinned an adorable but very cheeky grin.

'Wow,' said Jez. 'I am so pleased.'

'Is it very far to walk?' she asked.

'Not if we go straight down the countryside walk past the woods.'

'Will I be safe with *you* though? If you can fend off those ruffians you might take advantage of me,' she joked. Jez blushed again and Paula laughed.

'I didn't mean it you idiot. I'd only have to make you get the giggles and you'd be like putty in *my* hands.' Jez realised that Paula had been getting the gen on him.

'You'd probably be right,' he said and gave her a shy

smile.

'Brilliant. I will just go and lie to my mother!' As they strolled home Jez had asked Paula what the lie was.

'I said I was waiting for a lift from Jemma and her mum, and I knew she'd fall for it because I often get a lift from them when mum is too busy. So, she's gone off now to meet old Nige. I've got Jemma primed by the way so mum won't know.'

Once clear of the club they began their gentle countryside walk together. It had turned out to be a surprisingly warm and sunny late evening and that had put them both into a very relaxed mood.

'Mum was pretty evil to you tonight,' said Paula. 'I felt sorry for you at times. I know what it's like to be on the receiving end of her tongue so I'm sorry she's like that.'

'Don't worry. I need to be pushed hard to get better. Your mum is OK really, in small doses anyway!'

'You are really easy going, you know that don't you? Too nice for your own good.' Suddenly, Jez reached over and slipped his hand in hers. He hadn't thought about it, it just happened. He removed it quickly.

'Sorry!' he said. 'I really don't know why I did that,' he blushed yet again and looked away.

'No, it's fine.' And she put her hand back in his. Jez's heart was suddenly racing. Grinning from ear to ear they chatted gently about happier things than they usually did and then suddenly, without any thought he stopped, pulled her gently towards him and gave her a full-on kiss.

'Oh my God,' went through his head. 'What did I just do? She'll kill me.' But she didn't, she just kissed him right back.

Then they did it again. And again. Then once more for luck.

'Wow. I thought that you didn't like me.'

'How could anybody resist that floppy hair and your smashing innocent smile. I've fancied you since I first saw you. Some of the other girls think you are hot too, or at least very warm, but won't admit it. That's why they were so keen to see you in those revealing trousers!' Jez blushed again

'I'm going to run out of blood at this rate! Those bloody trousers! How could I have made such a spectacle of myself?' Paula grinned at him again and he realised that he didn't care so much now because it had clearly got him noticed. Still grinning he chatted gently with Paula until they were near to her house.

'I want to kiss you again.'

'Not here because mum might see. She can't know about us yet, but I have really enjoyed tonight, and I'm glad you feel the same about me as I do about you.'

'Are you my girlfriend now?' Jez had suddenly asked, out of the blue, before returning to his normal, hesitant self. 'Bloody hell, *now* what have I said?' It was as though he was no longer in control of his mouth, and he felt strange and embarrassed. 'That was a bit forward,' he thought, and he was about to run away but she replied quickly.

'I think I *might* be your girlfriend, but then you would have to be my boyfriend. So will you be my boyfriend?'

'But we have only just met. How do I know that you don't just want me for my body?' He'd heard that in a comedy show and now seemed a good time to say it.

'Don't be daft, and I've seen most of your body anyway.

I'm serious. I *have* fancied you since I first saw you. Everybody else prefers your friend John but I like you better. I like the idea of you being my boyfriend!'

'Of course I will be your boyfriend. But how come you've seen most of my body?'

'Jez, you play badminton in a polo top that's too small for you, you wear shorts that flap around when you jump about, and you don't wear underwear. A blind man on a galloping horse would have seen most of your body if he watched you playing badminton.'

'Oh dear,' is all that Jez could think of to say to that but instead of apologising again he added 'How do you know when you are in love?' I've never thought about it before, and I didn't expect to have to think about it tonight.'

'I think we just found out,' said Paula.

'Then I think that I really do love you,' said Jez.

'Don't be so bloody soppy,' said Paula.

'OK,' laughed Jez

'But I want to be soppy, just for a while anyway.'

'Alright, but just for a little while or I might go off you.' Paula said that with a giggle.

'Now you are being soppy,' said Jez, still very red in the face. 'So, boyfriend and girlfriend then?'

'Yes. Oh, and I'm 16 next Tuesday by the way.'

'Great. Are you having a birthday party?'

'I am, but not till dad gets back from the oil rigs in about 2 weeks' time. That's not why I told you though! Bye.' With that she was off, and he watched her till she was safely opening her front door.

'What did she mean?' thought Jez. 'Why would she go out

of her way to tell me that she's 16 next week when she's not having a party? Perhaps she wants me to buy her something.' While he continued his stroll home, he had wondered what John would think about his girlfriend. 'Girlfriend', he thought. 'I really like the sound of that,' and he had found himself smiling yet again. John! His teasing. His comments to Jez about his lack of a girlfriend and how it was time he "got laid". "Got laid"! Suddenly he realised what Paula had meant about being 16 and he blushed massively. And he wished he hadn't been wearing just his polo top and his tight white shorts.

Chapter 4. *Really* getting to know her.

Jez now felt as though he had left his old but cosy world of school and badminton and he had now moved into a different space. He couldn't think about anything else but Paula. When he got home, he had gone straight to his room and changed out of his kit before he saw his mum. He needed to wind down a bit. At dinner his mum spotted the good mood.

'Was coaching good?' she asked.

'Very,' was all that he needed to say for his mother to smile at him again but, despite her happiness, Jez couldn't mention his relationship to his mum or to John. Not until after Paula had told *her* mum anyway but, despite having told nobody, it was still the only thing on his mind and the whole of Friday had turned out to be a bit of a blur to him. 'Relationship,' he thought. 'Wow!' He still felt as though something had taken over his mind *and* his body. 'Am I now supposed to buy wine and chocolates or something? Do I have to dress like the "Man from Milk Tray"? Should I get some aftershave?' He only had a gentle fur on his chin, but he could shave it off anyway. John was never in love with his girlfriends, they only met up for fun and sex so he wouldn't ask his advice. He thought that perhaps he should read some books on love, or sex, or both. But he decided not to bother with any of that and just go with the flow. He might have got it wrong anyway, it was still possible that Paula was just teasing him.

He didn't get to see Paula that Friday which actually suited him. He would have struggled to pretend he didn't know her, at least as well as they had known each other yesterday! 'What a shame we have to keep it all a secret,' he thought.

'I got you some condoms,' said John, out of the blue, as they chatted during break.

'What?' said Jez. 'How the hell could John know about me and Paula? Surely he couldn't know.' Thinking this made Jez realise that John was still teasing him. 'Sod off,' he said, yet again, to John. 'Why would I want some condoms?'

'I walked past the club last week and watched some of your game against Mrs. Jones. I have seen the way she looks at you. She definitely has the hots for you, and you really must get some better fitting kit because you seem to be advertising everything there mate.' This had all been rubbish of course. He had been nowhere near the badminton club. 'Take the condoms. I keep telling you that it's time you got laid.' Though he was genuinely trying to help him, Jez hadn't seen anything positive in what John had just said. 'Time you had some fun,' John added as an afterthought.

'Don't be so bloody silly. She is old enough to be my mother and she's a real a dragon anyway. She doesn't have the hots for me and I certainly ain't keen on her. You can use the condoms yourself.'

'I've got plenty so don't worry about that. After your

display in those trousers the other day I thought I had better get you the large ones by the way. They're in the very bottom of your haversack, just in case she can't resist you.' He had walked away before Jez could reply.

Jez blushed again and thought some very evil thoughts about what he might do to John next time he saw him. The normally mildly spoken Jez came up with some proper profanities, surprising even himself. It was a good thing nobody was around to hear him, and he decided that something really had taken over his mind. Jez had been so angry about this whole teasing thing that he didn't play badminton that evening. He would normally have played against John, but since John wasn't in his good books, he had decided not to play at all.

The weekend had looked like it might be a bit dull for Jez. The weather wasn't great so he couldn't go out on his bike as he would often have done on a Saturday. He wasn't in the mood for music, or for hanging out at John's house where they had got into the habit of playing video games. John had a ZX Spectrum, and they had played 'Formula One' quite a lot. Today though, after his week with Paula, Jez's thoughts were with her, and what he could do to impress her - he didn't want to lose her now. So that Saturday morning he had, unusually for Jez, gone into town and wandered around the shops in the new shopping centre. He wandered past the fancy clothes shops, but he hadn't felt brave enough to go in there, so he went into "Baker's Oven", where he bought himself a pasty for his lunch, which he was still eating when he strolled into Debenham's. This had really incurred the wrath of some of the shop staff in there because

Debenhams was a very posh shop and they had made him finish his pasty at the door before letting him in! After eating it he gave the bag to a member of staff and he then began his investigation into adult shopping by going into the Menswear department. He felt odd going into menswear; he still thought of himself as a teenager, but there wasn't a "Teenagerwear" department! He started looking at the clothes.

'What would impress Paula?' he had thought, before realising that he really had no idea, so he looked around at the clothes for a while longer but eventually he decided that he would bring her with him if he bought any clothes for himself. He had been too shy to walk past the bras and stuff to go into the ladies' wear department on his own so he wasn't buying clothes for Paula either. He wandered over to the 'scent' department where the assistants wafted smells under his nose on little bits of cardboard. He hadn't liked *any* of them, whether intended for him, though he didn't yet use aftershave, or for Paula. He ended up wondering why the world needed so many different perfumes anyway.

Having given up on Debenhams, he wandered about the remaining shops until he reached a narrow lane that contained the town's jewellery stores. He wondered whether a stylish watch might be a nice sixteenth birthday present because Paula could keep it forever and remember their early courting days. There were two shops in that lane with watches in the window. One contained watches with names like Rolex and Omega and the prices ranged from about *five hundred* pounds to about *eighteen thousand* pounds. The other shop window contained brands like Sekonda and Accurist, and the prices ranged from *nineteen* pounds to *one hundred and twenty* pounds. That was an eye watering price difference, especially since he had thought that they all looked alike, and he couldn't afford any of them anyway. So that wasn't going to work for him either.

He finally realised that he wasn't very good at this, and he decided that, maybe once he had forgiven John, they could wander around together, and John could help him buy something nice for Paula. Better still, once she had told her mum about her relationship with Jez, he could wander around with her. He ended up deciding that he wouldn't buy anything yet, even with John. He could come out with Paula to buy some perfume or something on the day of her party, or perhaps just after that. Better not upset her mother!

"A tale of two Windows" came suddenly into his mind while he was thinking about those two jewellery shop windows. Paula loved English literature and he knew that Dickens had written a book called "A tale of two Cities." Once they could go out together, he could invite her to investigate a "A tale of two Windows", and she would be impressed by that idea. Jez was rubbish at English literature, so he had felt impressed that he had had the idea at all. 'I hope she doesn't choose a Rolex though,' he thought to himself.

What he finally had bought before leaving the shops that day was some new kit for badminton, and he decided that he would get it from the men's section of the sports shop, just to make sure that it was suitable!

(Day minus 11)

Jez had woken up on Sunday to a very sunny morning and so he decided that, after breakfast, he'd go out on his bike. He hadn't been sure why he wanted to cycle that day, but he set off at about 10.30 with a packet of sandwiches and a drink. Once he had set off, and he was pedalling along, he realised that he had no idea where he wanted to go. Ordinarily he would be out with John, but he was still annoyed with him, so today would be a solitary jaunt, and he decided to be truly independent and not make a plan at all. He had deliberately kept away from the woodland path, and from anywhere near to Paula's house, in case she saw him and gave the game away to her mother. It occurred to him that he should maybe have kept those shiny, thin trousers to wear while cycling, but then he had thought better of it. He'd only get embarrassed if somebody looked at him!

After a while he found himself by the river and so he decided that it was time for his lunch. He dismounted near to a sandy stretch of riverbank and sat down to eat. He had been enjoying his meal for a while when he heard raised voices coming from just over the adjacent mound of sandy earth. One was a man's voice with a broad Scottish accent and the other was an older man with a local accent. He could only hear snippets of conversation.

'...told you, ...many .... I don't want any more.'

'You'll .... you're told or mah boys will ....'

'I've .... no ....'

'Boys!'

Jez heard a shout and decided that he ought to take a look at what was going on. He could always clear off quickly on his bike if needed. He had set up his bike as a ladder against the sandy mound, which he began to climb for a better view, but he slipped while part way up and came crashing down, sand flying everywhere as he landed. The screaming pair must have heard that crash because he had heard *"Run!"* as he began to pick himself up. Jez realised that he was shaking but he dusted himself down and hid. The sand had partially covered his bike as the mound had given way, so it wasn't really visible. After about 10 minutes he decided that whoever had been arguing had probably gone so he dusted himself, and his bike, down. He peered around very carefully before setting off and, deciding that the coast was now clear, he joined the main road that ran alongside the bank before picking up some speed. He had already made his mind up that he had better not cycle straight home in case he was going to be followed by the gang.

After a detour via the town's only sweet shop he had returned home and got cleaned up before telling his mum about his adventure. He had finished describing the events at the riverbank to her, leaving out some of the ruder words, when she turned to him and said, 'You do realise what was going on there don't you?'

'Yes mum, it was probably a drug dealer trying to sell some stuff to that old man.'

'Although I'm proud of you for doing what you did, do you think it was wise to try to intervene?'

'I wasn't trying to intervene mum, I just wanted to know what was going on. Maybe it wasn't wise though.'

'Promise me you won't get involved with things like that again. Just call the police if you see something. You're too valuable for me to lose. You're the only man in my life since your dad died.'

'I promise mum.' She smiled at him, but this made her realise that he was possibly growing up faster than she had thought and that he might be finding other reasons to leave home before she knew it.

(Day minus 10)

Monday turned out to be a fairly ordinary day and being "in love" hadn't changed the real world for Jez. He had to endure Geography twice that day, but he also had maths. Today, Miss von Hofmann was talking about triangles, sines, cosines and tangents, which would lead on to arcsines, arctangents etc.

'Wir sprechen von Dreiecke', she said, and proceeded, legs apart and with hands together pointing at the ceiling, to do an impression of a triangle. This had begun well but it had all gone wrong when she had tried to change the triangle into one with a right angle so that her class could see how the length of the hypotenuse changed as the angle changed. This hadn't worked very well and she managed to lose her balance. She had looked as though she might fall over but she managed to steady herself just in time. Unfortunately, this act of steadying happened just in front of Jez and when her glasses fell off they landed right in his lap. This time Jez had been the only one not in hysterics with laughter and was, as expected, extremely embarrassed as he handed them back to her. Miss von Hofmann had seen the funny side of it though and it lightened the day for all of them, especially for Jez who was still rather distracted because he had arranged to play badminton against Paula that night, and he was anxious in case things had changed between them. He had brought his new kit and he hoped that Paula would be impressed.

That night the game had turned out to be a good one, or so he had thought, but her mother had been there and as she watched with her dragon eyes, she had moaned at them both constantly. To make things worse, she had ordered Paula to go straight to the car, paid the fees and then given Paula a lift home immediately afterwards.

Jez had felt so let down because he had thought about Paula all weekend and now, she was gone. He had still been wondering what he would get her for her birthday, and he really really wanted to talk to her, and to walk home with her, again.

'Had Paula got her mother to give her a lift home on purpose because she was having second thoughts about him? Did she really like him or was she teasing him? Was she just going to report his kissing skills back to her mates? And did she notice the new kit he was wearing?' He had wanted desperately to see and to kiss Paula again and he felt really frustrated.

(Day minus 9)

The following day he chatted to Paula at morning break. She had kept her distance and they had a "polite" chat during which they had made arrangements to meet that evening, not to play badminton but just to walk home together. This had made him feel a lot better and he could hopefully chat to her and discover what she might like for her birthday. Her mother was coaching somebody else that night and Paula had lied that she was going home with Jemma again. Jez couldn't wait and the rest of the day had proceeded very slowly. They had met up a few blocks from school, keeping well away from the badminton club in case they were seen, and they soon began their walk home.

'I've been thinking about you all weekend, you are so gorgeous,' is how Jez had started the conversation with unusual boldness.

'Anyone would think you were chatting me up,' replied Paula.

'Might be,' he replied. Paula laughed and the conversation had then flowed with ease. They had talked about yesterday's game of course. They had enjoyed it, unusually Jez had won, just, but they didn't particularly care about that at the moment. The chat had continued, each saying potentially wind-up things to each other between comments about the game but once clear of school, and in the countryside, she had taken his hand, pulled him towards her and planted a massive kiss on his lips.

'It's my turn this time,' she said. He said nothing but he *did* respond with more kissing.

'Lovely,' is all he could think of to say after that.

'You are a twit,' was her response.

'But a loveable twit?' Paula gave him a friendly wack on his shoulder and they both laughed. Jez then suggested that they follow the woodland path through the trees that night. He didn't know why, the idea had just come to him as they passed the entrance to the woods, but then it was more private than the path so maybe they wouldn't then be seen snogging!

'It looks a bit dark in there,' said Paula.

'It's fine when you get in because your eyes get used to the light. It's sheltered from the rain too so it's usually nice and dry in there. And it's warmer,' said Jez. 'I often walk along that path, especially when the weather gets bad.'

'What about the ruffians?' said Paula with a laugh.

'Ruffians? Oh yes, but you are with me tonight so I can protect you. Oh, and did you notice my new kit yesterday?'

'Yes,' said Paula. 'It doesn't flap about like your old kit did and it's not nearly as revealing. I liked the old ones better.' She giggled.

'I think I prefer my new kit for exactly the same reason,' he laughed. 'Are we going in here then?'

'OK,' Once in there she found that Jez had been right. It was actually quite cosy in there and she spotted a few squirrels and a rabbit as they had walked. Some birds were singing, and she had heard an owl hoot. The leaves on the trees were just beginning to change from green to brown and the area had a sort of relaxing feeling about it, as though they had gone off on a romantic foreign holiday.

'This is lovely,' she said. 'The path is a bit overgrown though so does it not get used much?'

'I don't think many come this way at all and I never see anybody along here. I think a few local lads come down here with a torch on a Saturday when it gets dark though,' and he pointed to a little pile of empty beer cans, 'but I never see anybody.' Paula smiled and on their route through the woods she spotted a flat-topped grassy mound.

'That looks cosy, let's have a rest there.'

'OK, provided that I get a kiss as well as a rest,' he said boldly. The grass was really soft and dry. It was a bit long but not prickly at all, so they decided to lay down and have a bit of a cuddle. Now in each other's arms they gazed at each other for a while before more kissing ensued.

'Have you remembered?' asked Paula suddenly.

'Remembered what?'

'My birthday. It's today.'

'Sorry, I forgot. I did remember your birthday was coming soon and I had a look around the shops last Saturday. I did know that it was on the way, just forgot the actual day. I can't believe that it has come around so fast, so I haven't got you anything. I would have got you some chocolates or something if I had remembered. Happy birthday anyway.'

'Don't worry, said Paula, 'I have plenty of presents at home. It's you I have been waiting for, and you can start by giving me a kiss.'

They embraced and kissed, for what seemed like ages. Jez's heart was beating like a drum.

'START with a kiss? What else could she want?' He hadn't had to wait long for an answer from Paula.

'So, you didn't remember that it's my 16th birthday? There I was expecting you to turn up today, all dressed up and prepared, complete with some condoms, to help celebrate my birthday!' Paula said that with a put on, huffy air.

'What!' That sentence had been like a bolt of lightning through Jez's frame, and he sat up. He could almost feel his hair standing on end.

'Condoms! She said condoms so she wants to have sex with me, and she wants it now. Bloody hell.' Through a very red face, and with a heart beating ten to the dozen he said 'But I had no idea you were that keen on me. I've never done it before, and we've just come from school and so I'm not prepared. I thought that you would want a hotel room or something, like they do in films. Shouldn't I shower or something first? I'm a bit grubby and I'm sweaty with all this excitement.'

'You are no sweatier than I am,' she replied, 'I'm excited too, but that's the worst come on line ever invented Jeremy Carter. Actually, I want to get a bit sweatier and how can you shower around here? Unless we go down to the river and you strip off and I throw water over you?' She giggled again.

'Now that is a proper chat up line Paula, and I'd love to go down to the river and strip off, provided you do the same,' said Jez, now a little more confident. He put his arms around her waist and whispered something surprising (to Jez!) into her ear.

'That would be perfect but not without a condom,' said Paula, now a little taken aback by his sudden boldness, her arms wrapped around his neck. Jez's mind was racing. This had all been so fast. He desperately wanted to have sex with Paula, he loved her, and she wanted sex with him. But no condoms! But then she might be teasing him? She could have brought some herself if she really had meant it so perhaps she was leading him on, knowing he wouldn't have any, and she would report back to her friends. He was suddenly filled with doubt again and he wondered what

John would do in this situation. 'John! John had said...'

'Wait a minute,' he said to Paula. Heart still pounding he had thought back to what his mate John had said about putting condoms in his haversack. 'Had he been serious? Had John really put some condoms, size large, in my haversack? That's what he said he had done wasn't it?' He quickly rifled through his haversack, and from right at the very bottom he pulled out a pack of condoms, size large, exactly as John had said the other day. He really had put some in there!

'You did bring some then you lying sod,' said Paula. 'You were intending to have your evil way with me all the time. I must see you in a different light now Jez Casanova Carter!'

'No, seriously, it was a joke from John.' He told her all about the conversation they had had about her mum, about how she would likely have the hots for Jez, and how John had said he had put those condoms in his haversack, but that Jez hadn't believed him. He was delighted when she laughed and laughed.

'You with my mother? She's really strong you know. You wouldn't survive! Or at best you'd need a fortnight to recover. So, nobody knows about *us* then?'

'No', replied Jez. 'I really didn't think that you would want actual sex with me, I thought you were just teasing me. I'm not a hunk like John.'

'Pillock! Get them condoms open before it gets too dark to see what we are doing.'

'We'll have a kiss and cuddle first,' said Jez, slightly anxious now because Paula was probably about to see him totally naked, and he wondered whether darkness might actually have been his friend.

'Only after you help me off with these,' said Paula.

In what seemed like a flash the sex was over. So fast in fact that they decided to use another of the condoms John had given Jez.

They stayed together for quite some time afterwards. Everything had all been perfectly natural, so Jez needn't have worried, and he realised that he didn't need aftershave and smart clothes to get the girl he wanted. He just needed the right girl. They decided that they would have to think up some excuses for being late, it was gone 5.30pm and beginning to get dark in the woods.

'I love you so much,' said Jez. He couldn't believe he had just said that, but that was how he felt. He thought about how lucky he was and how much his life had changed in the space of two weeks. He didn't need to envy John any more. He now had all he wanted. Paula was a dream and so beautiful. 'Sorry I didn't get you a birthday present.'

'Don't worry, best birthday of my life,' she replied.

'It's not all a trick so you can tell your mates all about me now you've seen me naked, is it?' said Jez, suddenly.

'Certainly not,' said Paula, and planted a huge kiss on his nose.   'And you are not going out with me just to score one over John?' asked Paula.

'John has nobody that compares to you. You are all I want. I don't need to tell anybody anything by the way, not till you say so. Then I will put an announcement in the paper. Headline news – Jez and Paula are in love.'

'Soppy apeth,' said Paula, and they kissed again.

Jez was in a bit of a daze as he walked home with Paula and all too soon, they had reached the end of the path.

'I will tell mum about us after my birthday party,' she said. 'Secret till then?'

'Yes,' said Jez, though he had really wanted to tell everyone, especially John. He especially wanted to thank him for making that night possible!

Chapter 5. More coaching.

(Day minus 7)

Coaching day had come around again and so Jez had had little else on his mind all day. At the end of the school day, he changed into his kit and set off, racquet poking from his haversack, towards the club.

'Nice racquet,' he heard somebody say. 'Worth a few bob I reckon.' Jez turned around to see one of the fourth-year yobs looking at the handle poking out from the corner of his haversack.

'Not worth anything,' Jez had replied as he speeded up his walking. He wasn't going to run from this idiot, but he wasn't going to lose his racquet either.

'We'll find out then,' said the yob as he lunged at Jez. Jez was too quick for him though and as the fourth-year lad went to grab the handle Jez deftly spun round so that the handle swung *towards* his attacker. The idiot wasn't expecting that, and as it swished towards him it caught him just below the eye. There were times when not being tall was an advantage for Jez! This angered the lad, but Jez now had a head of steam, and he used his haversack to whack the lad in the stomach just by reversing into him. Again, this wasn't what the yob was expecting and all he did in return was to yell 'It's probably crap anyway.'

Jez had been really anxious in case the idiot would get his mates and come after him later, but he needn't have worried. Nobody was going to admit that he had been beaten by somebody with Jez's build!

Five minutes later Jez and Mrs Jones had begun playing against each other as usual, but Jez realised that tonight was a bit different. She was laughing while playing and she actually complemented him on some of his skills. She had still moaned on about him being a bit weedy, but Jez decided that things were looking better for coaching. Paula was there watching but she had been keeping her distance. She had had to go shopping with her mother after practice and she knew Jez would be disappointed, as indeed was she. It was raining though, and she hadn't fancied snogging outside anyway. Jez had walked home as usual and his new kit got wet, but he didn't care, and anyway he had followed the woodland path where it was drier. He smiled when he saw the little flat topped grassy mound and, as he passed it by, he remembered what happened the last time he had seen it.

(Day minus 4)

The following day was a lovely sunny autumn day, and it was surprisingly mild. Paula was thinking about Jez on the way to school. She had decided that she wanted to see him that night, but she couldn't tell her mother about him, so she thought of a ruse.

'Jez wants to play against me tonight,' she said to her mum.

'OK. Make sure that you don't pick up any bad habits.

You know he can be sloppy at times. You're not getting sweet on him, are you?'

'Mother, we've been through this before. There's a much better selection than him at school.'

'Good,' said her mum. 'Unfortunately, you can't though because it's going to be a busy day for a Friday, and I am coaching until six tonight. So, you can't play because I can't give you a lift home.'

'I'll get Jemma to persuade her mum to give me a lift. She can wrap *her* mum around her little finger.'

'Unlike me,' said Marjorie. 'You wouldn't get around *me* so easily!' Paula smiled.

'OK then, you *can* play, but remember what I said about picking up bad habits and be back home early, no stopping off to shop or pick up lads!'

'OK mum. I leave picking up lads to Jemma anyway.' Paula smiled as she said that.

Soon it was home time and Paula and Jez met at the club for their badminton game.

'We don't need to play for very long tonight, do we?' said Paula with a smile. Jez's heart began to thump again.

'No, I don't think we need a long game at all.'

The game was very enjoyable for both of them, and they felt that no bad habits had been passed to each other. The walk home afterwards was just as eventful as the previous Tuesday, and they were sad when they had reached the end of the path. They had to say farewell to each other at about 5.30.

'Till next week then,' said Paula.

'Till next week then,' said Jez, very formally.

The weekend passed very slowly for Jez. For the second weekend in a row, all he could think about was Paula, about how he wanted to tell everybody about his girlfriend, especially John, and how he wanted to take her to see his mum and how happy she would be. At least he and John could talk on equal terms now – Jez had heard so much about John's girlfriends and soon it would be his turn. In the event he didn't seen John at all because they both had lots of homework to catch up with, so Jez, like John, had busied himself with that.

(Day minus 3)

On Monday, Paula hadn't been available to play against Jez because it was the day of the school trip to a local Roman Fort, and Jez wondered whether the world wasn't trying to keep them apart. He had played badminton with John that night and, unusually, John had beaten Jez.

'You seemed distracted,' John said to him after the match. 'Missing the lovely Mrs Jones perhaps?' he joked.

'Piss off,' had been Jez's reply. 'Just a bit tired today. I did a lot of homework over the weekend.'

'I don't believe you,' replied John, but what John *had* been thinking never came to light.

(Day minus 2) October 1st

Jez and Paula had managed to get to play badminton the next day and he had walked her home again, complete with a new pack of two normal sized condoms. Paula had got away with the "I will come home with Jemma routine" again and the weather was very fair though a little cuddle now and again to warm each other on that October evening wasn't an unpleasant thing for either of them. Everything went exactly as they planned, and with fewer nerves this time, they were able to enjoy each other's company in a less hurried way. After they had used their second condom Jez turned to Paula with a peculiar question.

'In films, when the men and women go to bed together, they only seem to have sex once. Obviously, you can't see what they get up to, but it really does seem that they only have one go. We always do it twice, is that normal do you think?'

Paula had always been struck by the way that Jez talked like a little boy sometimes, and she realised that that was a part of his charm. She was also surprised that here was a young man who always expected her to know things that he didn't, and she suddenly realised just how fond of her he had become.

'Jez, we have only had sex on three occasions and yes, I know we've always done it twice, but I think it's traditional at our age. It's usually older people that you get to see in films, and they get worn out quickly.' This sent them both into a fit of giggles. 'You haven't been watching porno movies with big John, have you?'

'No. I've never seen anything like that, and I don't want to. Have you?'

'No,' she replied, although she did have her fingers crossed.

'I'm not old or worn out so I want to do it again,' said Jez.

'What now? Steady on, and much as I'd like to, we

haven't any condoms left *and* it's very late!'

Jez looked at his watch. 'You're right,' he said. 'We'd better get dressed!' While getting dressed he suddenly added: 'Why did you call him big John Paula? Is that what all you girls call him?'

'No. He is quite tall, but I just mean that you seem to look up to him for some reason.'

'Not any more I don't,' he replied with a smile, and he realised that what he had just said, without thinking, had really been true. He gave Paula a hug.

'What was that for?'

'Nothing,' replied Jez, though it really wasn't.

As they approached the end of the path Jez and Paula separated and, as always, he watched Paula until she was safely going in through her front door. Today though he suddenly felt uneasy as he watched her do that. He couldn't work out why he felt that way, maybe he was worried that her mother was beginning to suspect, maybe he was ailing something, but he had definitely got powerful butterflies in his stomach.

'Why do I feel uneasy, what's wrong?' he thought. He continued on home and had his tea, but that feeling of anxiety remained with him all of that evening.

(Day minus 1)

On Wednesday, Jez and Paula had chilled as usual though they did chat at afternoon break. He was still suffering from anxiety, and he had the distinct feeling that something horrible was going to happen to his relationship with Paula, but he decided to say nothing to her. After all he had thought that yesterday and here she was today, and they were both absolutely fine. They parted and they promised each other that they would meet up tomorrow for their (now usual) walk home.

(Day 0)

Badminton coaching (and sex) day had finally arrived again, and Jez was in a really good mood. He had showered extra carefully and walked to school full of anticipation for the day ahead, the feelings of anxiety having left him. He had bought another new pack of condoms (since they had used up all the previous ones) even though buying condoms had been thoroughly embarrassing for him. He had bought them at the chemist's shop and the assistant had asked him all sorts of questions and stared at him over her glasses. He knew that his hairdresser sold them, but he wasn't walking into there just to buy condoms. There'd be loads of men and boys waiting for haircuts and they would look at him knowingly. Had he ever gone into a supermarket he would have realised that they could be bought there without any such problems!

Thursday morning had been perfectly normal, it had gone well and, as usual, he met Paula at afternoon break but, as he approached her, he could see that she looked upset.

'Jez I can't come to badminton tonight. Mum says I have to wait in for the carpet fitter. I am so angry.' That massive feeling of anxiety returned to Jez, as though he would never be able to see Paula again. He was crestfallen.

'I knew it,' he thought. 'It was all too good to be true.'

'What? Do you think she suspects? Has somebody told

her?' he said.

'Nobody knows. She can't possibly know.'

'Why do you have to wait in for the carpet fitter?'

'Because he can only come at about 4pm today. If mum stayed in to wait for him, she would have to cancel your coaching.'

'Then let her cancel the coaching. We can walk home together because she will be busy waiting for the carpet fitter.'

'It's too late to tell mum now so I really am going to have to go home with Jemma today, straight after school.'

'I want to kiss you now.'

'I want to kiss you so much Jez. Not in public though. It's my party next Thursday. I'll tell her just before that. My dad should be home by then and he will calm her down, he's good at that, and then we can be open and tell your mum and all our friends. Then we can kiss whenever we like, but we'll keep the sex a secret though.'

'OK. I can wait until tomorrow,' lied Jez, and they said their goodbyes. They parted without the usual smiles.

'Are you going out with him?' asked Jessica, another one of Paula's mates. 'You meet him a lot.'

'What that toerag? I have to talk to him because my mum's his coach and we have to arrange his sessions.'

'I think he's cute' replied her mate.

'Really?' said Paula. 'I'll set you up if you like.'

Jez was feeling *really* anxious now, as though he would never see Paula again. He kept telling himself that the cause of the anxiety he was feeling was just the disappointment of not seeing Paula tonight, and that they could pick up where they left off tomorrow. But it was no good. He couldn't break that feeling. He didn't even enjoy his coaching session.

Chapter 6. Missing.

(Day 1)

That memorable October Friday had started out as a normal, quiet day at Jez's school, the morning had been fine and dry, and an autumnal chill had started to creep in, but not much else of note seemed to be happening at all. Things livened up a little at lunch time though when a police car was spotted driving in through the school gates. Only a few students had seen it, but word soon got around. The reason why they were there was a big mystery. Perhaps it was a talk from the police, but there had been no notices about it. The reason for the visit seemed even more puzzling because the staff didn't seem to know why they were there either. Perhaps they were here to arrest somebody!

Nothing seemed to happen with actual police officers until about 2.15 pm when Jez's friend John was called to see the deputy head. John, wondering what on Earth this was all about, was soon knocking on the deputy head's door. Mr. Johnson called him in.

'John, you're not in any trouble, we just want to ask you some questions, or rather Sergeant Bulmer here wants to speak to you.' Sergeant Bulmer introduced himself to John and the questioning began.

'John, you are friends with Jeremy Carter, aren't you?'

asked the sergeant.

'Yes'

'Did you see him at school yesterday?'

'Yes.'

'What did you talk about, not general chit chat, but anything that you wouldn't normally discuss?'

'I really can't remember to be honest. We just chatted about stuff.'

'Did he say what he was doing after school?'

'No, but he always has badminton coaching on Thursday after school.'

'Did he go to coaching yesterday?'

'I suppose so, but he didn't mention it which is odd because he usually talks about nothing else on a Thursday. Perhaps he was a bit down when I think about it, but then he had been unusually happy lately. Is he in trouble?' The sergeant didn't reply to that but continued with his questions.

'Did you see him go to his badminton practice?'

'No.'

'Have you seen him today?'

'No. I haven't seen him at all today. Is he absent?' No reply.

'Where does he go for his badminton coaching?'

'He always goes to the university badminton club whether he is playing or being coached. He sometimes gets me to play there but I am not very good. Actually, he has a new coach, Mrs Jones her name is, and he told me that her daughter goes to this school. She's called Paula and is in the year below us. He sometimes talks to her at break to make arrangements for his coaching nights so maybe she saw him there. Why do you want to know? Where's Jez?' Again, the sergeant didn't reply.

'Did you see Jeremy at all last night John?'

'No because I was at a party.' This was the first lie John had told during this interview. He had actually been in bed with a very attractive 20-year-old called Tiffany, a young woman that he had met on Monday evening while on the bus into town. He had seen her as soon as he got on the bus, and he had been delighted when he spotted that the seat next to her was empty. Of course, he had to sit next to her. For her part, Tiffany had been attracted by a mature looking lad in school uniform, so they had got on rather well. That had only been 3 days ago, but she had invited him to her house last night to get to know each other, and there was only a brief amount of chat before they had decided to go to bed together. But of course, he wasn't prepared to tell the sergeant any of that.

'Was Jez at the party?'

'No. He had badminton coaching.'

'So, as far as you are aware, Jeremy had no plans to do anything last night, except to go to his coaching session and then to set off for home?'

'Yes.'

'Does Jeremy have any enemies, or is there anybody that he has fallen out with recently? Anybody that might want to play a trick on him or do him harm?'

'No. Jez is one of those annoying people that you can't argue with. He never answers back, and I have never known him bear a grudge. He's impossible to fall out with.'

'Then thanks John, that's all for now.'

'I'm not going until you tell me where Jez is, and why you have asked me all these questions.' This time the sergeant did answer John.

'Jeremy Carter did not return home last night, and his whereabouts are still unknown. If you remember anything about yesterday that now seems unusual then contact the police immediately and please, you must not talk about this interview with anybody else.'

'So, I can't talk about what you've just said? You wouldn't be here though if Jez was OK so is there anything that *you* aren't telling *me*?'

'Jeremy is probably absolutely fine. We don't consider anybody missing until they've been gone for at least twenty-four hours. He just didn't come home last night so he's likely got drunk somewhere and doesn't want to face his mother. Don't worry.'

'You can go now John,' said Mr. Johnson. 'Remember, don't talk about this interview with anybody at all. Not yet anyway.'

A very anxious John left the room. Not only was Jez missing but his parents might find out that he had lied to them. They were already suspicious because, though he had showered before he left her house, he still smelt of Tiffany's perfume. He had told his parents that he was at a party and that some lads had got drunk and sprayed scent around. They had seemed to have believed that but now they might not. He had also told them Jez was at the party so he could see trouble looming. Where the hell was Jez?

Ten minutes later Paula had been sent for and after she

had entered the room she received the same blunt questioning, but the sergeant did have a few extra questions for her.

'Do you usually go to badminton practice with Jeremy?'

'Yes, but only since my mother began to coach him. Actually, I go with my mother, but I usually watch them play, or sometimes play against Jez myself.'

'It sounds as though you are telling me that you didn't go yesterday.'

'That's right, I wasn't with my mother while she coached Jez last night.'

'Was there a reason why you weren't there?'

'Yes, the carpet fitter had to measure up in our house last night, so I had to go straight home to let him in. Mum couldn't do that because she was coaching Jez.'

'And you arranged all this with your mother yesterday?'

'Yes, she told me in the car on the way to school.'

'So how *did* you get home last night?'

'I always go home with my friend Jemma and her mum if my mum can't take me. They live near us, and they drop me at the door. I did that yesterday.'

'So, you went home straight from school, and you didn't see Jeremy after school at all?'

'Yes, that's right.'

'Does Jeremy have any enemies, or is there anybody that he has fallen out with recently? Anybody that might want to play a trick on him or do him harm?'

'I don't know him well enough to answer that. He seems really forgiving to me, and I can't imagine him falling out with anybody.'

Paula was allowed to leave but given the same warning that John had been given. She was now very very anxious, and she was shaking. She couldn't talk to anybody about it and that made her feel worse. It was really awkward telling her friends that she wasn't allowed to talk about what the police had said to her.

*   *   *

On Thursday night, Valerie Carter hadn't initially been too concerned that Jez had been late home because it was badminton coaching, and he was often late, but by 7.30pm she had felt that something was wrong. Where had he got to? His dinner had dried up in the oven and it was unusual for Jez to not get back in time for his tea, but she couldn't think where he might have gone. She wondered how to go about looking for him, but she knew that Jez only had one real friend, and that was John Cummings.

They had lived next door to the Cummings when Jez and John were at primary school, but John and his family had moved to the posher end of town when Jez was 11. She knew where they now lived, but she didn't have their phone number so she thought that she might go up there to see whether Jez was with John. But then she realised that Jez didn't have a door key so if he returned home, he wouldn't be able to get in. By 9pm though she was really worried, so she decided to go to see the Cummings and to leave a note on the door for Jez. If he returned, he was to wait for her because she wouldn't be out long. She arrived at John's house at about 10.15pm.

'Valerie, how lovely to see you. Come in. You look terrible, is something wrong?'

'Is John at home Mrs. Cummings? Jez hasn't come back from school, and I'm really really worried about him.'

'No Valerie, John's not in, he's out at a party and he said he wouldn't be back till late. Since it's already gone ten, and it's a school night, John shouldn't be too much longer. Jez is probably at the party with him.'

Valerie considered this and she supposed that she hadn't realised that Jez was growing up, but that she would be cross with him for not telling her where he was going.

'If he comes back with John he can stay here for the night and I will ring to tell you, or you can stay here and wait for them if you like.' Valerie replied that she thought it better to be home when Jez returned.

Once she had got home Valerie went to bed but she didn't sleep, and no phone call came from the Cummings.

On Friday morning there had still been no sign of Jez, so she telephoned his school and told them she was worried about him. She didn't say that he had been missing since last night, but she did ask them to ring her once he had been to registration. The school receptionist phoned her back at about 9.30am. Relieved to hear the phone ring she answered it quickly, but she had to sit down when the secretary told her that Jez hadn't yet turned up for school. They said that they were sure that the explanation was simple and that she wasn't to worry. She realised now that that probably wasn't true and as soon as they had rung off, she called the police.

'Don't worry Mrs. Carter, your son is likely to return

home soon,' said the desk sergeant at the police station. 'He'll turn up looking very sheepish because he's been out somewhere that he shouldn't be. That's what usually happens when sixteen-year-old boys are reported missing.'

'Honestly sergeant, Jez really wouldn't do that. If you knew him, you'd know that it's not in his character at all.' Valerie went on to describe Jez at some length. She had sounded so upset that the sergeant agreed to alert all available officers in case Jez had collapsed in a doorway or something. He also promised to ring round the hospitals in case somebody fitting his description had been admitted. Valerie thanked the officer and rang off. She was now absolutely beside herself with worry. Where on Earth could he be?

By 1pm on Friday afternoon all of the necessary phone calls had been made, but the police officers had found nothing. Detective Inspector Roberts had been advised that there was a potentially missing boy and, after studying all the details, he decided that he ought to visit Jez's school. It was Friday, and by Monday anything could have happened to Jez, and student's memories might then have faded. That was when he had summoned sergeant Bulmer and asked him to do his usual school visit to interview the missing boy's friends. Following that visit to the school, and after considering the answers he had received from those friends, Valerie had been assigned a family liaison officer, and Jez was officially declared missing.

That evening Paula's mother picked her up from school as

was usual for a Friday, but Paula was unusually quiet during the journey.

'Anything wrong love?'

'No. I'm just tired.'

'Perhaps you should have an early night then Paula.' They continued their journey home in silence until, as they approached their house, they could see that there was a police car waiting.

'Now what's that about?' said Marjorie. Paula recognised sergeant Bulmer, but there was another man inside the car with him. The two men waited for Marjorie and Paula to approach their house before getting out of the car, but once Marjorie was at the door they were out before she had unlocked it, and detective inspector Roberts held up an ID card while announcing himself and the sergeant.

'May we come in please Mrs. Jones?'

'Of course you may. What's this about?' she asked, as they entered the house and gathered in her spacious hallway. The officers didn't reply at that point, so Marjorie decided that she must break the silence.

'Shall I make some tea? This is my daughter Paula by the way.'

'We've met,' said the sergeant. 'No tea for us thank-you.' Marjorie stared questioningly at her daughter.

'You've met?' she mouthed as she beckoned her visitors to follow her into her rather large lounge. She had just invited them to sit down when the questions began.

'I understand that you are a badminton coach at the university badminton club. Is that right?'

'Yes.'

'Did you coach there last night?'

'Yes,' said Marjorie.

'And did you coach a young man named Jeremy Carter last night?'

'Yes, I did.'

'And how was the training?'

'The same as usual. He's quite a good player but he loses concentration and he's a bit weak in the upper arm which stops him having full control of the shuttlecock. What's this all about inspector?'

'When did the young man leave the club Mrs. Jones?'

'It would have been at about 4.30. We both left at about the same time, which is a bit earlier than usual, but I had to phone my daughter to find out whether the carpet fitter had been to measure up for some new carpets. Again inspector, what is this about?'

'Jeremy Carter did not return home last night and his whereabouts are still unknown.' Paula tried to look surprised but had to look away to hide her expression. 'His mother is very worried.'

'She must be,' said Marjorie. 'This is very worrying for me too, have you no idea at all where he is?' Neither the inspector nor the sergeant answered. For men that asked a lot of questions they didn't seem keen to answer any.

'How does he get home after practice?' asked the sergeant.

'He walks,' said Paula.

'Yes, he does,' added Marjorie, keen to remain the focus of these questions.

'Does he always walk home do you know?'

'Yes, he does. There isn't a direct bus and he told me he likes the walk. He always goes home the same way,' said Paula.

'How do you know that?' asked her mother, crossly.

'Because he told me one day after his coaching and he asked me to walk home with him. He described his route home because he said it was really nice and he thought that describing it to me might encourage me to go with him. He said it was a lovely path, but it was sometimes lonely on his own.' Marjorie grimaced at the thought of Paula with Jez on a potentially muddy and lonely path.

'So, if he has described his walk to you, would you actually be able to give us details of his usual route home Paula?'

'Yes, I would.' The inspector asked her for a description of the route and Paula gave him full details, as far as she could remember. Paula had then offered to take the two men to show them the way, but the officers refused to allow that and told her that she mustn't make that journey herself.

'We will search the route ourselves to see whether we can find any clues as to his current whereabouts,' said the sergeant, who then used his radio to talk to the family liaison officer that had been assigned to Jez's mum. They explained that a search of that path would be underway soon, but before leaving they had a few more things to add.

'Was anything unusual about him yesterday, about his behaviour or anything that he said?' The inspector looked at both of them enquiringly, but Paula and her mum just shook their heads.

'Please don't talk about this to anybody,' said Inspector

Roberts. 'It's important to not let anything be known to the public, especially since Jeremy has only just been missing for 24hours. He could be with a friend or many other places like that, so please don't worry either.'

After the police officers had left Paula had been expecting a further grilling from her mum, about how she knew Jez's route perhaps, but there was none. Later they had both eaten dinner with little appetite and saying very little to each other.

At about 7.30pm that evening and armed with the information they had gained from the school and from their visit to Paula and Marjorie Jones, two officers had been sent to search for any clues as to Jez's whereabouts. Those officers had begun by searching the route that Jeremy usually used to get home. They had initially been fairly casual about the search because lads usually turned up after such disappearances, but it was at about 9pm that two police officers had arrived at Mrs Carter's door. *They told her that they had found the body of a young man.*

Jez's mum identified that body late on Friday night.

Chapter 7. Concern.

The police had wanted Valerie to wait until the following day to look at the corpse, to wait until it had been tidied up, but she insisted that she couldn't because she needed to know for sure one way or the other. After the identification, Valerie had been taken home by another support officer who offered to stay the night with her, but Valerie had refused that offer.

For the second night running she had barely slept, rather she felt as though she were sleepwalking into a massive empty space. She didn't really cry though until Jez's new trousers arrived in the post on Saturday morning, and she sat and sobbed into the packaging.

Early on Saturday morning, before either Marjorie or Paula had had breakfast, there came a knock at the door. Marjorie opened it to find a female PC at the door who announced herself as WPC McKenzie. She showed Marjorie her ID and asked whether she could come in. Once in the lounge she asked them both to sit down, and she sat down herself. She advised them that she had some very bad news for them and then she very gently told them that Jez's body had been found. She gave them a few moments before adding that his body had been found hidden in the bushes along the route that he had probably taken to go home on Thursday night. Paula rushed upstairs. WPC McKenzie then asked Marjorie whether she was OK.

'Thank-you officer. I am, as you would expect, quite distraught, but I had better check on my daughter. She will be less able to cope with that news than I am.' Marjorie found her daughter sitting quietly on her bed.

'Are you OK Paula?'

'What do you think? We've just been told that somebody we both know, knew, has been found dead, and you expect me to be OK?'

'I didn't mean OK like that. I wondered whether you needed some support and it's all I could think of to say.'

'You'd better go back down to see whether they need anything else.' Marjorie returned to WPC McKenzie, but the officer could offer no more information and she told Marjorie that officers would be in touch if they needed anything else. She said that they had decided to tell her and Paula the news because they had been close to Jez, but that they must not make any of this public. After asking Marjorie whether there was anything else that had occurred to her about the last time she had seen Jez, she prepared to leave. Marjorie said her goodbyes and then just sat down and stared into space while the WPC let herself out.

* * *

Valerie spent most of Saturday trying to make sense of it all. 'He must have lost his footing and fallen.' A vision of his body on that slab returned to her. 'He had a mark on his chin so perhaps he had tripped. If only his dad were still alive, he might have made all this make some sort of sense. He might even have been with him to save him! I must tell Emma, but then I don't think I can do that just yet. When the police have released the body perhaps.'

* * *

Marjorie and Paula went out separately on Saturday afternoon. Once out of sight of her mother Paula hadn't known what to do with herself so she just walked and walked. She kept seeing his face, remembered how bashful he was when they made love, how he wasn't keen to get undressed in front of her in case she was disappointed, how he was shaking when he first helped her to undress. She was now beginning to wish that she hadn't become involved with him at all.

Marjorie was also deep in thought. 'He was so sweet about everything so what could he have been up to fall like that? He walked home that way every day so how could he trip and die? Now I feel sorry about the way I coached him, perhaps I shouldn't have been so hard on him.'

Jez's sister Emma, in her university accommodation, was now starting to feel a bit better. On Thursday evening, at about 6.30pm, she had been with a friend and, while they had been preparing for the start of the university term, she had had a panic attack. She had been in a terrible state; she felt that she needed to speak to her mum, but her friend Lisa had taken her back to her flat and stayed with her until she calmed down enough to talk. By 8pm though she was still in a bad state, so the university nurse had been sent for. The nurse gave Emma some pills which calmed her down, and eventually Emma had fallen asleep. On Saturday she thought about calling her mum but decided not to worry her. She found that she was wondering how Jez was.

'Probably the tablets,' she had thought, as she tried to get on with her day.

The police officers arrived at the Jones's to go through all of the events again. It was Sunday morning this time and the same questions had been posed:

'Had they remembered anything new? Was anything different about his behaviour that night? Was he meeting anybody did you know? Did anybody seem to be acting suspiciously around the courts during their last match?'

'He was murdered,' muttered Marjorie. She then said it again, louder this time. 'He was murdered, wasn't he?'

'We have reason to believe that the death was suspicious, but we can't positively say that he was murdered yet,' said the Sergeant. 'That's not official either so please keep that under your hat too.' Marjorie had a peculiar triumphant look about her, but Paula's anxiety had just got even worse.

The police left them at about 11.45am and Paula and Marjorie stayed apart until lunch time. Neither had eaten that lunch with much enthusiasm.

At about 2.30pm on Sunday afternoon there was another knock at the Jones's door. Marjorie answered and this time she found a middle-aged woman standing there. The woman looked as though she hadn't slept for days, and she looked really sad and forlorn.

'Are you the Mrs. Jones that coaches at the badminton club?'

'Yes,' said Marjorie. 'Who are you?'

'My name is Valerie Carter. Can I come in?' Marjorie realised that this must be Jez's mum and her heart skipped a beat.

'Of course. Come in. Go through to the lounge – just on the left.'

Marjorie offered Valerie some tea, which she gladly accepted.

'Paula, make some tea will you, and bring some biscuits.'

Valerie sat down and looked at Marjorie through swollen red eyes.

'I had to speak to somebody, and I hope you don't mind me coming here, but I'm Jeremy Carter's mother and you must have been the last person to see him. The police asked me not to speak to anybody about his death, but I have to, or I'll go mad. Why is he dead? What happened to him? Why Jez?'

Valerie had looked terrible as she asked these questions. Marjorie didn't reply to her straight away but instead she left her to calm down until the tea arrived. Paula brought it in, and Valerie drank as though she hadn't had anything for days.

'Valerie this is Paula, my daughter.'

'Hello Paula. I have a daughter too. She has just left for her second year at university. She's doing English literature.

She doesn't know about Jez yet.' She drank more tea. 'Did you know Jez Paula?' Marjorie glared at Paula and shook her head slightly.

'I sometimes saw him at school to make arrangements for when mum coached him, and I sometimes watched him play, but that's all. I had better go now because I have homework to finish.' Valerie attempted to smile at Paula, but it didn't really happen.

'What can we do Mrs Jones? Jez is dead and I need to do something to keep busy or I will go mad.'

'Call me Marjorie please, but what *can* we do Valerie? The police say we shouldn't even talk about it to anybody, but I agree, we do have to do something.'

'I want to see where he died,' said Valerie.

'Are you sure that you want to do that Valerie? It might be upsetting and anyway we don't actually know where he died, we do have an idea where they found him but that doesn't mean he died there.'

'Doesn't matter. I need to do something. I need to see…' Valerie didn't finish that sentence and Marjorie waited for her to regain some composure. Valerie had finished her tea, but the biscuits had remained untouched when Marjorie shouted for Paula to come downstairs.

'Yes mum?'

'Paula, you told the police about the path that Jez took to come home?'

'Yes, he told me one day at school. I remember once you offered him a lift home and he said he liked to walk. I think that I remember his route, along that country path I think.'

'Come on Valerie, shall you and I walk along that path?

We can start from the badminton club end, see what we can find?

'Yes. That's a good idea and it might help me come to terms with things. I hope that I will be strong enough when I get there. Shall all three of us go to support each other?'

'Not me. I do need to finish my homework. You do remember the route don't you mum, or shall I write it down for you?' said Paula

'Yes, I remember what you told the police. I will just get my coat.'

Marjorie picked up her car keys and they drove, in silence, to the badminton club. Once there, Marjorie had parked up before taking out her OS map, which they studied together. They settled on the route that Jez must have taken before setting off, and they followed his route slowly, and completely in silence.

They found the countryside route easy to follow and they decided that it must have been a well-used path because the ground was hard. Once they had got to a point where they could see Valerie's house, they realised they must have missed the point where his body had been found, so they stopped. They trudged back the way that they had come, again little being said until Valerie broke the silence.

'Was our Jez good at badminton Marjorie? It's all he ever talked about at home.'

'He showed promise,' was all that Marjorie said in reply. The trudge back continued and after a while Marjorie spotted some white striped tape across an entrance to the adjacent woodland. Should she mention it to Valerie? She thought it best not to, but as they continued there was a second entrance where there was more white tape. This time Valerie had seen it.

'Why is that taped off do you think? Could he have been down there? He wouldn't walk through there surely? It's dark in there now and it would have been darker still at that time of night.'

'It might be where they found him,' said Marjorie. 'But we aren't allowed to go past the tape.'

'That's the place!' said Valerie. 'I just know it. I want to stand here for a while. I think he might have gone into the woods through that entrance and stumbled somewhere or met somebody.' She stood there for a long time, her facial expression changing now and again, but then, suddenly, she just said 'Will you take me home now, please?'

'Of course Valerie.' They walked back to the car but said very little to each other. Though Marjorie had said she would take Valerie home she actually took her back to her own house instead. She thought that she might need some company and Valerie's house might hold too many memories just at the moment. Once there, Valerie began to speak.

'What happened to Jez? Did he fall or did somebody do this to him? I want to find him, make whoever caused his death to know what he's done.'

'Maybe between us we could do some investigating and see what we can find,' said Marjorie.

'I'll help too,' said Paula.

'Paula! I didn't know that you were listening.'

'I can ask around at school. Somebody might have seen something. Somebody else must come home the way Jez did and I could start tomorrow.'

'Paula, it might be dangerous to do that,' said Valerie.

'I'll be fine. It might help me too.'

'Alright,' said Marjorie. 'We can't tell the police though, unless we do find something.'

Valerie went home feeling slightly better. She said she would ask the neighbours whether they had seen anything, and she would speak to everyone she saw coming along that path tomorrow because *they* might have seen something. Marjorie would do the same at the other end of the path, the end that began at the club. Paula would ask around at school and between them they decided that they had to try this or go mad while waiting for the police to do their job.

Chapter 8. Investigating.

(Day 4)

Students arriving at school on Monday morning had been surprised by the announcement of a special assembly, even more surprised that it had been scheduled for *later* that morning. At about 9.45am, the school had been brought together but in two halves, because they couldn't fit all the students in the hall at the same time. The deputy head had taken the assembly.

'You will no doubt be wondering why we are having an extra assembly in the middle of the morning. It is a very difficult thing when we have to announce that somebody from our school has gone missing, but I have to tell you that nobody has seen Jeremy Carter of our lower sixth form since last Thursday evening. He was last seen at badminton practice on Thursday so if anybody has any information as to his whereabouts, please speak to me as soon as possible.'

This same announcement was repeated for both halves of the school with a more serious tone being adopted for the upper school students.

It had been quite a brief assembly but lots of muttering took place as the students left for the start of period two. Very few youngsters in the assembly hall had known Jez personally, but that hadn't stopped them inventing reasons for his disappearance:

'I reckon a pervert's got him,' laughed one.

'He's run off with that Miss Spinks from the office, I would have given the chance!' said another.

'Probably tripped over his shoelaces and got amnesia,' added another.

'He's dead, or dead drunk,' was also heard that morning.

'Drugs,' or 'left with his boyfriend,' or 'the dog's killed him,' or 'a whale has eaten him,' and so on.

The school quickly got back into its normal routine after the assembly but at morning break Paula looked for Jez's friend John. She had had to ask around a lot before finding him because sixth formers didn't generally mix with the lower school and she had had to sneak into the sixth form common room too, but it was there where she found him, sitting in a corner and, unusually for John, he was by himself.

'Are you John, Jez's friend?'

'Yes. You are Paula aren't you. I saw Jez talking to you a few times. Were you two going out together?' It had seemed to be all that John thought about at that time and Paula was a bit taken aback by the abruptness of the question.

'He was being coached by my mum and we used to talk about arrangements sometimes but that's all. It doesn't mean that I am not worried about him though so did you see him on Thursday? Did he seem different at all?'

'You sound like the police! Yes, we chatted to each other after lunch, and he *was* pretty excited last Thursday. He was going to badminton, and he was more excited than usual in the morning, but he was quieter when I saw him in the afternoon. I wondered whether he had something extra planned.'

'Did he say that he had planned anything? Was it a girlfriend maybe?' She just managed to hold back on her emotions as she asked this.

'He never said. I don't think he had a girlfriend, but he probably wouldn't have told me anyway because I had been teasing him about your mum. Sorry about this but I said she might have the hots for him. I even bought him a pack of condoms to make him feel a bit more uncomfortable if she tried it on with him and I put them in his haversack for him. But that was the previous Thursday.'

'I am sure mum didn't see him like that.'

'Sorry,' said John.

'Do you know where he is?'

'No,' replied John. 'I didn't even see him go to his badminton coaching which is unusual.'

'Who else knew him?'

'Nobody really. He is a quiet lad. Hang on a minute, you said *knew* him. Is he dead? Do *you* know something Paula?' Paula became flustered.

'I don't know anything to be honest. We hoped that *you* would. My Mum knows his mum and we thought we might try to help find him, like amateur detectives.'

'Oh. Well good luck. He's a good mate really but I'm sure that he's OK.' With that he got up and, with no further explanation, was gone. Paula had to sit down. So much was buzzing round her head about the night Jez died. She really wasn't coping with this at all, and she arrived 10 minutes late for her first lesson of the afternoon. She lied that she had been unwell in the toilets.

During lunch time and afternoon break Paula had 'bumped into' many people who were in Jez's year or in her year. The conversation had always been very similar.

'Do you know Jez Carter?'

'Who? Oh, you mean the missing lad?'

'Yes. Did you know him?'

'No. What did he look like?'

'Longish dark hair, centre parting, not very tall and with a soppy grin.'

'Oh him! The lad that everybody looked for because he was wearing see through trousers one day?' Paula groaned inwardly. Then some had added:

'Sorry he's missing though.'

'Are you his girlfriend?' Some more comments were less pleasant, for example:

'Oh, the lad in the sexy trousers!'

'I thought he was gay. Only a gay boy would wear those trousers.'

There were many other derisory comments and Paula had to tell her mother what little she had found out in the car on the way home. She missed out the bit about the ill-fitting trousers.

'Those bloody trousers.' She remembered the day he had worn them and, becoming increasingly angry with her school mates, she realised that her boyfriend had been at the school over 5 years, and all that most people remembered about him were those bloody tight trousers. It meant that, without those, and that incident of teasing, nobody would have noticed him at all. She felt desperately sad for him and wondered how many people would notice if *she* was no longer at school.

Valerie had slept badly again, and she couldn't face breakfast. Jez should have been sitting opposite her in his dressing gown, waiting for his skin to dry off fully after his shower, but he wasn't there, and she realised that he was never going to be there again. She sat down and just looked into space for a while, but then she realised that she'd need to ring work. She was anxious about ringing them but, in the event, they had been very understanding. They told her to take as much leave as she needed. So, instead of heading out to work, she gathered together a picnic chair and a flask of tea, and took them out to the lane that led to the badminton club.

She had managed to persuade herself that it wasn't *her* Jez that was dead, and she felt a little better. Instead of trying to find Jez's killer, she was helping the police to find the killer of another teenage lad. She did realise that, rather than catch people this early in the day, she would have been better off asking people that regularly walked there in the evenings, but doing this now kept her mind off the difficult stuff that was to come. She hadn't yet told her daughter about Jez, and she was dreading having to do that. Being four years older than Jez she been a proper big sister, so she would be devastated.

Valerie remained in place for nearly three hours and chatted to everybody that passed her, including a young constable, but eventually it had become too much for her and she returned home.

It had been a bit more difficult for Marjorie to carry out the same task at the badminton club end of the path. On one hand she didn't begin until after 3pm so at least she was probably asking the right people but, while Valerie had the advantage of being Jez's mother, Marjorie wasn't received as easily. She had ended up telling people that she was helping the police with their enquiries, not a lie as such because she wasn't actually pretending to be a police officer, but even then, few people had actually told her anything useful.

Marjorie called on Valerie at about 7pm that evening to compare their findings, but she found Valerie to be in a bad way. She clearly hadn't eaten much, and the room was dark and cold, so Marjorie made her some tea again. She had hoped that a drink would help Valerie begin to feel a bit more talkative and it seemed to work, and now that Valerie looked a bit brighter Marjorie began by asking her how the "chatting to walkers" had gone.

'People were lovely, but none had seen anything that night. Some gave me names of people that they knew would often walk along that path at teatime, and I have written them down. The paper's over there.' She pointed to her sideboard. Marjorie read those with interest and found that there were five names on the list, three had addresses but two didn't, though one had a "thereabouts" description! 'I'm sorry, I haven't asked you how you got on,' said Valerie. 'Forgive me but I'm not being a good host tonight.'

'Don't worry, I understand. This must all be terrible for you.' Marjorie paused. 'I only got one name, but I know where she lives. Shall we go to see these people tonight?'

'Not me,' said Valerie. 'I couldn't face any more. I don't mind if you go and see them, perhaps tell the police what you find, but I don't like it here at the moment so I might go away somewhere. I can't even bring myself to tell Emma. Not yet.'

Marjorie could see that Valerie needed some space and, after some general chit chat and more commiserations, she left. She now felt terrible herself.

'Poor Valerie. How would I feel in her position?' she wondered. 'I only have Paula, though I do have my husband. What would I do in her place? I really have no idea. What a terrible business.' In the car going home she did some thinking and she realised that all she could do was to help find out who killed Jez. At least Valerie could then look Jez's murderer in the eye and ask him why he had done it. That might help her come to terms with her loss and move on. 'Loss,' she thought. 'What an awful word. Nobody should have to deal with the loss of a loved one, especially not a youngster.' She had a determination now to find out what had happened to Jez, with or without the approval of the police.

(Day 5)

Jez's school had been unusually subdued on Tuesday morning because the announcement of Jez's disappearance had really begun to sink in, and staff and students had become quiet, worried and very anxious. This wasn't something that happened to *them*, was it? People disappeared in TV crime dramas; it didn't happen in real life, did it? But Jez hadn't yet reappeared. Where was he?

The police still hadn't made it generally known that Jez had actually been found because the circumstances of his death had begun to raise some concern. The pathologist had found saliva in the region of Jez's chest and genitalia, but they had found no semen. Though he had a bash to his jaw and a bigger one to his forehead, the state of his lungs suggested he had suffered from a lack of air at some point, though they couldn't be sure whether the asphyxiation or the blow to the head had been the cause of his death. It seemed that he had died slowly, over a period up to a day perhaps. (They added in their report that they hoped that he had been unconscious during that time). It was also found that his fingernails were full of dirt, as though he had been scratching at the ground before he died. There were a few traces of lipstick around his mouth and, though he was wearing his kit of white tee shirt and white shorts (with nothing else underneath), his lower body was grubby, as though his clothing had been removed, he had lain (or been placed) on the ground, and then his kit had been put back on. The sides of his arms were lightly scuffed, suggesting that he might have been held down while face up, the ground keeping his rather thin arms beneath his body. The police had recovered his haversack, which had contained only his school clothes and some schoolbooks, and they would need to go through those with his mum. He had some loose change and some condoms in his pocket. He was clearly expecting, or had had, a sexual encounter at some time that day. They would need to speak to his pals and his mother about that.

Marjorie meanwhile had been doing some planning. She had the list that Valerie had written out for her, and she decided that she would have to start her investigations by talking to those people. Between 10 am and 12pm on that Tuesday she had no coaching, so she found a quiet cafe, ordered coffee and a Danish pastry, and studied the list. It read like this:

Erica Briggs and her dog Eric, both quite elderly.
Geoffrey Smithson and his dog Fred. They were memorable because he and the dog had the same colour hair: a sort of brown colour.
Maureen Davidson who walked home that way after work. Same time every day – about teatime.
George Dickinson, a rather shady character that people kept away from.
Freda Bainbridge and her dog Pickles. She ran the local chip shop and was well known. She walked Pickles every day before the evening shift at the chip shop.

Her own information had added nothing, comprising only of Erica Briggs and her dog Eric. She decided that she would be wise to see the women first and ask them whether they had seen anything that night. The men would only be "interviewed" if nothing came from talking to the women. After she had eaten her pastry and drunk her coffee, she left the cafe and went about the rest of her day as normal. She conducted three coaching lessons that afternoon, but none had been particularly good students and she kept comparing their performance with that of Jez, which annoyed her. By the end of the afternoon, she had felt unsettled, and she couldn't work out why. Was it because she now felt that she had been unnecessarily hard on Jez? Felt sorry perhaps? This made her more determined than ever to try to help the police. 'Wasn't it Agatha Christie's Jane Marple that said suspects would talk more freely to an old lady who knitted, than to the police?' Marjorie wasn't old, and she didn't knit, but maybe she could use her feminine charm to help her. 'I'm good at that,' she thought.

She decided to begin her visits immediately and she would start with Erica or Maureen. At that time of night Freda Bainbridge would already be at work in her chip shop.

That evening Paula had been very quiet in the car during her drive home with Marjorie. 'You seem down tonight,' she said to Paula.

'Jez is still dead mother,' Paula replied. 'Everybody at school is very sad and worried about him even though they don't yet know that he's dead, but you don't seem to understand that.'

'I thought he wasn't very popular?' said her mum.

'He wasn't popular, but he wasn't *un*popular mum. He didn't have many friends, but people didn't dislike him. He was quiet and didn't mix much, but he's still one of us and he's missing.' Marjorie had felt impressed by this camaraderie.

'Never mind love. I can tell you that I am going to help

find out as much as I can about what happened to Jez that night and I have Valerie's list of suspects to help me to begin. The Game is Afoot.'

'Mother, this isn't a game,' shouted Paula. 'Jez is DEAD. It's real so why the hell are you playing games?'

'The Game is Afoot is what Sherlock Holmes would say before starting an investigation, Paula. I said it to show you that I am really determined!'

'Oh.'

'Will you help me then Paula? I want to start tonight.'

'No. Definitely not. I appreciate what you are doing but count me out. I want nothing to do with it. And don't take any risks mum.'

'I won't,' she replied.

Back in the house Marjorie ordered a takeaway for both of them which didn't take long to arrive. Marjorie divided up the food which they ate in relative silence.

'How are the prawns Paula?'

'Fine.'

'Enough rice?'

'Fine.'

'There's cheesecake for dessert.'

'Fine.'

After having eaten only a little of the cheesecake, Paula went up to her room without speaking to her mum. A little later Marjorie prepared to leave for her evening "work".

'I am going out now,' she shouted as she left.

'Fine,' shouted Paula.

'Fine,' thought Marjorie, and she set off with her road atlas to find 81 Elmwood Grove, to talk to Erica and maybe to bark at Eric. On the way she had wondered how she would approach Erica. Should it be 'Hi Erica' or 'Hi Mrs. Briggs, or was it Miss Briggs?' She decided to stick with Erica. Then there was the introductory words to think about. 'I was given your name by Valerie,' etc. etc. She decided that she would wing it when she got there.

Elmwood Grove turned out to be easy to find and she gave a sharp knock on the door of number 81. Eventually, an elderly lady opened the door. Marjorie had been pleased that Erica smiled when she introduced herself and relieved that, despite her age, Erica wasn't deaf. She heard Eric barking.

'Hi. My name is Marjorie Jones, and I am helping the police with their enquiries into the disappearance of Jeremy Carter. He attends Basingrove Secondary school, but he disappeared last Thursday. I used to coach him on a Thursday night and was probably the last person to see him. His mother Valerie tells me that you often walk along the same path as Jeremy, and we wondered whether you had walked your dog along there last Thursday. Perhaps you saw or heard him as he walked home.'

'Would you like to come in for some tea dear? I've just made some.'

'Yes please, I would love a cup.' Erica's home was small and dainty. Marjorie was shown into the living room and Erica went into the kitchen for an extra cup and saucer to add to the china that had already been laid out on a small coffee table. The room was brightly painted in pale greens and oranges, a throwback to the nineteen seventies perhaps.

There were photographs of lots of young men on shelves around the room and while most of the men in the pictures looked quite young, the photos themselves looked much older.

'I see that you are looking at my menfolk.' Erica looked pleased with Marjorie's interest.

'Menfolk? Are they your nephews or sons maybe?' asked Marjorie. Erica roared with laughter.

'Neither', said Erica. 'All ex fiances.'

'There looks a lot of them,' said Marjorie.

'There's nine' said Erica with some pride. 'The most recent is from almost 10 years ago when I was sixty-seven.'

'You said "ex" fiancees. Do you mind my asking what happened to them?' Marjorie was feeling anxious in case they were all dead.

'Don't mind at all. Left every one of them at the altar. I was a beauty once you know but it took them all so long to propose that by the time it came to the wedding, I had found somebody much better looking!' She laughed again. Marjorie didn't know what to say.

'Don't worry dear,' said Erica. 'I wouldn't have been faithful to them anyway, and they have all been married since. I still get Christmas cards you know, and they bring their children to see me sometimes, at least while they are young. That one,' and she pointed to a colour photograph, 'was the most recent. He was 28 and I was 65 when that was taken. Wasn't he good looking Marjorie? But I was a proper Joan Collins then too and we had fun together. He didn't take long to find a proper bride when I left him though. He's already got three kids, all still under five. I love them all.'

'Did none of them mind that you jilted them?' asked Marjorie, worried now that they might have tried to murder Erica or something similar.

'No, not at all. I didn't *actually* leave them at the altar, except for Tim bless him. He was very good about it, he just said not to worry, and we enjoyed the reception anyway; the food was lovely, and we danced to the excellent band. I broke up with the rest of them in time to cancel the wedding.'

Marjorie was rather stunned by this, so they sat with their tea for a while but, after a short pause, Erica said 'Do you want to see the rings?'

'Rings?' asked Marjorie.

'Yes, my engagement rings. You don't think I gave them back, do you?'

'OK,' said Marjorie and Erica went to her sideboard and pulled out a faded old blue leather covered box. It had gold tooling on it, and it looked as though it might be over a hundred years old. Marjorie was beginning to wonder whether it might contain a small pistol or something. Erica opened it and showed her the contents. Marjorie was amazed to see eight, obviously very expensive, rings in a fitted velvet interior. There were two empty spaces.

'Wow,' said Marjorie. 'Why only eight?'

'I had to sell one because I fell on hard times. I kept the best ones though.' More laughter.

'What about the other space, there's two spaces but you only sold one.'

'I never did fill that one. I suppose there's still time though.'

'They look really expensive!'

'Yes, they were. My mother gave me the box, but I got the filling!' and she laughed heartily yet again.

'Are they safe in that sideboard?'

'Here, you're not from the insurance company are you, here on false pretences, asking about a missing boy as a smoke screen to check up on my security? If you are I'll set Eric on you.'

'No, of course not,' but she reminded Erica of the real reason for her visit.

'Oh, the missing boy. My niece told me about him yesterday, but I can't help you because I always walk Eric before the school kicks them out, so I won't have seen anything. I don't want to meet any school kids because Eric bares his teeth at them.'

Marjorie thought that Eric would struggle to terrify a trifle but continued anyway.

'So, did you see anything or anybody out of the ordinary last Thursday? Maybe pacing up or down or looking shifty perhaps.'

'No, I really didn't. It was quiet all last week in fact. I'm afraid that I saw nothing that would help you. What was he like, the boy that's missing?' A Knot appeared in Marjorie's stomach.

'Pleasant enough,' she said. 'He needed a lot more practice to make his badminton really good though.'

'You said *needed* a lot more practice. Do you think he's dead then?'

'I don't know.'

'Was he a good-looking boy?' asked Erica.

'She's man mad,' thought Marjorie.

'I didn't really notice,' she replied.

Marjorie stayed for a few more minutes longer to be polite, they talked about the price of coffee and other mundane things and how disappointed she had been with the summer this year, but Marjorie hadn't been sure whether to believe anything Erica had said to her. She had to admit though that, at this stage anyway, she really didn't think that Erica had attacked or attempted to abduct Jez!

After that slightly barmy introduction to amateur sleuthing Marjorie decided to drive to the nearest pub because she needed to use the facilities and she fancied a gin and tonic anyway. She thought about Erica as she drank.

'Was any of what she said true? Had she really never seen Jez? You'd notice a lad in white PE kit with a badminton racquet sticking out from his haversack. But then she did say she deliberately avoided school kicking out time.' Perhaps she would cross her off the list of suspects.

Ten minutes later she was outside Maureen Davidson's door and this time she found herself in front of a very modern looking 1950s semi-detached house. The owners had obviously wanted a new look to the house and they had clearly spent a lot of money by installing new aluminium windows and door, and they had rendered and painted the brickwork in a pale cream colour. She had already decided to use the same introduction as with Erica. Eventually, after a second knock, the door was opened but this time it was on a chain.

'Hi. My name is Marjorie Jones, and I am helping the police with enquiries into the disappearance of Jeremy Carter. He attends Basingrove Secondary school, but he disappeared last Thursday. I used to coach him on a Thursday night and was probably the last person to see him. His mother Valerie tells me that you often walk along the same path as Jeremy, and we wondered whether you had walked your dog along there last Thursday. Perhaps you saw or heard him as he walked home.'

'Show me your Police id,' said Maureen.

'I don't have a police id because I am not a member of the police force. I am merely helping them to establish some facts.'

'I'll get my husband,' said Maureen 'he'll see you off.' She closed the door. A few minutes later Maureen's husband Don arrived at the door. Marjorie repeated her introduction.

'But you're not from the Police so what are you up to?' Marjorie explained that Jez had gone missing after her coaching session with him, and she felt obliged to offer assistance. The police were very busy, and they would need all the help they could get. She pointed out that she was probably the last person to see him alive.

'So, you are his killer then,' said Don, looking very pleased with himself. Marjorie gave him one of her stares and, after he had visibly shrivelled somewhat, he thought for a while before letting her in.

'Come on in then, don't mind my wife. She likes a bit of peace at night.' Marjorie found herself in a thoroughly modern living room with one of those Swedish Hi-fi systems that spread itself along the top of a low, Danish style sideboard, and a very smart TV. She remarked on how pleasing the room was and Don softened even further. It was very much *his* design of room because he said that his wife Maureen had always just gone with the flow.

'Maureen!' he shouted. Maureen arrived, but not immediately.

'I was just making some tea pet,' she said, and then thought she had better offer some to Marjorie. A few minutes later they were sitting down in comfortable armchairs with a small coffee table each.

'Marjorie was probably the last person to see that missing lad alive,' said Don. Maureen started to say that she must be the murderer, but Don piped up with 'Done that one love, sorry.' But then he added 'I thought he was reported missing, but you are talking about him as if he was dead? So, is he dead or missing, which?'

Marjorie gave a non-committal answer to this, and Don had seemed satisfied. She had actually begun to warm to them and began to tell them all about her coaching, how Jez wasn't actually that good but that he would likely improve with time.

'Then this must be difficult for you,' said Maureen.

'It is yes,' said Marjorie, suddenly finding herself close to tears. She blinked them back and carried on with the questions, but it seemed that Maureen had neither seen nor heard anything that night. She had never walked along the secluded part of the woodland path because it wasn't safe for her on her own and she didn't know anybody that would venture in there unless they were up to mischief like those lads that drank down there on Friday and Saturday nights.

Don had told her about those and when she walked home on a Friday she did so quickly, just in case they had started early.

Marjorie, feeling that she had heard enough, commented on how helpful the couple had been and that she would pass on this information to the police if they needed it. They parted on friendly terms and Marjorie headed back to the pub for another gin and tonic.

She sat for only 10 minutes with her drink because it was getting late, and she had decided that she had to see at least one more from the list that night. She didn't have Geoffrey Smith's address, only a "whereabouts" but after knocking on a few doors she learned that Geoffrey was quite well known, as was his dog, Fred. She soon had his address, and she was there within minutes.

3 Lampton Drive turned out be a very old, white painted, farmhouse type building. The door was hard, and it had hurt her hand when she tried the loud knocking she had used with her other "suspects". She decided to bring some sort of knocker with her if she was to continue her investigations beyond tonight.

'Suspects,' she thought. She was beginning to enjoy herself doing this. Perhaps she would write a book about her experiences when she had finished.

Geoffrey answered the door quite quickly and she was greeted by a brown eyed man with a broad smile and a thick mop of very bright brown hair. Padding along behind him was a small dog with a thick mop of very bright brown fur. They really could have been related!

She began as before:

'Hi. My name is Marjorie Jones, and I am helping the police with enquiries into the disappearance of Jeremy Carter. He attends Basingrove Secondary school, but he disappeared last Thursday. I used to coach him on a Thursday night and was probably the last person to see him. His mother Valerie tells me that you often walk along the same path as Jeremy, and we wondered whether you had walked your dog along there last Thursday. Perhaps you saw or heard him as he walked home.'

'Would you like to come in for some tea my dear? I've just made some.' Marjorie had said that she would love some tea, and in she went, but then deja vu hit Marjorie.

'I have already heard that tonight, haven't I? I know that I have tried to use an identical greeting but to get an identical one back was weird. It was Erica wasn't it who said those exact same words. I'll keep that for my book...'

'Love some,' said Marjorie as she went in. There was indeed freshly made tea, complete with two cups and saucers, on a table in the front room. The room was decorated in muted tones of green that clashed with the furniture slightly, but actually suited the age of the building. Geoffrey invited Marjorie to sit down, and he poured the tea. Marjorie wondered why there were *two* cups.

'It's nice to meet you dear but when do we start?' asked Geoffrey.

'Start what?' asked Marjorie.

'You know what. Don't be a tease,' said Geoffrey. Marjorie was getting worried now.

'I really don't. Were you expecting somebody tonight?'

'You know I was. Be a good girl and let's get started. Shall I get the box?'

'I assure you mister Smith; I do not turn up to men's houses to "get started" and it's some years since I could have been regarded as a "girl". I don't know what box you are talking about.' Geoffrey smiled at her.

'Are you sure? Perhaps you want to wait until we've had some tea. Do you want a biscuit? I have some nice ones in the kitchen, or a cake perhaps. We will need to keep some refreshment to have while we have some fun.' Marjorie wondered whether it might be time to leave but just then there was a knock at the door. Marjorie heard faint voices, Geoffrey's and those of a woman. Geoffrey returned to the living room looking very sheepish.

'I do apologise Mrs Jones. I *was* expecting a lady tonight, but it was actually Shirley here that was sent by the agency. So, you really do want to know what I know about that missing lad?'

'Yes,' said Marjorie. Geoffrey popped into the kitchen for another cup. The three of them sat drinking tea for a while and then Marjorie began her questioning, but the answers were disappointing.

'I'm sorry, but though I often walk Fred along that path it's never at school closing time, and I certainly wasn't out that Thursday. I do sometimes speak to a bloke called George if he happens to be along there during the afternoon. A Scottish chap in his early thirties he is with a sly look and a terrifying grin. I wouldn't like to meet him in the dark and away from other people! You never know what he might do.'

Marjorie considered this for a while but then began to chat with Shirley, who turned out to be an avid sports fan, mainly tennis. They spoke at length about Wimbledon and Roland-Garros, having both attended events there earlier in the year. After a while though Shirley remembered that she was there to be "company" for Geoffrey and so Marjorie had to cut short her gossiping. Just as she was leaving Geoffrey had asked whether Marjorie played trivial Pursuit. Marjorie replied that she didn't, but this did allow her to establish that Shirley had belonged to an escort agency that specialised in providing company for single men that liked to play card and board games with attractive women. Shirley's speciality had been Trivial Pursuit!

Marjorie had gone straight home after this, but she decided that she needed a shower before retiring to bed!

Chapter 9. Joe.

After the shower, and while lying in bed, Marjorie had decided to telephone her friend, or rather her husband's friend, Joe.

'Hi Joe, it's Marjorie.'

'Oh. Hi Marjorie. Nice to hear from you, but it's a bit late and we are in bed. Is everything OK?' Marjorie replied that all was well with them and probably OK with her husband though she hadn't heard from him for a while. Then she told him about Jez.

'Sorry to hear about that,' said Joe. 'It must be difficult for you being the last person to see him.'

'That would be his killer Joe,' said Marjorie.

'He's dead? You said he was missing.'

'Sorry Joe, I shouldn't have said that because the police told us not to tell anybody, but they *have* found his body.'

'Hell no. How old was he?'

'Joe, please forget I told you any of this because the police want to release details themselves, but Jez was just turned sixteen.'

'Wow, very sad. I *will* keep what you said a secret, but why are you ringing *me* then?'

'Are you free tomorrow morning?'

'To do what exactly?' Joe didn't often get asked this by his friend's wife, especially when Dan was away.

'I am helping the police to track down people that might have seen Jez on the night he disappeared, and I am calling to see a chap called George tomorrow morning. Are you available to come with me if he turns nasty?'

'That's Wednesday, isn't it? Not first thing. I might be able to make 11 o'clock ish. I'm going shopping with Trish, but we usually get back in time for morning coffee. You're welcome to join us then.'

'Thanks Joe. What I'll do is to visit George on the way to work then ring you if I need you.'

'OK but be careful. I have to go now; Trish wants me to put the phone down.' They said their goodbyes and Marjorie felt that she should really be getting some sleep, but she decided to make some notes first. Amateur sleuths seemed to do that in novels and she wanted some notes for when she wrote her own sleuthing novel.

Erica Briggs: Marjorie decided that Erica was a dead end. She obviously didn't see anything, nor was she aware of anybody else that might be able to help. Probably lived in a fantasy world if the truth be told. Told a good yarn.

Maureen Davidson: Aggressive woman with a slightly less aggressive husband. They both seemed deeply suspicious of the world and if there was anything to be seen that night Maureen would have gone straight to the police. She said she didn't see anybody but an old woman that night (probably Erica Briggs). She described her and the dog Eric, so Marjorie believed her.

Geoffrey Smith (and his dog Fred): Geoffrey Smith had been a rather lovely but lonely middle-aged man. She found that she had liked him, and Shirley. It seemed that he wouldn't be able to carry out anything as complex as an abduction or a murder, and he was too busy with his "bought in" social life to bother schoolboys.

She was very interested in what he had said about a character called George though, the one that had intimidated Geoffrey. Was he the George Dickinson on the list? She put her notes down and slept deeply. In that sleep, she could see Erica as an old lady who still kept a lookout for a suitable chap, preferably a youngster, which to her meant between 30 and 50. To her, Jez would have been a child, and she would have smothered him with love in the form of fizzy pop, cakes and biscuits.

Next, she envisioned Maureen, who walked that way after work because she actually wanted to meet students. She missed not having her own children and hoped that she might chat to a few of the girls. This rarely happened and she would have avoided Jez if she had seen him because teenage boys were nasty things and Maureen wanted nothing to do with them.

Marjorie hadn't dreamed about the fairly gormless Geoffrey, and she woke feeling restless.

Paula had got up before Marjorie on Wednesday morning and was in the process of eating breakfast when Marjorie entered the kitchen. Marjorie was surprised to see how organised everything looked.

'Morning love.'

'Morning mum.'

'Anything exciting happening at school today?' asked Marjorie.

'Mother!' is all that Paula managed before returning to her room, but it had taken a full ten minutes before Marjorie had realised why that might have upset her. The next she heard from Paula was the sound of the front door closing rather loudly as she left for school.

After eating her own breakfast, Marjorie headed out for work rather earlier than usual. She had decided that she would call on George Dickinson on the way to the badminton court, provided that she could find his house. She had been given a rough description of where he lived, and she felt sure that she would find him, but in fact it hadn't been that easy. She had knocked on quite a few doors before she had finally been told that George lived in a remote cottage about half a mile from where she had parked. Five minutes later she found herself outside number 3, Pressington Row. This was an ancient looking stone built house with a slightly unkempt look. She wondered what had happened to numbers 1 and 2 since she couldn't see any other buildings along that fairly remote lane.

She knocked on the door and, after a while, it was opened by a big, heavyset man of about 30. She had expected a loud booming voice to match his stature but instead a deep but slightly squeaky voice with a broad Scottish accent greeted her.

'Aye? What?'

'Hi. My name is Marjorie Jones, and I am helping the police with enquiries into the disappearance of Jeremy Carter. He attends Basingrove Secondary school, but he disappeared last Thursday. I used to coach him on a Thursday night and was probably the last person to see him. His mother Valerie tells me that you often walk along the same path as Jeremy, and we wondered whether you had walked your dog along there last Thursday. Perhaps you saw or heard him as he walked home.'

'You're kidding right? You want to talk to me about a missing lad? Get lost.'

'If I could just come in?' said Marjorie.

'Listen love, if you came in here, you might not get out alive.' Marjorie laughed.

'You are joking, aren't you?'

'No, I'm not. Now clear off.'

'I'll be back later with my mate Joe.'

'Do that. I'll look forward to it.' And with that, the door slammed shut. Marjorie's heart was beating ten to the dozen. This wasn't what she had been expecting but she remembered what Geoffrey had said.

"A chap in his early thirties with a sly look and a terrifying grin."

'This didn't happen to Jane Marple,' she thought. 'Did George mean what he said? Should I come back with Joe later? I think I'd better ring and ask his advice first.'

Marjorie telephoned Joe at about 11 o'clock, and she had been pleased to find that he was back at home with Trish.

'Joe, could you come with me to visit George?'

'Yes, if you want. When?'

'Now if you could and wear your white muscle vest.'

'What?' said Joe. 'Why would you want me to wear my muscle vest? What's going on?'

'I'll tell you on the way. I'll come and pick you up.' Joe turned to Trish.

'Marjorie wants me to go with her to visit a man she thinks might have something to do with a missing lad. She said to wear my muscle vest.'

'What the hell?' said Trish. 'Sounds properly kinky to me. Are you sure that you should?'

'I'll listen to what she has to say in the car. Then I'll make up my mind.' Marjorie arrived about 10 minutes later and the door was opened, but it wasn't Joe that stood before her.

'Hi Trish,' said Marjorie in as cool a voice as she could manage.

'Hi Marjorie. What are you up to now?' Marjorie quickly told Trish about her first 3 interviews and told her that she wanted company while visiting George. After a few minutes thought, Trish invited her in.

'Are you sure that this is OK and will Joe be safe?' asked Trish.

'Yes, I'm sure that he will be fine,' replied Marjorie and both she and Joe, in his very tight, white vest, got into the car, despite Joe having said nothing at all! Once in the car Marjorie told Joe what George had said.

'Shouldn't we call the police?' asked Joe.

'No, it'll be fine. When he sees your muscles he'll know I mean business and let me in.'

'Oh dear. I might have muscles but that doesn't mean that I can fight off hefty men,' said Joe.

'You'll be fine, don't worry.'

They were soon knocking at the same door that she had found earlier that morning and, again, it had been opened by the man with the broad Scottish accent.

'I said I would be back,' said Marjorie. 'This is Joe.' George spent a while looking at Joe's handsome face and bulging muscles.

'*He* can *definitely* come in. *You* can if you behave.' For the second time that day Marjorie had been utterly astonished by what George had said. She should have been anxious at this point, but she seemed oblivious to the danger that she might be putting herself, and Joe, into. Once they had both stepped inside, they were led into a dark but very large living room. Seated on one of three settees were 2 quite burly men, both wearing black, and on the walls there were a number of paintings and photographs of very scantily clad men. Marjorie couldn't believe her eyes but began to speak anyway.

'Thank-you for agreeing to see us. This is an interesting room. Are the two men in black your friends and would they go out with you during your afternoon walk?' This was an absurd line of questioning, but Marjorie couldn't see that, and she was becoming hopeful now.

'These are mah boys,' had come the reply, in his broad Scots accent.

'Your boys?'

'Aye. They look after me, but no they don't come out with me when I have my walks, at least not both together.'

'What do you do for a living George?'

'I don't know what business it is of yours,' he replied, 'but I do a bit of this and that. Sometimes this, sometimes that, and sometimes the other.' He gazed at Marjorie while he said, 'the other' and squeaked a peculiar laugh. At this point reality was beginning to set in and Marjorie had finally realised that Joe would be no match for George's "boys".

Marjorie thought she had better get this over quickly and asked whether he had seen or heard anything that Thursday night. George said that he walked that way most days "for fun" and that he liked the atmosphere along there.

'So, you did walk along there last Thursday night?' pressed Marjorie.

'I did but I was busy later that day, so I had mah walk early. Frantz over there was with me, weren't you Frantz.'

'Aye,' came the reply.

'Frantz is from Yugoslavia aren't you Frantz?'

'Aye,' he said, again in a voice that almost shook the room. Marjorie didn't think that George's "boy" sounded at all Yugoslavian and doubted whether that was actually his name.

'And were you looking for boys?' said Joe suddenly, pointing to the pictures on the walls. Marjorie looked at him in astonishment and suddenly felt a bit panicked in case George took the question the wrong way. This input from Joe hadn't been expected and George looked oddly at Joe and stared at him for a little while.

'Ah know what you're getting at Joe,' said George. 'But look at the pictures Joe and look at mah boys. They are all men. Men like you, Joe. Men who are totally masculine and know what they are.' He gave Joe a look that scared Marjorie. 'Ah call them mah boys but I like men. Men over 21. I even like mah women on the older side,' and he looked over at Marjorie with that leer of his. 'Ah've seen you before haven't I Joe? You seem familiar somehow, doesn't he boys?'

and he gave Joe another threatening look.

'Doubt it,' said Joe.

'Then ah think we are done here now,' said George. He turned to Joe and said 'Call in any time Joe. It would be lovely to see you again, if you ken mah drift Joe.'

Marjorie thanked him and she and Joe left, quite quickly. Once through the front door they heard the three men in the house laugh heartily.

'Did you believe any of that?' asked Marjorie.

'No,' said Joe. 'But you thought he might be intimidated by me? He seemed to me to be teasing me, and you!'

'He did didn't he. Well you are gorgeously teas-able. I need a drink.'

'So do I,' said Joe.

'My place for a Scotch?' asked Marjorie.

'Haven't we just had one of them? My place for coffee I think!' replied Joe.

Chapter 10. Joe and George.

What Marjorie didn't know before calling Joe is that he and George had indeed met before, just the previous week in fact. That meeting had been very memorable for Joe, for all the wrong reasons: he hadn't expected that it was the same George that Marjorie had wanted him to visit and, had he known, he would have refused to go with her.

Joe had been a child of very wealthy parents and had enjoyed a lovely childhood. He had been given everything, *including* love and affection, so he had wanted for nothing. This hadn't turned him into a "spoiled" child though; he had been a happy and tolerant child who enjoyed life to the full, trying everything he could but not trying to use his wealth to gain popularity. He had done all the things that rich people seem obliged to do; he had been skiing in the Alps, holidayed in the Mediterranean and had worn the best clothes, although that was only when he had to wear fancy stuff; he was actually happiest in jeans and tee shirt. He was an only child which had actually helped his parents decide which school to send him to. They chose the local comprehensive for him over an independent school because they wanted him to have a wide range of friends from different backgrounds. This had worked very well, and most in the school admired him for his determination and achievement. He excelled in football and was an OK scholar, getting enough grades to go to university. He could have gone to Oxford or Cambridge because his parents had the means, but he chose to go to Warwick university to study mathematics and statistics. He thought that it might help his future employment prospects – it had certainly been the "in thing" to study at the time.

At university, as in life generally, being good looking can make you instantly popular. It's a sort of added value thing where you not only have good friends, but friends that are nice to look at too. Joe fitted into this category very well and, upon arrival at Warwick, was soon a member of the various groups that form at university. Obviously, he had played football as a carry on from his school days, but he had also been attracted into a drama group and a rowing group. By the end of his first year, he had been described as the best-looking man in his year, most muscled and the one most likely to become prime minister.

Though he didn't need any money, he actually got a job during his first long summer break, which he was surprised to find he rather enjoyed. So, at the start of his second year, he had been full of beans and ready to go.

Despite his popularity, Joe didn't have a steady girlfriend while at university, he just hadn't seemed to click with any of the young women he had met. He had many flirtations and flings, but they generally hadn't lasted long, and he usually parted from the women amicably. He did enjoy a drink though and he had spent increasing amounts of time in the pub during his second year. This also meant that he would more frequently have gone back to mates' digs for toast and a natter afterwards, and that is where he had first met cannabis. Unfortunately, as his second year had progressed, this had become an increasingly popular friend to Joe. Whilst under the influence his usual reserve would completely disappear, and he would sometimes have no idea what he had been up to while fuelled by the complex mixture of alcohol and drugs that he had eventually ended up using. Unfortunately, his drugs habit became progressively worse and, by the end of his second term, he had moved onto class A drugs such as cocaine.

Cocaine had made him feel euphoric, energetic, talkative, mentally alert, and hypersensitive to sight, sound, and touch. He had liked this. Unfortunately, it had made him rather sex mad too, which meant that he would sleep with anybody who offered themselves: he had increasingly regarded sex as an antidote to the misery he felt once he had come down from his wakened state while high. This even meant that he had been the target of a gay drug dealer who got more than just money for the drugs he had sold to Joe.

Fortunately, his parents weren't stupid, and they had instantly seen that all wasn't right with Joe when, at the end of the academic year, he had gone home for the long summer break. He was so agitated that they couldn't miss the signs – he would be in a foul mood then go up to his room, just to return looking more responsive and surer of himself. After much research and heartache his parents had sat him down one day and given him a choice. They could either lock him in his room with nothing but bread and water for 14 days as full "cold turkey", or they would pay for him to go to rehab. Joe hadn't been on drugs for long and he had realised that he was an addict but hadn't been able to think of a way out of that evil cycle of dependency. He was actually pleased that his parents had noticed and had given him a way out of this misery, and he chose rehab. His parents made the arrangements and, after a difficult two weeks, they had taken him to the clinic and hoped that they could return to pick up their son soon.

Unfortunately, it had taken a very long time for the treatment to work for Joe and he ended up having to postpone his return to university for a full year. The benefit of this was that it had given him the opportunity to alter his friendship groups, and for the effects of his dependency to be removed as much as possible.

He finished his degree with a straight pass, with which he was satisfied, he had met Trish in his final year, and this time he had felt a real bond with his girlfriend, so they had married a year after his graduation, and they settled into a nice house in Basingrove, where they had both found good jobs.

The problem was that, for a while at least, he needed an occasional "smoke" to stay off the harder drugs, and so he had found a dealer that supplied Basingrove residents. That man was called Jean-Paul Trafiquant, clearly a manufactured name so that dependents would know his job. Joe had bought the odd batch of cannabis from Jean-Paul but had stopped after being married for about eighteen months. Drugs were gone, Joe was clean, and he didn't see Jean-Paul ever again.

Nor could he because Jean-Paul was dead; he had crossed the wrong people when he had chosen not to pay for a delivery of what he considered to be substandard substances. His body was never found but George Dickinson had taken on his "delivery round". He had acquired Jean-Paul's lists of clients and suppliers and was doing very well out of it.

One day he reached Joe's name on his list, and he sought him out. His phone number was easy to find, and he had telephoned him one evening at home.

'Hi Joe, George here. I want to offer you some business.' Joe assumed that George had been directed to him by his company.

'Sure, what type of business are you in?'

'The sort of business you need.'

'What do you mean?'

'You are on my list,' said George.

'What list would that be?' asked Joe, still in business mode.

'Jean-Paul's list.' Ice began to run through Joe's veins. That wasn't a name he had wanted to hear again, ever. He tried to bluff it out.

'I don't know a Jean-Paul.'

'Oh yes you do, and I hope that you remember that Jean-Paul always had a little man with him during your "purchases" Joe because he was a photographer, and I have quite a few pictures here Joe. I know what you look like, I know where you live, where you work and I know you will want to resume your business with me, now that Jean-Paul is dead, won't you Joe. I'm looking at a very clear photo here where I can see you with the very tall, blonde Jean-Paul and you seem to be shaking hands, if you get my drift Joe.'

Joe was shaking with fear, and he had to sit down. There was no way he was getting back into drugs. He thought for a while and supposed that he could just buy them and not use them, but he couldn't afford that now. He didn't earn enough for that, and his parents were no longer in a position to help.

'No. I don't need them now.' At that point Trish appeared and asked whether he was OK. He had sounded upset. 'I'm fine,' said Joe. 'I've just learned that an ex-colleague has died. Don't worry.' Trish had said she was sorry before leaving him to it.

'Would that be the lovely Trish Joe?' said the voice on the line.

'Look,' said Joe, 'I am going to the gym in about 15 minutes. Meet me there in half an hour, in the car park at the back?'

'Certainly Joe.'

'How will I know you?' asked Joe.

'I will know you Joe,' came the reply, in George's broad Glaswegian accent.

Thirty minutes later, Joe was sitting on the low wall at the back of the gym. The gym had recently installed CCTV at the front and sides of the gym, but Joe knew there was not yet any at the back. He was nervous and angry. He had formed a sort of plan, but he didn't know what to expect, and he had realised that he might have to adapt it as the conversation went along.

'Hi Joe. Lovely to see you.' The voice made Joe jump. It was as if George had appeared from nowhere.

'Leave me alone. I'm clean now and I don't need any of this. If you don't leave me alone, I will report you to the police.' In response George said 'BOYS,' and the two men appeared, as if by magic.

'I might end up in prison you think Joe? Well, I might, but these two will still be available. They know where you live, and they might seek revenge for their loss of income.'

Joe had been disappointed with this response, but he had been expecting it.

'I won't buy any drugs. I would rather you kill me. Going back to drugs would kill me anyway and then you wouldn't get any money from me at all. Just get it over with, do it now.'

'Now don't be like that Joe. It wouldn't be you that mah boys would do harm to, and surely, we could work something out. What if I just sold you a little cocaine Joe. And you could maybe sweeten the deal a little?'

'No cocaine because that would definitely kill me. And what do you mean by my sweetening the deal?'

'You and your supplier enjoyed each other's company at university Joe. I have photos of that too.' Joe's heart sank.

'I only did that to get the drugs, and only when out of my head. No way will I sleep with you.' George produced a photo of Trish.

'What if I deliver those photos of you and Jean-Paul to your lovely wife?' He showed Joe more photos, photos which made Joe feel quite sick.

'Look, go away now. I will think about this, but I won't go back to drugs. What if I just offer the deal sweetener? You look fairly clean and healthy for a drug dealer. I have done it before. I'd prefer that over the drugs. I will find a place for us.' George looked Joe up and down.

'Well pretty boy, that's an interesting offer, and I must admit that I'm very tempted, so why not let me go away and think about it Joe. I will work out a deal and ring you tomorrow, at work I think Joe. Don't want to upset Trish do we. 11.30 sharp. Be there.'

George's "boys" had already vanished, and George was gone pretty quickly too. Joe watched a small white car driving away. He had been left shaking and his mind was racing. He didn't go into the gym that night, he spent the time on that wall, thinking about what to do next.

At exactly 11.30 am next morning Joe's phone rang in his office at work. He had made sure that his office would be empty, he had cancelled his appointments for around that time, and when he answered the phone, he heard George's voice.

'Good morning Joe, lovely to hear your voice again. I have given some thought to our little discussion of the other evening. You do remember that conversation don't you Joe?' Without waiting for a reply, he continued. 'I would indeed like to accept your offer of a deal sweetener Joe. I have thought about it quite a lot since we spoke and I think it could be beneficial for both of us, if you know what I mean. You do know what I mean don't you Joe?' Again, George didn't wait for a reply.

'As it happens, I am free on the afternoon of Thursday 3rd October for a few hours. We could carry out the transaction then could we not Joe?' Again, he didn't wait for a reply. 'I have one specification though Joe, I expect you to make at least one purchase from me, if you ken my drift. You'll be OK with that won't you Joe?' Again, no waiting for a reply. 'I will ring again at the same time next Wednesday morning, which is the day before our meeting. You can fill me in with the details that you have worked out then. That'll be fine won't its Joe?'

He rang off. Joe felt as though he had been in the front row of a Billy Connolly comedy routine but had only heard part of it. He actually laughed at the thought. 'This is serious though and I must get to work.' He picked up the receiver of his desk phone, which was still warm from his previous conversation. He dialled and the call was answered quickly.

'Can I speak to Cheryl please?' asked Joe.

'Cheryl speaking, who is that please?' came the reply.

'It's Joe, remember we were at university together and Trish and I bumped into you back in March? We went for coffee and chatted for ages?'

'Of course, hi Joe, how are you? Still gorgeous I suppose, and the lovely Trish, how is she? We really got on, didn't we? Was that really back in March, doesn't time fly?'

Joe wondered whether Cheryl was related to George! He finally got a word in and said 'Yes to all of those. And are you well and still with your husband whose name I can't remember?'

'Yes, to both of those Joe. So why are you ringing me out

of the blue like this, and while we are both at work, you are still at work aren't you Joe?'

'Yes, at work but I wanted to ring you without Trish hearing.'

'Are you chatting me up Joe?'

'No, if I weren't married I would, believe me, but I wondered whether the offer of your old flat was still on? You said we could borrow it if we were up in town for a party or something and didn't want to drive back.'

'Course it is Joe. You aren't cheating on Trish, are you?' she said laughing.

'No, of course not,' said Joe but his stomach did turn a bit. 'On Thursday 3rd we are going up to a preview of the grand opening of our new office block. It's up there near to your flat, and we'd both like to drink because the sparkling wine will be free. Since it's daytime we don't want to get on a bus while we are drunk, so we wondered whether we could just bed down at your place? You've seen our new office block haven't you, right next to your flat.'

'Yes, we've seen it. My neighbours will be pleased when it's finished to be honest because they are making so much dust and noise. Certainly you can stay there. The flat's going up for sale soon though, so look after it.'

'We sure will,' said Joe, suddenly feeling a bit brighter. 'Can I collect the keys on Wednesday afternoon and return them on Friday? I might find a spare bottle of bubbly to leave behind.'

'Of course you can. Stay for some coffee too. It'll be lovely to catch up.' Once the goodbyes had been said, and the phones had been put down, Joe began planning *exactly* what he would say to George Dickinson.

Chapter 11. The recording.

That evening Joe had got home to find that Trish hadn't yet returned from work. 'Handy!' he thought and pulled down the loft ladder that led to their large attic space. He knew just where that video camera was. He hadn't used it yet because he and Trish didn't own a video recorder, but there was that Betamax professional machine at work that would record for over 3 hours. The camera had a microphone on the front which would be very handy, then there was the long cable. 'Excellent,' he thought as he packed the camera back up in its box and hid it in the boot of the car. He had just finished that when Trish returned in her Mini.

Joe went to see Cheryl at 12.30 pm on Wednesday 2nd October, the day before Jez was murdered. He had asked at reception for Cheryl and was shown into her office and he was a little concerned because Cheryl looked busy. But she stopped work when she spotted Joe and they had enjoyed a quick hug and the usual how are you type stuff before Joe asked her to come out for lunch. He said that it was his treat for the loan of her flat.

They laughed a lot during lunch – looking back at university life through rose coloured glasses had been a tonic for both of them. At 1.45 though Cheryl said that she really had to be back at work, so she handed over the keys, they made their goodbyes, and both returned to work. Actually, though Joe *had* headed in the direction of work, he had then turned off and headed for Cheryl's flat. Her directions had been really clear, and the journey had only taken him 10 minutes. Joe parked and went straight up a slightly dingy set of stairs to the flat, which turned out to be a studio flat – one big sitting room containing a bed, the kitchen area and a large settee. The only additional room was a shower room with a toilet.

After a look round, and studying all the options, he set to work. The flat had hot air heating with vents about a third of the way up the wall. He turned on the heating and found it to be a bit noisy. It also seemed to blow air all the time it was on, so that it heated the air until the room thermostat said it was hot enough, then the fan continued to circulate air until the room chilled, and then the heating came back on again. He was delighted by this because it created a constant background sound which would mask any noise from the video recorder. Next to the door there was a locked cupboard that had a bookcase sitting on top. Both were quite hideous but that didn't matter, so he went back to his car and came back up with the camera and recording equipment. He did this in two stages; the Betamax machine was really heavy so that came up first, the camera and some tools had to come next.

After a short rest he began his preparations. These had

taken all afternoon but by the time he had finished there was nothing to see. The video camera sat neatly at an angle with books and ornaments either side. If you were looking for it, you might just have seen it, but Joe thought George would be too busy to notice. He had moved the furniture around so that if George's "boys" came with him they would have to look away from the camera to keep an eye on George and Joe. The Betamax machine was locked in the cupboard (which Joe had had to alter slightly with a file and a small saw so that no wires could be seen) and was effectively invisible.

He carried out a dry run by laying on the bed and doing some writhing about. The recording system worked like a dream. He even chatted to himself to see whether the sound could be heard. He was delighted by the results. After hiding the tools in a drawer, he left the flat and returned to work.

George had telephoned Joe exactly as promised on Wednesday morning and Joe was shaking while he told him where to find Cheryl's flat. He told George that he had decided to make a small purchase during their meeting, and they could decide the size of that after they had finished "Joe's sweetener", depending on how satisfied George had been with that. George told Joe that he was sure that his contribution would be most stimulating, and that the purchase could be quite a small one. Again, Joe had the distinct feeling that he was listening to a sketch by Billy Connolly. Part of it sounded funny, and he realised that Billy Connolly could read out a set of directions and it would sound funny, but today it didn't manage to raise a smile from Joe.

George had said that he would meet him outside Joe's new office block at 3.10pm on Thursday. They would greet each other like clients, with a warm handshake and a hearty hello.

George was punctual, and they entered Cheryl's flat at about 3.15pm that afternoon. Joe explained to George that he would need to be quite drunk before anything could happen because he wasn't gay, not even bisexual, and that he had only engaged in the practice with his previous suppliers because it was the only way that they would give him his drugs. Joe had added that he was pretty off his head when those transactions had taken place and that he would need to be the same today. What he hadn't told George was that he had already had 10 mg of a sedative drug that afternoon, just to relax him enough to be there at all.

Joe and George sat on chairs facing each other and Joe started to talk about his university days. Though he was now 30 those days had seemed like yesterday. He told him about his wealthy parents who made his life so comfortable. He explained how they had paid for the rehab and that he'd been clean since, barring the cannabis he had got from Jean-Paul. He even explained how his parents' wealth had virtually disappeared due to his dad's ill health and that was why he could no longer afford to buy drugs, even if he wanted them.

George sat patiently waiting through this chatter and they drank some of the whisky that Joe had brought, Joe much more than George. Eventually George declared that it was time for action, and they undressed. Joe said that he needed to pee first, so he went into the shower come toilet where he had hidden the remote-control switch. This was on a long cable and Joe was pleased that the fashion of the day was to carpet these types of room. The cable was thin, and it was easily hidden under the carpet, even the inline switch couldn't be seen. He activated the recorder and rejoined George.

By about 6pm George had become bored with Joe. Joe seemed legless with whisky by then anyway, and totally incapable of even standing up. George suggested that since he had brought some cannabis and cocaine that Joe should buy some. He could have a special price on account of the enjoyable evening. Joe bought some cannabis and they sat for a while before getting dressed. George had very kindly stayed with Joe to make sure that he was OK and he and his boys, who had sat and watched the whole thing, departed at about 8pm.

After they had left, Joe sat for about 30 minutes while the sedatives and alcohol began to wear off. He lit a fire and burnt the cannabis, hoping that it wouldn't affect the birds too much. He had to shower and have coffee and some food first but, by 10.30pm he was taking down the camera and wires, and he finished by removing the video cassette from the machine. They were soon all packed away in his car boot, which he locked. He then locked the flat and eventually caught the late bus home.

He had George, and his boys, on video tape. He smiled and felt the tension drain away. When he got home, he found Trish already in bed. Through a drunken haze he told her all about the office party he had been to and how drunk he had become. She had laughed at him, watching his many attempts to get into bed, where he instantly fell asleep. He slept very very soundly indeed that night. On Friday morning though, when he woke, he had felt very poorly, spent much of the morning in the bathroom and didn't make it into work until late afternoon.

Chapter 12. The announcements.

The desk sergeant telephoned the head at Basingrove school on Tuesday morning and asked whether some officers might hold an assembly at the school on the morning of Wednesday 9th. He advised the head that there was bad news for the school, and he carefully told her that Jez had been found dead, and that they were treating his death as suspicious. It's a good thing that she had been sitting down because she took that news rather badly.

'Oh dear, how extraordinarily sad. A young man, just becoming old enough to venture out into the world on his own, to be so cruelly cut down like that, it doesn't bear thinking about.'

'Indeed,' said the sergeant.

'Of course, you must do what is necessary. I must admit that I would find it terribly difficult to make those announcements myself because I should be all over the place, I think. May I tell my staff beforehand sergeant?'

'Yes, the inspector has already suggested that you do that, but not until just before the assembly. We don't want his death made public until tomorrow.'

'Of course, Sergeant. I will hold a special staff meeting before the assembly. I must make you aware though that our assembly hall cannot hold the whole school at once. We normally hold assemblies in year groups. Might I suggest that we tell years one and two together in a first group, then repeat with the second group being third and fourth years and hold a final assembly for fifth year and sixth formers? Would that be acceptable to you sergeant?'

'I will need to check with the inspector first madam. He isn't available right now so can I suggest that if you haven't heard from me by 6pm today that the inspector is happy with your proposal?'

'Of course, sergeant. This is all so terrible. Do any of his friends know already, perhaps in the course of your enquiries? His poor mother......'

'Jeremy Carter was taking coaching from a Mrs Jones. Since she was the last person to see him before he met his murderer, she, and her daughter, have been told, as will be his close friend John. He is to be interviewed tonight so he will be told then. They have all, or will all, be asked not to make any of this public until we say so. I must ask the same of you as well please.'

'Of course, sergeant.'

'The inspector will arrive at your school at about 8am in the morning to go through the arrangements, if that is fine with you.'

'Certainly. Oh dear. I wish you the best of luck with your investigations. I must now work out how to tell my staff. Goodbye sergeant.' The sergeant put down the receiver. He would be accompanying inspector Roberts tomorrow and he wasn't looking forward to the assembly either.

At "O" level, Jez's friend John had done OK at school, but not as well as his parents would have liked, so his father had had words with him at the start of sixth form.

'I do try to work at school dad, but there are too many distractions for me to concentrate.'

'You mean that there are too many girls fussing around you at school!' John didn't reply.

'Either way John, you must catch up at home, so I have organised some extra history tuition for you. I think that you are getting lazy, and so I have been through the Yellow Pages and found a tutor for you.' John hadn't been very keen on that, but he said he would give it a try. Miss Fielding had been duly appointed and she had first arrived a week into term with a proposal for two visits a week. The family agreed, the tuition began, and they were given John's dad's study in which to work.

What his dad hadn't known was that John knew Miss Fielding. She was head of history at his school, and was the envy of many of the girls, and the fantasy of many of the lads there. She was about 28 with long, shiny mousey hair that framed her face perfectly. She had perfect white teeth and a very attractive smile. She applied very little make up and wore casual clothing, usually a mid-length skirt and a striped rugby top which emphasised her ample bosom, and the lads would sit wondering about her bra size. They had even organised a bet to see who could get nearest to the actual size. One day they would find out (they hoped) and winnings would have to be paid out.

John wasn't taught by Miss Fielding, so he hadn't seen

much of her at school, but he had placed bets on her bra size. John's target since turning 16 was to sleep with as many women as possible before he settled down with just one. He loved sex and it was easy for interested girls to get him to bed. He had certainly never made the first move, but he hadn't considered that women like miss Fielding would have had him on their radar.

He did have a thing for older older women though, which is why he had been so quick to suggest Marjorie might have a thing for Jez. He was actually a bit jealous, and he had fantasised about Mrs. Jones, even though he hadn't met her. He was now fantasising massively about Miss Fielding, and the concentration on work that his dad had wanted wasn't really happening at first. She eventually turned out to be very strict and she had worked him very hard, so after a while he stopped seeing her as a fantasy and more of a slave driver.

One evening though she was wearing a flimsy blouse, and he just couldn't stop staring. He couldn't help it; he had tried not to, but she was just like a magnet for his eyes. Miss Fielding noticed and glared at him. He really couldn't help it though, and he could actually see the very bra that they had all made bets on.

Miss Fielding had arrived, as she usually did on a Tuesday, for John's tuition, but at this point neither John nor Miss Fielding had known anything about the impending announcement of Jeremy's death, so to them it was just another evening of tuition. His parents had gone to the theatre that night and left John in charge of the house.

'Remember your tuition is tonight,' his mum had said as they left. John groaned, but that night Miss Fielding arrived in a similarly flimsy blouse.

'My parents are out tonight,' said John. 'Can you let me off tuition tonight?'

'No,' said Miss Fielding and took his hand and lead him to his dad's study.

'Does she know what a turn on this is?' thought John. Miss Fielding asked if she could use the bathroom while John got his books and other paraphernalia ready. John agreed and sat down to work. When she returned though John thought she looked different somehow. As they began working, she kept leaning forward and John's eyes were drawn down as well as forward. She was no longer wearing a bra! He was sure she had one on when she arrived, he always checked. She must have taken it off in the bathroom. He found himself staring. He couldn't concentrate on anything else.

'John,' said Miss Fielding having noticed his stare. 'That's really not acceptable. We must get *something* done before your parents get back. When *do* you expect them to return?'

'In about 2 hours,' said John.

'Really?' said Miss Fielding. 'My husband is away at the moment, so we are currently both alone.' John's heart had started to race.

'What had she just said? Her husband is away. Why would she tell me that? Was she getting flirty? She had taken off her bra – she knew I would notice!'

The answer soon became obvious when she got up, moved to John's side of the desk, and sat next to him.

'The girls at school tell me you like older ladies John.'

'Do they?' he said, almost choking over the words. She put her hand on his knee.

'Hell,' thought John, but did the same to her.

'You wouldn't be trying to get me to bed, would you?' he said, expecting her to slap him about the head, deny it and demand that he start work.

'I have heard stories about you from the girls at school,' she said. 'I have often wondered whether they are true.' John's heart had begun to race, and he put his hand around her neck and pulled her gently towards him. He had been delighted when he felt no resistance, and they kissed for a while.

'So, what do the girls at school say about me then miss?'

'That's for us to know and for you to wonder.'

'I need to go to the bathroom. I need to pee,' he said, after considering that answer for a while.

'Don't be long,' she replied.

Once in the bathroom he locked the door and, after a quick wash, he couldn't help but notice that her bra was on the floor.

'The size!' he thought. 'My chance to win that money.' He picked it up and he studied it carefully, but then he was bitterly disappointed. 'Damn. Why don't they put the size on women's bras?' He put the bra back where he had found it and returned to Miss Fielding feeling unusually apprehensive. Was she leading him on, just to say no? Then he thought about her husband, who might very well kill him.

'Oh well, here goes.'

'Where's your room?' asked Miss Fielding.

'Over there.' John pointed across the landing.

'Take your clothes off in here,' she said, 'I want to check you out first, see whether what the girls have told me is true.'

'OK,' thought John. 'I wonder what the hell goes on in sixth form history lessons?'

'I will if you will,' he said aloud.

'Certainly,' she replied. They spent a while eyeing each other up and neither seemed disappointed.

'You have a double bed,' she said as they entered his room, both completely naked. John couldn't believe his luck, him and Miss Fielding! Whilst enjoying their first embrace John had thought about what was happening. Could he tell his mates, should he even tell them? He decided not to. They wouldn't believe him anyway. And then he forgot about any of that, at least for a while, but it was while they were in the throes of passion that the police arrived. There was a loud knock at the door.

'Shit,' said John. The knock had been persistent, so John got out of bed and looked through the curtains. He saw that it was the police.

'You'd better answer the door,' said Miss Fielding.

'My clothes are in Dad's study! Sodding hell.' He quickly found some trousers to put on before running downstairs to open the door, rather out of breath.

'May we come in?' asked the inspector.

'Sure,' said John and he led them into the living room. The inspector couldn't help noticing the sweat running down John's chest.

'You look rather warm,' said the inspector. 'Are we disturbing you?'

'No. Just been on my exercise bike upstairs.'

'Ah,' smiled the inspector.

John was surprised when the inspector had insisted that they both went somewhere to sit down. He suggested the dining room.

'We are here about Jeremy Carter.'

'Oh good.' John had assumed that they had come to tell him that they had found him. He had been wondering where Jez could have got to.

'There will be another special assembly at your school tomorrow,' said the inspector. 'I am very sorry to tell you that Jeremy has been found, but I'm afraid to also have to tell you that he is dead.' John went as white as a sheet. He thought he was going to faint, and he put his head on the table in front of him.

'Dead?' he eventually asked, just to make sure he had heard correctly.

'I'm very sorry, but that is indeed the case. As his best friend we thought we ought to tell you before we announce his death in an assembly tomorrow.' He paused for a while. 'Are you OK?'

'Yes, I will be in a minute, just shocked. Does his mum know? How did he die? Where did he die? Did he suffer?'

The inspector interrupted his questioning.

'His mother does know but I can't answer any of your other questions yet because we really don't know. Please don't tell anybody else about this. We want to tell the whole school together tomorrow.' John looked stunned; he really had thought that Jez had stayed out somewhere or, at worst, that he might have been abducted or something. It really hadn't occurred to him that he might be dead.

'Will you be OK? Would you like Sergeant Windsor to stay with you a while?' Ordinarily John would have loved the strikingly beautiful Sergeant Windsor to stay all night, but this time he said no. He said that he would be fine, but he had some thinking to do.

As he was was about to leave the inspector turned to John and told him that if anything came to him about Jez's behaviour that day, or if he thought of anything else at all, he was to contact them immediately. He also told John that if whoever was upstairs with him had heard any of the conversation, he was to swear them to secrecy. John actually blushed, rare for him, but he said that he would do just that.

Once the police had gone Miss Fielding came into the living room. John was just sitting, staring into space. She was now fully clothed, including the bra.

'Are you OK?' she said. 'I am so sorry to hear about Jeremy.'

'Thanks,' said John.

'I will stay a while with you if you want, or I can go if you'd prefer.'

'Stay a while please,' said John.

'I'll make you some something to drink,' was her response.

While they drank coffee John told Miss fielding a bit about Jez, how they had been best friends for years, almost their entire life. Then he asked her whether she had known him. Miss Fielding had replied that she hadn't taught Jez, but she had seen him around the school, sometimes with John.

'Nice looking boy,' she said.

'Jez didn't think he was good looking,' said John ruefully. 'Even I could see there was something about him that women would like. Perhaps his problem was that he was comparing himself to me.' Miss Fielding looked at him. He looked devastated about Jez. His comment hadn't been because he was arrogant, he had genuinely thought it be true and perhaps it was. John was gorgeous, and perhaps Jez set had his sights too high because of his friendship with the best-looking lad in the school. Jez hadn't realised how handsome he was becoming. She felt desperately sad for both of them.

'What happened earlier in your bedroom,' she said as she was leaving, it didn't happen did it?'

'No miss,' said John. 'After the way it was cut short, I'm sure that I couldn't finish it now anyway.'

'Yes,' is all she said.

John told his parents about the police visit when they got home that night, and they were shocked and saddened. They asked the usual questions, which John answered, and he then went on to tell them that the police would be announcing Jez's death at school the next day. He told them that he didn't think he could face that, and they accepted that he should take the morning off. John was glad that they had agreed to that because he knew that he would need time to adjust to his new situation.

For a while he sat thinking about his friendship with Jez, the daft things they had done together, the fairly constant teasing Jez had got from him, those condoms in his haversack etc. when he had suddenly wondered how Mrs. Jones was taking the news. He even considered the notion that perhaps she really had fancied Jez, and that she had smothered the little fellow with her voluptuous body.

Seemingly popular now, John had a visit from another woman late that same night. Earlier that day Marjorie had realised that she hadn't interviewed any of Jez's friends in the course of her enquiries. She remembered that Jez had a friend called John, and Paula had said he sometimes played badminton against Jez, so she was able to get his address from the club records. Armed with this information she turned up at John's house about thirty minutes after his parents had returned from the theatre.

She knocked at the door of their house and explained to John's dad why she was there, giving her "I am helping the police with their enquiries" routine. Mr. Cummings said that John had been interviewed by the police more than once, and he felt that he had now had enough for one day. John had just had some devastating news and he was now missing his mate and so he should be left alone.

'That's alright dad,' said John appearing suddenly. 'I *would* like to speak to Mrs. Jones. Jez told me a lot about her.' Eventually his dad agreed, and they were lead through into the study.

'Hi Mrs Jones. Jez talked about you a lot and it's nice to finally meet you, but I have just been told he's dead.' John had to pause at this point. He was expecting her to gush with sympathy, but he was disappointed.

'We know,' said Mrs Jones. 'I just wanted to know whether you had remembered anything at all that might help us find his killer.' She took his hand. It was warm and clammy, and he was taken back to when he had teased Jez so mercilessly. This was a slightly creepy woman with "come on eyes" and John suddenly felt that he had done his friend an enormous wrong with his tormenting, and now the suggestion that Jez should accede to any advances she might have made to him were so totally wrong that he just pulled his hand from hers and stood up.

'No there's nothing, and I'm really tired and pretty upset too, so if you don't mind, I'd like you to go now.' Marjorie looked rather stunned but said 'OK' and rose to leave. John had led her to the front door, and they had said their farewells, when his mother appeared.

'That was quick!' said his mum.

'That was Jez's badminton coach and she's nosing around about Jez's death.' He had to pause again. 'I don't know why she came to look me up because I've told them all I know.'

'You look done in John. You'd best get to bed.'

'Yes, I think I will go up. Goodnight mum.'

Sleep didn't come easily to John. He just couldn't cope with the news that had arrived that night. Jez had always been there, all of his life they had been together, and in many ways, he had been like a brother to him.

'What had happened to him and why, who had killed him and why did he find Mrs. Jones so creepy?'

He was beginning to think that he would never recover from his loss, and he decided that if they did find Jez's killer, he would stand first in line to shoot him. He finally managed to fall into a very restless sleep at about 3 am.

Chapter 13. School assembly.

The inspector turned up at the school at exactly 8am and the time for the very sad assembly was drawing near. The head had hastily arranged the pre-assembly staff meeting but she was not looking forward to it at all. The staff themselves had been surprised to hear about an unexpected staff meeting, and an assembly, but a few had already worked out what it might be about. Miss von Hofmann was particularly anxious because she had missed the little floppy haired lad who kept getting the giggles in her lessons. She hoped that it wasn't the terrible news that she feared most. The staff meeting began at 8.35am.

'I am sure that you will be wondering why we are having this extra staff meeting, but I imagine that many of you have realised that it is about the missing boy Jeremy Carter.' The head had to pause for a moment after the mention of his name.

'It is with great sadness, and with great difficulty, that I have to announce to you that Jeremy's *body* was found by the police last Friday night.'

There was a gasp from the staff and the head had to pause again to recover her composure. The staff then sat in absolute silence. His form tutor had already been told about the news in a private meeting before the staff were to be told, but even she was visibly upset by the announcement. There were a few questions from some of the staff before the meeting had to come to a close:

'How will the students be told?' asked his geography teacher. This gave the head the opportunity to outline the planned arrangements for the assemblies.

'Will there be a book of condolence?' asked another, to which the reply was yes. The head then suggested that a photograph be extracted from last year's fifth form group photograph and blown up to stand, with a candle, next to the book, which would be placed in the foyer. Students and staff would be able to sign it during breaks and lunchtimes.

'Does the whole school need to be told about this in an assembly?' asked Miss von Hofmann. She had recovered her composure now and had realised that really it was only fifth and sixth form students that needed to be told formally. If the police were making the announcement, she assumed that it was to jog students' memories of last Thursday and hopefully produce new leads. 'Surely just one assembly of fifth and sixth form will be enough? Younger members of the school will soon hear about it from friends and family, and they will see the book of condolence.'

'I think that is very wise,' agreed the head. 'I will put it to the inspector who is in my office now. Please wait while I check with him.'

She wasn't gone long. He agreed that only fifth and sixth form needed to be in the assembly, which was now set for 9am, no staff needed to be present and only fifth and sixth form students need attend. The day would be absolutely normal for the rest of the school, or at least as normal as it could be under the circumstances.

There was absolute silence as detective inspector Roberts entered the assembly hall. Form tutors had already told students that the assembly was about a very serious matter, and a few had already worked out what it was about. Inspector Roberts stood on the stage until the last few youngsters had finished entering the assembly hall. He was flanked by two uniformed officers, Sergeants Bulmer and Windsor. None of the teaching staff were there, not even the head, but Mister Johnson, the deputy head, was standing at the door making sure that order was being maintained. Once the last students had entered, he closed the doors and he watched from outside, waiting for a sign that the officers had finished.

Sergeant Bulmer's booming voice rang out, demanding quiet from the assembled young people, even though they had been unusually quiet anyway, and Inspector Roberts began. He announced his name and rank and introduced his fellow officers, together with their rank. A wolf whistle was heard as sergeant Windsor was introduced. She was used to this and her glare, alongside that of sergeant Bulmer, prevented any more attempting a second try.

'I want all of you to cast your minds back to last Thursday,' began the inspector. 'A member of this school called Jeremy Carter attended school as normal. He was a quiet young man, and we believe that he didn't speak to many others during the day, but he was present in all of his lessons, and everything seemed quite normal. After school we believe that he went on his own, to the university badminton club where he took part in some coaching. He left there at around 4.30pm to go home, but he never got there. He wasn't seen on Friday either, or a thorough police search was carried out. He was found late on Friday night but, unfortunately, he wasn't found alive.' He paused while this sank in. 'Some of you here knew Jeremy, Jez I believe he was known as, so you will be shocked and saddened by that news.' He paused again and murmurs went around, some blowing of noses was heard but the inspector continued.

'We believe that there were suspicious circumstances surrounding that death. We would like anybody that saw Jez that day to come forward and talk to my officers. Anything, no matter how trivial it might seem may be important, so rack your brains. If you spoke to him, we want to know what was said. If you saw him after school, or after coaching, we want to know where. Sergeants Bulmer and Windsor will return here during lunchtime today. The headteacher has agreed that they may sit in the entrance hall where I understand a book of condolence will be opened today. The only way we will be able to work out exactly what happened to Jez will be to know precisely what he did that day, who he met and where he went.' He paused again and gave a signal to Mr. Johnson who came into the hall and stood next to the inspector.

'I am sure that you are as shocked as we are to hear this news. We knew that Jez was missing, but we all hoped that he would be found and returned to us in due course. This is not the outcome we wanted, and we are as saddened as you must be, but I think you will all agree that we must find out what happened to Jeremy, and that if anybody is guilty of doing him harm then that person must be brought to justice. Please give the police all the help you can. As the inspector said, we are opening a book of condolence today, it will be in the entrance hall and lunchtime will be extended by 15 minutes for the rest of this week. We will hold a minute's silence now to remember Jez.'

The silence was perfect. Not a cough, not a splutter or a whisper, nothing. At the end the deputy head asked students to 'lead off from the back.' It was an unusually quiet exit for an assembly.

That afternoon Miss von Hofmann had to teach the group that would have included Jez. It was very difficult – she kept looking at the space where Jez would have sat, the chair now empty. She wondered whether she should say something about Jez, but she couldn't, it would just be too upsetting. From that moment nobody from that group sat in that seat and Miss Hoffman decided to not speak in German in maths lessons anymore, and even if she did, she wouldn't mime the meaning with actions. In fact, it was a long time before she became herself again and made such entertainment in any of her lessons, though she did once forget herself in Jez's group's lesson. She suddenly realised what she was doing and stopped, tears in her eyes.

'It's alright miss,' one of the girls had said. 'We understand.'

Chapter 14. A review of the police operation.

The police officer that had found Jez's body on that Friday night was called Tom Hollingsworth. It was on October 4th 1985, and he would remember that date for a long time. Finding a dead body is never pleasant but, when it is the body of one so young, it can seem devastating. Tom had only been with the force for eight months and Basingrove station was his first posting. Detective inspector Roberts had offered him a day's leave after he had found Jez's body, but Tom wanted to help with the enquiries that would certainly now proceed. The inspector had asked to see him on Saturday afternoon.

'Tell me, Tom, exactly what did you find during your search of the woodland last night, and how you had found it? I realise that it was dark, and all you had was your torch, but be as precise as possible.'

'Well sir, the two of us had been asked to scan the whole area between the badminton club and the end of the path leading to Jez's house. We split up and I got the bit where the path splits into two. Officer Bradley searched the open path while I went into the woods. I thought it probably wasn't safe for a WPC to go into the woods by herself, so she stayed out in the open. To be honest sir, I wasn't keen on going in by myself either, but we are short staffed, and it was Friday night.' Tom paused for a while.

'Go on Tom.'

'Well sir, I have to admit that in the dark it was a very spooky place, owls were hooting, there was a woodpecker pecking and there was the odd movement in the trees. I tried to keep my wits about me, and I directed the torch beam everywhere while walking slowly. I kept looking back too, just in case somebody else was in there. It's probably because I was so terrified that I made sure the torchlight missed nothing. I didn't want to be pounced on by a creature or a mad bird, or even a pervert of some kind. It wasn't long though before I came to a sort of clearing with a patch of grass. The grass was flattened down and clearly someone or something had been lying on it, so I felt a bit wary. I couldn't imagine a young lad walking down there so I thought I'd have a quick scout around then be out. Thing is though sir, my torch light reflected off something white. I had no idea what it was, so I thought I'd better stand still a moment in case it was coming towards me. When I realised it wasn't going anywhere, I approached it and found the lad curled up under some bushes. It looked like he had vomited and fallen into the shrubbery next to the little path that runs through there. The vomit was nearer to the mound than the body, so perhaps he had been sitting there and felt ill. His haversack was near him but not right next to him, as though he had thrown it away or lost it in a struggle. I yelled *here* and WPC Bradley came running with her torch. She had radioed in while running to find me, so it wasn't long before the rest of the team arrived and did the photos and stuff.'

'Did you touch anything?'

'No sir, not really. I did feel his wrist but couldn't find a pulse. I checked his neck but felt nothing there either. I radioed the station and asked them to call an ambulance in case he could be resuscitated because he was still warm. They arrived before our team and they did what they could for him, but they pronounced him dead.

'Can you tell me anything else about the body?' asked the inspector.

'Not really sir. I was a bit cut up to be honest because it's the first dead body I have found, and with it being dark and all the noises....' There was another pause.

'Alright Tom, I think that will do for now. Go home and get some rest.' After he had thanked the inspector, he went off home. Tom hadn't been a great deal older than Jez when he had found the body, and the inspector had felt sorry for him, but he now needed to see WPC Bradley and he went off in search of her. Unfortunately, she wasn't on shift that day so he would have to wait until tomorrow to speak to her. It was time for him to go home now and, since he had to wait for the pathology report anyway, he had decided that nothing more could be done that day, and he left too.

Despite it's being a Sunday, the inspector went into work for a couple of hours the next day and he sent for WPC Bradley. 'The sooner the better,' he had thought, and he didn't mind the overtime. She had been expecting the call because Tom had alerted her already.

'Come in please WPC Bradley and thank-you for your time. I have spoken to Tom about your search on Friday night and I now would like your version of that evening.

Are you able tell me exactly what Tom found along that path?'

'Yes Sir. Tom had entered the woods at the badminton club end of the path, and I left him there while I continued searching the open path. I was becoming despondent because I hadn't found anything at all but then I heard Tom shout *here*, and I made my way to find him. I was near the exit of the woods by then and I entered them from that end. I had started radioing the station to ask for backup before I reached the woods' entrance, so in I went while on the radio. The body must also have been nearer to the exit than the entrance because I was soon with Tom. There Tom was, just standing looking at the body.' She paused and looked at the inspector.

'Go on please.'

'Tom was looking into some bushes. In there was a young man dressed in a white tee shirt and shorts. He looked as though he had been playing tennis, or some other sport, and somehow, he had ended up falling into those bushes. He couldn't have played anything in there so he must have been taking a short cut home or similar. He must have been sick because there was some vomit nearby and the smell was awful. His body was curled up, as though he was trying to get more comfortable. He wasn't tangled up though. If he'd fallen, he would have struggled to get out, wouldn't he? He'd be all scratched and his kit would be torn, but it wasn't. It was as if he had been thrown in there while already unconscious. He wasn't very big so it wouldn't need much strength to do that. We didn't touch anything, but Tom said he had felt his wrist and neck for a pulse but felt nothing. I checked too but there really was nothing. I felt his chest to see if it was moving. He was still warm sir, warm as you and me now. He must have just died. If we had found him sooner...' and she tailed off again. The inspector gave her a moment to recover.

'Where was his haversack?' WPC Bradley thought for a moment.

'I don't remember sir. I didn't see it. It certainly wasn't next to him, or I would have done. Did Tom see it?

'Yes,' replied the inspector, 'and we do have it. It was picked up by the photographer after she had taken the photos. It was quite a few feet from the body which is probably why you didn't see it. I just wanted to check that you hadn't moved it or anything like that.'

'But,' said the WPC, 'surely, he would have been wearing it if he had just fallen into the shrubbery, wouldn't he? It would have been on his back if he hadn't taken it off, so he must have been up to something in there. Maybe somebody was with him. Was his haversack open when you found it sir?'

'Partially,' said the inspector. 'One clasp was undone. It's not clear whether something had been taken from it or whether he had just left it like that.'

'He looked as though he had died in some agony sir. His face was set in a grimace. His hair looked smooth though, as though there hadn't been much of a struggle. He was so young....,' and she tailed off again.

'I think that's enough for now Bradley,' said the inspector. 'Thanks for your time, I may need to see you and Tom again though.'

As she was leaving, WPC Bradley stopped and said 'Do you think there was foul play sir? Was he murdered?'

'I don't know. I am waiting for the pathologist's report. We might know more then, but I don't expect that report until Monday or Tuesday.'

'Thanks sir.'

'So where do we go from here?' thought the inspector. 'A young man walks home along a well-used path every night for years. Then one evening he doesn't return home. He has taken a detour into the woods that night and met with his death. The first questions seemed to be these:

'Why did he go through the woods that night instead of following the open path? '

'Was he alone?'

'Why had he been sick. Was it drug related?'

'Why was his partially open haversack about 10 feet from the body and not with him in the hedge?'

Once he had received the results from pathology, he might be better able to answer some of these questions. Since he wouldn't get those results until tomorrow or Tuesday, there was nothing more he could do that day, so he went home in time to find the roast in the oven, and his wife and daughter playing badminton in the garden. That made his stomach turn. He couldn't work out why.

'Jez had played badminton that night, hadn't he? There must be a link between his obsession with badminton and his death, maybe he had met a fellow player along the route, maybe....' The inspector's thoughts trailed off because he had finally realised that he must stop thinking and start afresh tomorrow. His own family were the most important thing to him now on this Sunday; time spent with them was becoming increasingly rare.

The pathology results didn't arrive until late on Monday night, but they had made for very interesting reading indeed. Earlier that day though, wanting to get things moving, the inspector had arranged for two officers to tour the area around Jez's route home, and around the badminton club. One of those officers was Tom Hollingsworth, the young constable that had found Jez's body, the other being PC Marley. Marley had seen nothing but a few elderly folks walking their dogs, or out with grandchildren, so he had quickly gone back to the station, but PC Hollingsworth had stayed for a while longer and had come across Valerie Carter sitting with her flask of tea and some biscuits. She was sitting near to her side of the path, near to where Jez had been found. She had brought a little picnic chair and was well wrapped up from the chill that had arrived over the weekend. They chatted.

'Good morning. You look comfortable there. Do you often sit here with your flask of tea?'

'No,' replied Valerie and she explained who she was and what she was doing.

'I am very sorry for your loss,' replied the PC, not sure exactly what to say.

'I just needed to take in the space Jez had trodden so many times when he was going to school. I'm thinking of going away for a while, so I just need this time in his space.' She did not mention that she was gathering names for

Marjorie.

'That is probably a good idea Mrs. Carter,' said the PC. He went on to explain that it was he who had found Jez on Friday night and expressed his sadness to her that somebody so young should die like that. He told her that he hoped she would learn to live with her loss, but that he realised that she would never fully recover or forget her son. Valerie's eyes filled with tears as she thanked the PC.

'I am glad that you found him so promptly,' was all she could think of to say. But then she added 'Thank-you for your thoughts and well wishes. I appreciate them and you're right, I will never get over losing Jeremy. You seem wise despite your young years. I imagine that your mother is very proud of you.'

All Tom could think of to say was 'I believe that my mum *is* proud of me,' and then added 'Well mind how you go,' as the sort of stock phrase he had been told to use when saying goodbye. He left her alone and continued his patrol, but Jez remained on his mind.

'If only we had got there sooner,' he thought as he left Valerie. 'Might have saved him then.'

The rest of his patrol had been quiet, and he had seen just a few people. The only thing that struck him as significant was that, later that afternoon, he had seen a man he recognised strolling along. Though he had recognised him he couldn't think of his name. The man had seemed very forward. 'Afternoon mah good man. I like to see that we are well protected by the law.' The accent was broad Glaswegian.

'Good afternoon to you too,' the PC replied. 'I must ask

some of my colleagues who that man is,' he thought. 'I have seen him before, at the station, I think. Yes, I'm sure that I have.'

Chapter 15. Computer searches.

Tom wasn't on shift on Tuesday, so it was on Wednesday morning that he had sat down at the station's new computer terminal to try to find out who the unpleasant Scottish bloke might have been. He carried out a search of all those arrested during the time he had been at the station which, fortunately, hadn't been long. He applied two filters: – aged 25 to 40 and originally Scottish. The computer had come came up with just two matches and those were Angus Thompson and George Dickinson. He noted down their addresses and decided to visit them in that order, Angus this morning and George this afternoon. He had logged off from the computer terminal and donned his helmet ready to leave when the elderly sergeant spoke to him.

'You off on your round this morning Tom or did that computer thing give you something exciting to do?'

'Just off on my morning beat sir,' replied Tom. 'I'm doing the high street today between Debenhams and the football ground. It's usually busy on a Wednesday morning.' Tom didn't mention his planned visit to speak to Angus and the sergeant hadn't enquired further.

After a quiet few hours Tom had found himself knocking

on the door of 11 Trentham Gardens to speak to Angus. The address had sounded very grand but there was nothing grand about the house, it had looked rather scruffy in fact. It was an elderly mid terraced house with a small garden to the rear and no front garden, the front door opening directly onto the street. He had to knock a second time before the door was finally opened by a woman wearing a dressing gown and who looked as though she had just got out of bed.

'*Now* what do you want?' she said, grumpily.

'Good morning,' said Tom. 'Is this the home of Angus Thompson and may I speak with him please?' He was good at remaining polite despite the hostile reception.

'It is his home yes, but not for long and he's not here anyway,' said the woman.

'That's a shame,' said the constable. 'May I come in for a chat about him?'

'No, you can't,' she replied. 'I ain't dressed yet and what do you want with him now anyway?'

'Will Angus be back soon?'

'Doubt it. And when he does, he'll be collecting these,' she opened the door to reveal two small bulging suitcases.

'Is he going away for a while?'

'He's already away and when he gets back, he'll be gone for good. He's in Edinburgh, shacked up with a woman called Doreen. Bleedin' silly name for a young lass but there we are. She's welcome to him.'

'Has he been in Edinburgh long?'

'Nearly 2 weeks.' Tom realised at that point that it couldn't have been Angus that he had spotted yesterday. 'And you've no idea when he might be back?'

'No but, tell you what, come in, give me 2 ticks to get me clothes on and I'll tell you about it.' Tom hadn't been keen on progressing the conversation further but thought he might learn something useful about Angus for future reference. He was shown into a surprisingly pleasant lounge that was bright and airy, and he could smell coffee. After what seemed like seconds the woman returned wearing a pink dress that looked as though she had been wearing it for weeks.

'It was like this,' she said. Tom was disappointed not to have been offered coffee, but he allowed her to carry on with her tale.

'He tells me we should go on holiday for a few weeks because he wants to go back home for a while. He has business to do up there so he says we could book a B&B and see the sights. I thinks "lovely", so he arranges the B&B, and we go up on the National Express. The B&B is nice, and we spend two days looking around Edinburgh. He has business on the third day but we was together on the fourth day. On the fifth day, Tuesday it was, at about half past 12, he says he's going out. He'd just left but I sees his wallet on the arm of the chair, so I runs after him with it. I just get out the door and he's going into a house three doors down. Now, he'd told me that he was going across town, so I was a bit suspicious. I goes down anyway and am about to knock on the door when I think better of it. He might be busy I thinks. But then I thinks he might be up to something I should know about, so I just opens the door without knocking. Well, you wouldn't believe it, I wouldn't unless I'd seen it myself. There he is, my Angus, getting undressed. And there she is,

Doreen, stripping off too. It was obvious what they were about to get up to, and in the hallway too. Couldn't even wait to get upstairs! Well, I was beside myself, but I went in, and I gave him, and her, a proper telling off. He didn't deny anything. Told me all about it.' She paused for effect.

'He'd only met her down the pub while she was visiting here hadn't he. They'd arranged the whole thing together, B&B just a few doors away so he could have me and her for a fortnight, randy old devil. I told *her* she was welcome to him. I told *him* that he was welcome back to my house, but only to pick up his stuff and how it would be waiting for him when he got here. But then he'd be gone for good. After I'd told him off good and proper, I went back to the B&B, and I came home. I packed his things for him when I got back, but I ain't seen him since.'

'Is he still in Edinburgh now do you know?'

'He rang me yesterday. Said he was still there. He said he was tired so wouldn't be back just yet. "Tired". Bleeding cheek. I'll give him tired when I see him! Do you want a cup of coffee constable?' Suddenly Tom wasn't keen on having coffee so he just thanked her, wished her well and was on his way.

'So, Angus hadn't been in Basingrove yesterday and it couldn't have been him that I saw on Monday, and he couldn't have seen Jez on the night of the third,' Tom decided that he would go somewhere for lunch then visit George during the afternoon. After a quick snack of a sandwich and a bottle of water he called to See George Dickinson early on that Wednesday afternoon. After he had knocked firmly on the door, he was surprised to see

George's face appear, in a rather ghostly fashion, through the partly open door. Once he had seen the PC waiting, he opened it fully.

'Why good afternoon constable. Lovely to see you. I *have* been popular today. To what do I owe the pleasure of this second visit constable?' PC Hollingsworth explained that he was investigating the disappearance of a young man and that he had seen George on Monday, near the missing boy's last known position. He went on to explain that he wondered whether George had been walking along that way last Thursday afternoon. George hadn't seemed keen to reply immediately.

'May I come in?' asked the PC.

'Why of course. Be my guest. It's open house today.' George led PC Hollingsworth into the same room he had allowed Marjorie and Joe to enter earlier that day. The PC had shown the same reaction to the décor, but he had already read in the database notes, from within the computer system, that George had thought of himself as a gangster, and he had modelled himself on the Kray twins, particularly Ronnie. The Kray twins had terrorised London in the 1960s and they were essentially identical twins, identically evil at least. They were involved in just about everything, armed robbery, protection, arson and murder. George had read all about them. Though identical, Ronnie had described himself as bisexual, Reggie as straight, so George had decided to be Ronnie.

'What more can I help you with constable?' said George. 'Your pals were here this morning. Have they not reported back to you yet?'

'What pals were they?' asked the PC. George told him about Marjorie and Joe.

'They must be from another team,' said the constable, having no idea what George was talking about. 'So, as I said outside, a young man went missing in the area of the woodland path that leads from the badminton club to this end of town. He disappeared last Thursday; Thursday 3rd. I believe that I spotted you in that area on Monday and I wondered whether it was a place you would visit often.'

'Ah do like to walk along there of an afternoon constable, yes. As I told the two that came here this morning, I usually walk along there at about teatime, but not when there are school children about. I certainly saw nothing unusual last Thursday, although my walk was early that day because I had a date. As a law-abiding citizen, I'd have been straight on the blower to the police if I had seen anything.'

He had just finished his sentence when a youngish fair-haired chap dashed in. 'I have divided up the coke and it's ready for del.........' He had blurted that out but then he saw Tom, though he had seen the uniform first.

'Whoops,' he said. Tom's mind was working quickly now. Hadn't the computer said, "arrested on suspicion of supplying drugs"? He didn't think that he could just let that comment pass.

'Coke?' said Tom.

'We enjoy a drop of Cola at this time of day. Darren here delivers it to the rest of my team, don't you Darren.'

'Yes,' replied the lad. 'Would you like some constable?'

'No thank-you, not just at the moment.' He returned to George. 'Before last Thursday, had you ever seen a dark-haired young man of about 16 walking along that way? We are trying to assign his movements to a particular time of day.'

'Have you ever seen anybody like that Darren?' He turned to Tom and explained that Darren sometimes liked to carry the shopping for George. 'He's a good lad.'

'No George,' said Darren, still looking sheepish.

'So, we can't help you then, sorry and all that. Darren, ask mah boys to come in, will you?'

'Aye,' said Darren. He was soon gone but two burley blokes had quickly replaced him and strolled over to the big settee.

'Thanks for your time then,' said Tom. 'I expect we will be in touch again.'

'Now why might you want to talk again?' asked George.

'Just routine.'

'Time for you to go then, busy man that you are. Thank all your colleagues for the hard work they do for us, and for keeping us safe.'

'Yes,' said Tom, suddenly anxious. 'And you have a nice day.' He decided to call the station before leaving so he reached for his radio.

'I'll just ring the station first, tell them that I'll be back soon,' but as he picked his radio from his lapel George shouted 'Boys!' The two men who had been sitting in silence suddenly jumped up, one grabbed Tom, the other grabbed his radio, and threw it against the wall. It hadn't broken, but obviously Tom couldn't now call for help.

'OK. Keep that radio as a souvenir of our chat if you like. I'll be off now though.'

'I think not constable,' said George. 'Not yet anyway. I have some plans you see.'

'Boys, remove mah friend here's uniform.'

'Shit,' thought Tom, and looked at the half naked pictures on the walls.

'Oh, don't worry your head constable,' said George, now fully aware of Tom's concerns from the expression on his face. 'You're not my type. I prefer older men. Men with more meat and age. Bit more experience if you know what I mean. Boys, leave him his shirt and underpants, and his socks.'

As soon as Tom had been stripped to his underwear, and had been locked in his own handcuffs, George turned to him and said 'I had nothing to do with that boy's disappearance you know, so I'm sorry you came here today. As it happens, I am sorry he's missing, but you and your friends are barking up the wrong tree. I had a date that Thursday, at it from about 3pm till late. It was a very memorable afternoon in fact. 'Nice drawers by the way!' he added as he looked Tom up and down. 'Boys, take our friend to the guest room. Make him comfortable.'

The guest room turned out to be a windowless, downstairs room, with a single light bulb. To make him "comfortable" they had given him a bucket and a glass of water. One of them had pointed to a shelf full of books and invited him to read one of them. They removed his handcuffs before leaving him alone but as they were leaving Tom asked whether he was going to be killed by George.

'If the boss had wanted you dead, you'd be gone already,' replied one of them. 'Relax. He will have plans for you. Call if you need anything, anything at all!' and Tom was left to consider his fate. Nothing in the police training manual had told him what to do in this situation. Or maybe it had, and he had missed it. He had just scraped through after all! Either way he was now very scared, and he had to use the bucket that they had provided. This is not what he had expected when he joined the police force of this allegedly quiet town. He looked at the books on the shelf. "Escape from Alcatraz", "Twenty ways to leave your lover", "Colditz", "Great Escapes" etc. The only thing that perked him up was that alarm bells would be ringing if his radio had lost connection with the station and that would mean that his colleagues might start looking for him very quickly.

In fact, nobody had been about to look for him any time soon because staff back at the station had been very busy that afternoon. There had even been some mild chaos because *another boy had just been reported missing by his mother!*

Chapter 16. Inspector Roberts' final visit to Valerie.

While Tom was in the company of George Dickinson, and was coming to terms with his new, enforced captivity, the inspector and his sergeant had called to see Valerie for their final chat. On the advice of the family liaison officer, she had decided to decamp to stay with her sister, and she had moved on Tuesday afternoon; her sister lived just a few miles away and her sister's husband was a very supportive man. She had felt a bit better about the situation by Wednesday and was wondering whether to ring Emma, her daughter, when the police officers arrived. The inspector had arrived with his sergeant they had brought Jez's things with them.

'My apologies for having to bother you again, but my sergeant here has the effects that were found in the woods *that evening*. We don't normally deliver belongings like this Mrs. Carter, but we wanted you to look at these items carefully. We understand you will need some time with them, but we will need to ask you some questions about them at some point. When you are ready, of course.'

'This is everything,' said the sergeant as he presented Valerie with Jez's belongings.

'Where's his badminton racquet?' Valerie had almost

shouted this and almost immediately. 'For four years I have watched Jez leave my house to go to school with the handle of his racquet sticking out from this haversack. I could watch it disappear as he walked down the lane. Where is it? It's not here. It should be right here, sticking out of the left-hand side of his haversack's cover. It's not here.' She burst into tears. The inspector had been deeply moved by this and had decided that now was not the time for further questions. 'We will go, just tell us when you are ready to talk,' he said.

'No, don't go.' Valerie almost shouted that too. 'Stay, please.' By this time her sister Beverley had come into the room to sit with her. Valerie sat quietly for a while and Beverley asked the gentlemen to sit too.

After calming slightly, Valerie turned to the two officers. 'That racquet was his dad's. Mark gave it to Jez when Jez was only 12. Mark knew he wasn't going to use it for much longer because his cancer diagnosis was terminal. He died just a few months later. Jez was devastated by the death of his father, but after a few weeks he became determined to be as good as his dad had been at badminton. He wanted to follow in his footsteps. It helped him grieve for Mark. That's really why he began to play badminton. He had only had a slight interest before then.' Valerie paused for a while and Beverley took her hand.

'Mark was a really good player. He played for the County in championships, but he never managed to become an outright winner. Mark got that racquet when he went to the All-England Badminton Championship in 1980. He went to watch that competition whenever he could, and he won that racquet in a raffle. It was signed by some good players from the championship and Jez never let it out of his sight. You often knew where Jez was because that handle was like a flagpole, especially when he was shorter than he is now. He took it to school every day, along with his tee shirt and shorts in case he got a game unexpectedly.' After a pause she asked to see his haversack. Through tears she pulled out his clothes, books, a few pens, a ruler and 2 shuttlecocks. 'His tee shirt and shorts?'

They were actually still being analysed for any traces of 'substance' likely to help the investigation. 'They are still on him,' lied the inspector. 'A white, slightly grubby tee shirt and a pair of shorts that seemed a bit loose on him.' Valerie smiled slightly.

'He wouldn't let *me* buy him new ones, but he bought those last weekend while he was out in town. He has 3 pairs of shorts so those must be the new ones.' She took out his clothes. 'He was never great at folding these,' she said. She noted that they were quite creased, as they usually had been, but then she looked in his pockets and examined the coins.

'There's £2.62 there Mrs Carter,' said the sergeant.

'Now why has he got these I wonder?' said Valerie. She was looking at a packet of condoms.

'Did he have a girlfriend, a boyfriend even, or was he just living in hope. Was there something he wasn't telling me? He has been very happy the last few weeks. Did he have a girlfriend inspector?'

'We had hoped you could tell us,' he said. 'Perhaps one of his friends would know.'

'There's John Cummings,' said Valerie. 'If anybody knows it will be him.' She then carefully folded the clothes, put them neatly into the bottom of his haversack and added the books, pens and ruler. She dropped the shuttlecocks, money and condoms on top of those and carefully closed the haversack. 'I don't want to open that again inspector. Do you need it back, like for evidence?'

'No Mrs Carter. It can stay with you now.'

'Thank-you inspector.'

'Does Jez have any other family Mrs. Carter?' asked the inspector as he was leaving.

'There's my daughter Emma, who is at university, and my sister Beverley and her husband. That's all.'

'Isn't it a bit early to be back at university?' asked the inspector.

'It is really but Emma likes to go back a week or two before the start of term, to get back in with her friends and to find a temporary job. She shares a house with some other girls.'

The inspector then made his goodbyes, and as he left, he heard Valerie say to Beverley 'Well well well. What on earth had Jez got himself into? I think I had better ring Emma tonight.' Out of earshot Valerie added 'She will be devastated. How am I going to tell her about this. There's just her and me now.'

Inspector Roberts had got back to the station at about 2pm to find the station far from its usual, calm self – the second missing lad was called Mark Buckingham and he was of a similar age and build to Jez, both below average height at about 5ft 5inches, and both with dark hair. Unlike Jez though, Mark had left school and he had two jobs, by day he stacked shelves in Tesco, but that was only for 20 hours a week, so for four evenings a week he also worked in the fish and chip shop in the high street. Exactly like Jez, he had failed to return home the previous evening. He had even followed a similar route home, though his was a longer journey because it also took in most of the high street, but it did follow the same country lane towards the end. Again, though being missing for less than 24 hours didn't usually mean that somebody had been abducted or murdered, the similarity to Jez's disappearance had the station worried and inspector Roberts had again become involved. Once he had been fully briefed, he decided that he must hold a meeting of all available staff that afternoon, and he scheduled that for 3pm. It actually began a little after 3.

'Well, here we go again. I hope that you all understand just how serious things have become, one dead boy and another missing, and both having used that path that runs from the badminton club to the west end of Basingrove. I have already had it sealed off in preparation for it's being searched again. This needs to be an incredibly detailed search, so sergeant Bulmer would you go there to do that, immediately after this meeting?'

'Yes sir,' replied the sergeant.

'And I think, Diederik, if you could attend with sergeant Bulmer it might be useful to both you and to us.'

Hoofdagent Diederik Claasen was a Dutch police officer who had been attached to the Basingrove station on an officer swap scheme that had been set up by the local council. In common with many men from the Netherlands, he was very tall and quite slender. Getting him a suitable uniform had been quite difficult when he arrived because few UK officers could match his 6ft 7inches height, at least not with a 32-inch waist! Inspector Roberts thought that his height and agile frame might make him particularly useful for this search and asked him to concentrate on the woodland part of the route.

'Of course, inspector.' Fortunately, like many people from the Netherlands, he could speak very good English, but he was pleased that the English version of "inspecteur" was so similar to that which he was used to using at home!

'So far, we know very little about Mark Buckingham. Worryingly, his mother, like Jez's mother, is on her own and she has two children, Mark who is 16 and an older daughter who is 19. The daughter is living away at university which is, again, strikingly similar to Jez's family. Mrs Buckingham did almost exactly what Mrs. Carter had done by phoning round or visiting Mark's friends on the night he didn't return home, but none of them could say where Mark could be. So, again like Mrs Carter, Mrs Buckingham had telephoned the place Mark should be today, in this case Tesco's in the town centre. Just as with Jeremy Carter, he hasn't turned up there either, so they said they would phone her when he appeared. She had contented herself that he might have a hangover somewhere, but then she had been worried enough to call us at 11.30am today.' He paused for a drink of tea.

'All we do know about Mark is that he is a fairly quiet lad who loves football and tennis, listens to music and plays the odd video game. This is all so similar to Jeremy Carter that I am worried that somebody is targetting individuals who fit this profile. Where Mark differs from Jez is that we know Mark has a girlfriend. We don't know who she is, but we need to find her as soon as possible. Sergeant Windsor, would you visit Tesco, after this meeting, to talk to people that know Mark and maybe find out who this girlfriend is?'

'Will do sir.' WPC Bradley had sat very quietly during this discourse but had then spoken up.

'Do you have anything for me to do sir?'

'Not yet, but I will do in time. You were very close to the case when Jez's body was found so perhaps stay out of this for a while, but I will need your input if a body is found, you and PC Hollingsworth. Where is Tom by the way? Anybody seen him?' There were shakes of heads, but nobody had any clue where he had gone, or the predicament he had found himself in.

'That seems to be about it from me then. Are there any questions or points of information from any of you?' There were no replies to this, so the inspector ordered that everybody in attendance was to meet back in that room at 4.30pm and to radio in if that wasn't possible. The meeting ended at 3.30pm exactly and the inspector spent the next thirty minutes in his office, just thinking.

'Two lads go missing within a week of each other, both similar in appearance, similar interests and almost identical home environment. What sort of chap would target such young men? I suppose there might be some form of perversion here, or they might be similar in that Jez's death may have been accidental – perhaps there is some new craze that none of us know about and there is an unexpected danger. Jez had been carrying condoms so it could be that they had both met up with somebody for sex, and maybe things had gone wrong. Perhaps Mark is Jez's killer!'

This had done nothing but make him realise that he was getting well ahead of himself, and they hadn't yet found out anything about Mark's disappearance. Guessing was pointless. At 4.30pm sharp, the inspector was back in the meeting room and all previous attendees had returned.

'Nice to see you all back, it's been a wet afternoon, so I imagine that you are glad to be back in the warm.' There had been agreement on that point.

'Sergeant Bulmer. You and Hoofdagent Claasen searched the path from the badminton club to the west end of town. I haven't heard anything, so I assume that you found nothing?'

'Indeed not sir,' replied the sergeant. 'Diederik searched the woods, and I searched the path. Then to make sure we had missed nothing we swapped, and I searched the woods while he patrolled the path. Nothing, not even a sweet wrapper. It's been very windy the last few days, so the place looked like it had been swept clean. Nobody's been down there today sir, or if anybody has been there, they have dropped nothing. It had started to become quite muddy by the time we left.'

'Have you anything to add Diederik?'

'No sir. The leaves are beginning to fall from some of the bushes and trees so I could see quite clearly that there were no bodies there. Just a sort of grassy hill, with very flattened grass. Maybe people had sat or played on that, but there was no sign of anything else.'

'OK. Sergeant Windsor, did you learn anything?'

'Yes sir, I did. Mark's girlfriend is called Harriet Bainbridge, daughter of the owner of the chip shop where Mark works. The chip shop is owned by a Freda Bainbridge, who is a rather fearsome woman, and the gossip is that she gave her husband his marching orders when Harriet was about fourteen, and that the divorce settlement gave her enough money to buy the fish and chip shop. The other snippet of information is that they have a little dog called Pickles which Freda walks every day before opening the chip shop. And you'll never guess where she walks him? It's only along the path past the woods, the very one we've just searched and where we found Jez's body.'

'Well, well well,' said the inspector. 'Good job there sergeant, this is yet another area where the two cases are linked. Do we know what time she walks Pickles?'

'The gossip is that she takes Pickles for his walk just before going to work to open the shop.'

'Does anybody know when that chip shop opens? We never have fish and chips unfortunately.' The general agreement was that it opened at 5pm.

'So, if she opens at 5pm she will need to be there to prepare at about 4.30pm, so I want an officer to meet her on her walk tomorrow at, say, 3.45. WPC Bradley, a job for you I think?'

'Love to,' said the WPC.

'Sergeant Bulmer and I will interview Harriet Bainbridge and Mark's mum tomorrow morning.'

The meeting had ended at 5pm and the inspector returned to his office to do some more thinking, but he got nowhere. What might have helped his thoughts was that WPC Bradley had waited for Freda on Thursday, as he had instructed, but the usually very predictable Freda hadn't appeared, nor had Pickles. She had then gone to see Freda at the chip shop and at her home, but she was nowhere to be found.

Chapter 17. What has happened to Mark?

Tuesday (Day 5)

It was Tuesday, and Freda Bainbridge had only gone down to the basement of her chip shop to do some stock checking, but, when she got there, she couldn't believe what she was witnessing. She would normally have been at the wholesalers at that time, but that day she had called into the shop and ventured down to the cellar because she felt sure that she already had too many bread rolls. She wanted to check before wasting money on something she didn't need. When she opened the door though, it wasn't bread rolls that first confronted her.

'What the hell?' In the basement were Mark Buckingham and her daughter Harriet in a very passionate embrace. Freda had known that they were going out together, but she thought it was just a teenage flirtation, and that they weren't all that serious. Certainly not sufficiently serious to be found in a passionate embrace while both were almost completely naked.

For their part the couple had been genuinely shocked to see her because they had believed she had gone up to the wholesaler for the bread rolls and fish cakes. They thought that they would be totally safe in here today; they had used this basement as a meeting place for their liaisons in the past, and always after Freda had gone out. They usually heard her return so they didn't see a need to lock the door, which they couldn't have done anyway because it was bolted from the outside.

Freda was furious.

'What the hell is going on here?' she shouted as the young couple rushed to find the clothes they had so hastily removed.

'Mum. I thought you were out!'

'Obviously! And you don't need to tell me what's going on because I can see that plainly enough, but what the hell do you think you are playing at?'

'You said that you didn't need to ask what was going on,' commented Mark, sheepishly, as he pulled on his trousers. 'We thought you had gone to the wholesaler's. You knew we were going out together and we are both 16 so we are doing nothing wrong. Harriet is my girlfriend, so this is perfectly natural, isn't it?'

'Not with *my* daughter it isn't, and certainly not in my basement,' she screamed. 'Harriet, get dressed and get upstairs. Start getting the shop ready for when we open.'

'Mum…'

'NOW Harriet. I will speak to you later about this, but at the moment I want to talk to Mark.'

'OK,' said Harriet and she complied moodily with her mother's wishes.

'So, for how long have you been screwing my daughter you swine?'

'Mrs Bainbridge, we have been going out for a few months now and we are quite serious about each other. I have a job and we want to move in with each other when I can afford it. You knew we were together, and you must have realised that we would get together like this eventually. It is 1985, not 1925 and we are both legally old enough. We have taken all the precautions we need to so we had thought it would be OK.'

'That's my daughter you are talking about, and I won't have this. *Do you understand*? I won't have this. Get upstairs now and help Harriet prepare the shop. I will think about what you have just said to me, and I will talk to you after we close.' Mark finished dressing and did what Freda asked. He wondered how he could make things right and decided that if she could see how hard he could work then she would relent, and that he could continue to 'see' Harriet. At the moment though it looked like his girlfriend would be lost to him if he couldn't talk Freda round.

The shop opened at 5pm, as usual, and they had a busy evening. At the end of the shift, Freda counted up the takings and she seemed delighted with the amount of profit they had made. Mark and Harriet hadn't spoken to each other, at least in Freda's presence, all night. They *had* both worked exceptionally hard; ordinarily Freda would have been delighted with them, but today they were in her really bad books. When the shop had been closed up for the night Freda spoke to Harriet.

'Go home Harriet. I will talk to you when I get home later.'

'Mum, talk to me now because we need to sort this out.'

'Home Harriet, go *now*. Mark, you stay there, I want words with you before you go anywhere.' Begrudgingly,

Harriet set off for home, leaving her mother and Mark to talk. Secretly she was extraordinarily angry with her mother, but she knew that she would have to hold her tongue. She did give Mark a full-on kiss before she left ('sod mother,' she thought to herself), and winked at Mark before leaving them to it.

Freda turned to Mark. 'Follow me to the storeroom downstairs. You can tidy that up for a start!' Mark did so and he chatted while Freda had stood and watched him work.

'I really do have the highest regard for Harriet Mrs Bainbridge. We haven't done anything that wasn't what we both wanted, and she *is* my permanent girlfriend. I don't want anybody else because your daughter is the best thing to ever happen to me, and we both want to be together.' Freda continued to watch with interest.

'We really don't want to upset you, and Harriet said she felt sure that you would understand why we have to get together in here. There is nowhere else for us, and it certainly didn't seem right to meet at either of our parents' houses. Will you please give us your blessing and understanding?' Freda said nothing more until the room had been tidied, and she told him that she was satisfied with his work, which she had been.

What Mark *hadn't* noticed though was that she had been standing just *outside* of the door all of the time he was working. This was the *only* door to the basement, and so the only exit. Finally, she spoke to him directly.

'See whether you still want to screw my daughter after a whole night in here, not a night of passion but a night in prison.' Before he realised what was about to happen, she had slammed, bolted and locked the door, and set off upstairs.

'Let me out of here. Please Mrs Bainbridge, *let me out, let me out*. Please, please Mrs. Bainbridge.' He heard the shop door close, and it was clear that she had gone home. Mark was severely claustrophobic, so he continued this rant for a full five minutes before beginning to really panic. 'Open this door, please, please, *please*, open this door. Please.' He could feel his blood pressure rising, and his muscles tensing even more. 'What the hell can I do now?' He kicked the door hard, then harder, then harder still, but it wouldn't budge. His panic was getting worse, and he pretty much lost control. He ran from one side of the room to the other, he banged on the door again, he ran into the corners, he jumped over boxes. His panic was now major, his heart was beating very hard in his chest, and he began to see stars. He looked for somewhere to lay down, in the hope of going to sleep. It was now gone midnight so he was tired anyway, but sleep wouldn't come. He turned off the light, hoping that if he couldn't *see* the room, he could ignore the fact that he was locked in with no means of exit, but that didn't work. The only window was a little skylight, which was a sort of horizontal window that was built into the path outside. It was really thick, reinforced glass and he quickly realised that there was no way he could remove that. He finally decided that there was nothing for it, but to make himself a sort of bed from cardboard boxes – he had done that with Harriet, but now it meant nothing, just a pile of cardboard, no longer a place of romance for both of them. He calmed himself slightly with the thought that Freda would have to let him out tomorrow because she would need the stock. In the meantime, he had plenty of cans and bottles of drink, and some bread rolls.

He tried to busy himself by turning a bottle into a urine container, which he placed in the corner, but he was still in a panic. He finally dozed off at about 4am but the sleep was troubled and very intermittent.

Once back at home, Freda spoke with Harriet. 'How could you let that creature near you Harriet. All the lovely young men in the world and you have taken up with him, even slept with him you tart.'

'Mother, I am *not* a tart. I have a boyfriend and we have been doing what girlfriends and boyfriends do, nothing more. How dare you call me a tart. We are just lovers mum, what the hell's wrong with that?'

'You are just infatuated with him, that's all. He will run away and leave you; you mark my words. Forget him.'

'I won't forget him, certainly not just to please you.'

'Well, he certainly won't be in the shop from now on anyway Harriet. I have given him his marching orders.'

'What! You cow mother.' Harriet ran up to her room.

'How could things have got like this? What is wrong with Mark anyway. He is gorgeous and sweet, really caring. Just what does mother expect, I'm a grown woman now and Mark is a grown man. I'll go to see him tomorrow. He starts work at Tesco at 10am and he works in the fruit and vegetable department, so I'll look for him there.'

The next morning Mark had woken up at about 9.30am and it was a while before he realised where he was. The memories came flooding back to him and he was gripped by panic again. As before, he thought that the way to beat this was to try to keep busy. It was fairly light by now so he could just about see without the light on, which helped him a bit. He had breakfast of a can of lemonade and some of the bread rolls that had caused the problem in the first place. There were quite a few of those so he wouldn't be hungry or thirsty, at least not for a while. After breakfasting he studied the door again. He already knew it was bolted, and presumably padlocked, on the outside but, unfortunately, the door opened inwards so he couldn't keep battering the door until the bolt gave way and, after looking at the door handle for a while, it was clear that trying to open the door by pulling on that would just break the handle long before the bolt outside gave way. 'There must be something I can do to escape, but surely Freda will need to open this door sooner or later to get stock, so she's likely to let me out tonight.'

Later that morning, Harriet popped into Tesco's Basingrove store. She had changed her mind and decided to go a little later than 10am because she thought it would give him time to get some work done. She headed for the fruit and vegetable section and hung around there for about ten minutes waiting for him to appear, but when he didn't arrive, she asked a member of the staff whether she had seen Mark.

'No, I haven't,' she replied. 'Mark didn't turn in this

morning, so his boss is furious, and I'm not delighted either because I have to do his shift and I've got all of this lot to put out.' She pointed at a large trolley load of potatoes and carrots. 'He'll likely get the sack for this.'

'What the hell has mother done with him?'

'What?' asked the Tesco assistant.

'Oh, sorry, nothing. I was just thinking that I had better go and see Mark's mum, see where he is. I know Mrs. Buckingham well, with Mark being my boyfriend, and she won't be at work because the shop she works in doesn't open on Wednesdays.'

'Well good luck then and tell him to get himself into work sharpish.'

'I will, thanks.' It was about 11am by the time she arrived at Mark's little house, and she knocked loudly on the door.

'Is that you Mark?' Harriet heard his mother shout. 'I'll box your ears when I see you…' The sentence hung in the air when she opened the door and found Harriet.

'Oh love, thank God you are here. Mark didn't come home last night. I rang your mother's shop when he wasn't back by 1 o'clock this morning, but she must have closed up by then. Come in love.' Mrs. Buckingham continued to talk while Harriet was removing her coat.

'Have *you* seen Mark today? I was hoping that he had spent the night with you and that he felt too sheepish to tell me, though goodness knows you've been going out long enough and I wouldn't really mind if you two were sleeping together. Where is he Harriet? Please tell me you know where he is.'

'I'm sorry Mrs Buckingham, but I haven't *any* idea where

he is. I left the shop before *he* did last night so I haven't seen him since about 11.30 last night. I went to see him at Tesco this morning, but he hasn't turned up there either.'

'Oh, love where can he be? I'm so worried. I heard about that schoolboy that went missing last Thursday. Oh God love, what if he's been attacked, or murdered or anything?' Harriet tried to calm her down.

'Perhaps he's fallen over and knocked himself out or something, or he's gone out with a mate and he's sleeping it off in somebody else's bed or a doorway somewhere. If he's found another woman you'll have to wait while I box his ears first, but don't worry, he'll be OK. Tell you what, I will go and ask my mother what time he left last night and we can maybe trace him from there.'

'Should I call the police?'

'If he isn't back by this afternoon then maybe you should, but if I do find him, I will let you know immediately.'

'Thanks Harriet. I won't tell his dad he's missing because he's in Germany on manoeuvrers, so I don't want to bother him until we know something concrete. Off you go now, I'll wait in in case he comes home because he didn't take his key yesterday. It's on the hall table with that daft huge keyring he has.'

'Don't worry Mrs. Buckingham, I'll find him.'

Chapter 18. Confrontation and panic.

Freda was in the house when Harriet got home. 'Mother, what the hell have you done with Mark?'

'Hello Harriet, I thought you were still in bed.'

'At 12 noon? Mother I asked you a question, what the hell have you done to Mark and where is he?'

'Calm down Harriet. The last I saw of Mark was last night. He went off a bit annoyed after I had given him his marching orders.'

'You've sacked him just because he is going out with me and now he's *missing* you old cow. And you expect me to be happy with that do you? You think I'll say never mind and find somebody else? Tell you what mother, when I do find him, I'm leaving here, and I'll live with him if his mother will let us. She isn't as bigoted as you, so she probably won't mind, and you'll have to find two new staff for your sodding chip shop.'

'Just stop right there Harriet. Is he really missing?'

'Yes, not that you care, and I'm going back out to find him.'

'Have some lunch first,' said her mother, finally realising how upset Harriet had become.

'I'll get some while I'm out. I tell you what, I'll go to the

"Newtown Chippy" for some chips, see how you like that!'
With that she was gone. Freda smiled.

'I think I'll leave the shop closed for tonight,' she thought. *'As a mark of respect for Mark.* I haven't any staff anyway and we did well enough yesterday to stand a day's holiday. I'll let him out tomorrow, and we'll see how he has enjoyed *two* nights in his prison.'

This meant that Mark had been wrong when he thought he would be out of his prison that night. Freda hadn't appeared that afternoon because, good to her word, she didn't open the shop at all. Instead, she pinned a note to the shop door that read:
"Dear Loyal Customers, it is with sadness that I have decided not to open the shop today. You may have heard that the police are looking into the disappearance of my lovely employee Mark. The shop is closed today as a mark of respect."
She had thought it clever that she had managed to get the word Mark in twice, and she laughed after fastening the note to the door.

By 5pm Mark had realised the shop wasn't going to open that night either and his claustrophobia began to take hold again. This time the panic caused him to really lose control. He banged on the door, shouted 'somebody open this sodding door,' really loudly several times, but it was no good. He had even tried shouting up through the little window, but it was too noisy outside for people to hear him. After this major claustrophobic attack, he had to curl up and try to sleep. He turned out the light and managed about thirty minutes of sleep but awoke in an even worse state. He had to find the light. Panic, thumping heart, where's the light switch? 'WHERE IS IT?' he shouted, but nobody responded. His heart was beating so hard he thought that, either it would leap out from his chest, or he was going to die. He had to calm down, so he curled up tightly again and managed some more sleep. He woke up at about 9pm and this time he was a little calmer. He had to get out of there but first he had to find the light.

'There is a faint light coming through the window, that must be the street light outside. So, if the window is that way the light must be…,' and he found the switch straight away. He looked around his prison. 'I have plenty of food and drink and there's even spare light bulbs.' Then he remembered that he had begun to cut a hole in the door! He calmed down.

Earlier that afternoon, Mark had remembered that his little penknife was in his pocket and, since he had nothing else to do and plenty of time, he had contemplated trying to cut a hole in the door. He understood that this would be a Herculean task, a penknife against an enormous, hardwood door, but it was worth a try. Enthused by the job in hand, his panic calmed slightly, and he began to scratch at the door with the point of the knife. This initially seemed to do nothing, but eventually he began to see a groove forming. Slowly the groove began to enlarge, and after about an hour, he was making progress through the wood. The door was heavy, so he was making very slow progress, but making progress he was, and he told himself that it would be possible to get through eventually. This had made him feel better, and he celebrated by helping himself to another bread roll and a can of lemonade.

Now that it had seemed that he would have to spend a second night in his prison he decided to resume work on the door, and to leave the light on all night, so that if anybody passed by, they would wonder why it was on. He drank a can of fizzy orange and ate some more bread. That had suddenly seemed like a feast, and he resumed his work on the door. He resumed the scraping, which calmed him slightly. When panic arose, he would stand back to examine progress, which had become faster as he got further into the wood. By 3am he was ready for bed, the hole had become big enough to see through, and fresher air was coming in. He knew exactly where the bolt was, and he had reckoned that he would get his hand through that hole tomorrow.

Mark resumed his work after his breakfast next morning. 'Let's get this straight,' he said aloud. 'I have spent two nights in here so today it must be Thursday! Let's see whether I can get two fingers through that hole by lunch time.' In fact, it turned out that he could do rather more than that and, after more scraping, which now seemed more efficient because he could use the blade rather than just the point of the knife, he was able to put his whole hand through and feel the bolt. It was heavy but he thought that he would be able to pull it back, if only the padlock hadn't been on! 'Sodding hell,' he thought, but when he thought about it, he realised that he should have been expecting that, so he wasn't too disheartened. All he needed to do was to prise the bolt off the door and he would be out of that room.

To even attempt that prising off, the hole would need to be big enough to get his whole hand and arm through, so after a late lunch (bread and cola) he set to work with renewed vigour. Having thin arms was now a bonus to him and, by early evening, he could get his penknife under the outside bolt. Unfortunately, his knife had felt as though it might break, and he realised that he must not let that happen, so he had to think of something else. At least he was getting some fresh air in now and he had begun to feel better than he had done since Tuesday morning, when he had been free, and with Harriet! He now needed to think of another way to get this door open.

He hadn't been at all surprised when the shop was still closed on Thursday evening, but he had now worked out a new plan, and that involved using the hole he had made as a hand hole. That way he could tug on the door without the risk of breaking the handle. He had made a start and he found that by pressing his foot against the door frame, while pulling at the hole, he could get quite a lot of force on the door. He had tried setting up a sort of rocking motion and after many rests, and many tugs, he could feel that the bolt was beginning to part company with the door frame. That was all he needed to give him some extra determination to get this done. Annoyingly, the bolt hadn't seemed to yield any more during the night, but in the early hours he couldn't sleep, and panic was setting in again. At 2am precisely he got up from his cardboard bed and gave the door a massive final tug. This time he heard a loud snap. The door had given nicely but it still wouldn't open! He suddenly remembered that there was another bolt, right at the top of the door pointing upwards.

'Damn.'

He wasn't yet free from that horrible prison and the panic rose within him again; he really had to sleep now, and he sank to the floor and managed to doze for a while.

When he awoke, he remembered what had happened and, in a fit of real temper, he gave the door a massive tug but this time he had noticed that bottom edge of the door appeared when he pulled at the hand hole. He now gave another massive tug on the hole *and* on the bottom edge of the door.

Crack, crack, tinkle tinkle.

The top bolt was much smaller than the main one and, being nearer to the hinge, it had been easier to break. The door opened fully now, and the panic drained from Mark like a tidal wave. He just sank to the floor outside that door and for the first time in ages he relaxed. He stared at the bolt on the floor and at the bigger one still stuck on its hasp at the side, the padlock now looking really stupid. He laughed, he couldn't help it, but he laughed again, then fell asleep right there in that doorway.

Chapter 19. Further investigations.

Earlier on that Thursday morning, Marjorie Jones had woken with a start. It was very early morning, and her alarm hadn't woken her, but when she checked the time, she realised that was because it was still over an hour before it was due to ring. She looked around the room. Her bed was still there, her dressing table, her bedroom, all was as it should be. She got out of bed, donned her robe and went downstairs to try to shake herself from her fear.

Marjorie didn't dream, at least she didn't think that she did. In fact, just like everybody else, she did have dreams, but she rarely remembered them, but this one was very vivid. So vivid that she was still shaking when she woke up. 'What the hell was that nightmare about?' she wondered.

She ran through the dream in her head. The main character in Marjorie's nightmare had been Erica, with Eric as the support. She had clearly had her investigations in mind as she fell asleep, and the dream began innocently enough. The elderly but slightly dotty old lady was out walking Eric, along that now infamous woodland path, it was a mild autumn evening and still daylight, but with the sun fading and casting long shadows.

Marjorie watched Erica walking Eric and she considered whether Erica really had jilted all those men, but she was surprised when the image reset, and she had to watch the same walk again, then again, then again. This began to worry her, but she recalled the film "Groundhog Day" and realised that she had to remember the scene, and then to deliberately try to change it, or she would be in this loop forever. With tremendous effort, Marjorie found that she *could* change the sequence, but she was alarmed to see that all she had managed to do was to make Erica angry. So, she tried again, but she only made things worse and, after several more reruns of the plot, she saw that she had joined in the sequence herself! Now, both Erica and Eric were chasing her, demanding that she stop looking for Jez's killer. Stubbornly, Marjorie refused, so each rerun found her more and terrified and, eventually, Eric had Marjorie's leg in his mouth, and blood had begun to flow. But then, in the very next rerun, Jez appeared. He was in his badminton kit, but it was dirty, his hair was all over the place, he had a large bruise on his chin and his skin was deathly white. Marjorie tried desperately to wake up, but her dream was having none of that, and now Erica had begun to laugh.

'Hi Jez.' Erica laughed after saying this. 'We got her Jez. Look, *she's* terrified now.' Marjorie had no idea what to make of this but then Erica added more. 'I told you it was worth dying, now look at her. And look at you! You'll make a lovely photo on my wall, handsome devil that you are.' Jez laughed.

'Look Marjorie. No muscles, weak arms, but it doesn't matter now because we are coming to get revenge. Don't worry.' Laughter began again and Eric began to bark, but then Marjorie heard 'Another one for my collection, I get them all eventually.' There was then a pause in the dream and Erica disappeared, but her voice remained, sounding very ethereal:

'Marjorie, you were too easy. Not enough strength in your arms. You can't get the shuttlecock to the far end of the court. Did you hear that Jez?'

'Get out of my face you old dragon, get some gym sessions, you haven't enough arm strength. 'He giggled uncontrollably after saying this and added, doing an impression of Miss von Hofman: 'Keine Notwendigkeit für John's Kondome jetzt (No need for John's condoms now). We'll pause while Carter recovers.'

At that point she woke with a start. She was shaking.

'What the hell was that about,' she thought. She knew that she didn't remember dreams, but this stayed with her, and she had to get up and out of her bedroom. She was still shaking while she made herself a cup of coffee. 'I must find out who really killed Jez,' she thought. 'Surely not Erica? But then what was the dream about, was it directing me to something that I have missed? Perhaps I need a more sophisticated plan if this sleuthing business is going to work.'

Marjorie had recovered by breakfast time and, after she had dressed, she looked again at her list of suspects.

'Why had she left off Erica? That daft tale about her ex fiances! Surely, she should go back to being a suspect; were those men in the pictures really all men that she had promised to marry, or had she murdered them? Is there now a picture of Jez on her wall?' She decided that she would have to go back and see her, and that it was time to rewrite her suspect list.

She decided that she wouldn't waste time visiting Freda Bainbridge. She walked Pickles before the evening shift at the chip shop and the chip shop opened at 5pm each day (except Sunday) so, assuming that the chip shop opened on time that day, she couldn't have murdered Jez. She would have to have been at the shop before 4.30 to get the fish prepared and battered, and the potatoes washed and chipped, so she could be removed from the list. Her list now still had just two names, *George Dickinson and Erica Briggs.*

'It must be one of those two,' thought Marjorie, although she still considered George the most likely to turn out to be a criminal. She had two coaching sessions that morning, one at 9am, the other at 11am.

'I have time to see Erica again at 10am, and whether he likes it or not I will visit George this afternoon. I'll see whether Joe will come with me again.'

She and Paula had breakfast, and little was said between them because Paula was worried about how school would be. Yesterday she had been in the assembly when Inspector Roberts had announced that Jez had been found dead. Her friend Jemma had been sitting next to her in that assembly and couldn't help noticing how upset she'd been. They met up at morning break.

'Rotten about Jez Carter, isn't it?' said Jemma.

'Yes,' is all that Paula could manage.

'You loved him, didn't you?' Paula began to deny that but then she had to answer.

'Yes. How did you know?'

'I didn't believe all that rubbish about you talking to him just because your mother coached him, and you've been so upset since he disappeared. How far had you got with him, had you kissed and cuddled, maybe more?' Having seen the look on Paula's face she didn't need to ask any more.

'Oh Paula, I'm so sorry. I had no idea you got as far as screwing him. You must be devastated. Was it just a fling or were you really in love?'

'Oh, Jemma we really were head over heels. How can you describe what we had as screwing him? Everything felt so right. There was nothing sordid or rude about the sex. It wasn't just "getting laid" as the lads say. It was perfect, and now he's gone. I loved him so much.'

'Will your mother help you get over him?'

'No. She doesn't know, she mustn't know, not now, not ever. Please promise you won't tell anybody else, please Jemma.'

'OK, OK I won't. Well, I wasn't expecting what you just told me Paula, but I'm here if you need me. I don't know how I'd feel in your place because I've never been in love.'

'What about Jermaine? I thought that you and he were already sleeping together?' asked Paula.

'That's not love. Not what you felt for Jez, I wouldn't care if Jermaine left me. It's just fun with him, I couldn't live with him forever so that's not love, is it?' Paula thought about that for a while and had decided that what she had with Jez really was special, and she felt full of regrets and wondered how she could go on without him.

Once apart, Jemma realised that she wasn't sure how she

felt now. She had always thought Paula to be quiet and reserved so she had been surprised by what she had just heard, and she had fancied Jez herself which made her feel really awkward somehow. She would keep Paula's secret though, just as she had promised.

At 10.10am precisely Marjorie was knocking on Erica's door, but unfortunately there seemed nobody in. 'Damn,' she thought. 'Perhaps I could go and see George again.' She found a phone box and telephoned Joe.

'Hi Joe,' she said when he answered his phone.

'Hi Marjorie. What can I do for you?' Marjorie outlined her plan to him.

'No, definitely not. Once was enough, and anyway I am at work. I strongly suggest that you keep away from him.'

'Why's that Joe? He didn't seem too intimidating to me.'

'Have you forgotten what he said to you last time? "If you come in you might not get back out". Surely you must be afraid to go in there on your own. Leave this to the police. Word has got out now that Jez was murdered so you don't need to be involved any more.'

'He was as nice as pie when you were with me Joe, are you sure you won't come to see him with me? I feel that I have to help solve Jez's murder. He was my student after all, and I liked him.'

'No chance Marjorie and look I'm really busy. Leave it to the police and don't ask me again, OK?' With that Joe rang off.

'Now what? It's 10.20. Perhaps I will just knock on George's door, and he might let me in, I could tell him that Joe is in the car. That will frighten him, Joe's presence seemed to do that very thing last time I was there.'

At 10.30am she was knocking on George's door and again, the door opened just a little, and the slightly menacing face appeared.

'You again!' he said as he opened the door fully. 'Go away, I warned you last time and I mean it this time.'

'But I have new evidence,' she shouted as he closed the door. The door reopened, partially. 'It incriminates you,' she lied.

'In!' he said, as he opened the door fully. That same door closed with a bang as she entered.

'Make this quick, I'm busy. I did not harm that lad so just what incriminates me? This had better be good,' he opened a door and shouted 'BOYS' and the two heavy blokes arrived and sat on the settee.

'Perhaps I was wrong,' said Marjorie. 'Maybe I'll just go.'

'Oh, I think not. You're going nowhere until you tell me what the coppers are fabricating against me. I told you I had nothing to do with that lad so why are they trying to pin it on me? And your boy isn't with you today, is he? Did he realise it wasn't wise to tangle with me again?'

'Look, there *is* some evidence, but it doesn't necessarily apply to just you, it could be anybody when I think about it.'

'When *you* think about it? So, you're not helping the Police at all. Are you a private detective or something? Or are you trying to extort money from me. If you are then good luck with that pal.' Marjorie saw that this wasn't going well so she headed for the door.

'Sit down, NOW. Boys!' She came back and sat down.

'Now you tell me, this minute, what evidence? If you

want to leave here alive, you'll tell me and be quick about it.' Marjorie thought for a while, but George had had enough.

'Now!' shouted George.'

'Alright!' shouted Marjorie. 'The lad died near where you walk every day, in the woods.'

'So? Lots of people walk past there every day. Just why does that mean it's me?'

'You were seen there that day.'

'No chance love! You've got your wires crossed there because I had an appointment that afternoon with a client. Isn't that right boys?' They nodded. 'It said on the news that it was Thursday 3rd October when he went missing. That's right, isn't it Marjorie?'

'Yes,' she conceded. 'But I actually saw somebody that looked like you on that Thursday.'

'Boys, tell this woman where we were on that day and what times we were there. Just to remind you though boys it was 3rd October 1985 and we were with a client between 3pm and 8 pm. That's right isn't it boys?' One of the men produced a small pocket diary which he ceremoniously opened. He leafed through to find the 3rd of October and he stood up and showed the entry to Marjorie, standing over her while he did so.

'And just what the hell were YOU doing along that lane while he was going home? Did you fancy him, kill him because he said no? You are a liar Marjorie Jones, and I will be as good as you are at inventing tales if the coppers come after *me*.'

'OK. That seems fair enough. I will tell inspector Roberts when I see him. I suppose that the saliva on his body isn't yours either.' This hadn't been a wise comment because it seemed to hit a nerve.

'What the sodding hell do you think I am? I am running my business and keeping myself to myself in this God forsaken town, and all I get is grief. Just because I sometimes enjoy the company of men, as well as women, doesn't make me a pervert. Your trouble is that you read too many stories. You do, don't you? You get ideas in your head, and they run riot. Why don't you get out and find the real murderer, I'll go with you if you like, my boys too, *but leave me the hell alone.*' With that he raised an arm and Marjorie thought he was going to punch her in the face.

'BOSS,' came a shout from the settee and George backed off.

'Give her an hour in the guest room boys.' But then, after a moment's thought he said 'Just a minute, there's the dark room isn't there. Put her in there to "develop" for exactly 60 minutes then bring her back to me.'

The boys helped the now blindfolded Marjorie to walk up the stairs. She was shaking as she walked. The dark room turned out to be a plain room on the first floor with no windows and only one door. It was more of a walk-in cupboard. Once in there her blindfold and ear plugs were removed and one of the men had a chat with her.

'Look Marjorie, George isn't a nice man, so you really shouldn't be here taunting him. He actually was with a client when he said he was. He knows some important and very dangerous people, but he is a man of his word, so if he said an hour then that's all you'll spend in here, but be warned, if you tell anybody about this room, or even that you called here today, he will make your life, and that of your family, hell. Is that perfectly clear? I will only tell you once. Leave that lad's killer to the police, you clearly aren't working with them, are you? Just a clever woman who thinks she's Sherlock Holmes or Jane Marple.'

Marjorie was surprised by the eloquence of that message. These two were obviously educated men, and she warmed to them. She wondered what they had done to be in George's employ, but she believed what she had been told, and she began to shake a bit less. 'You are right. I coached Jez and I really thought I could make a difference. Apologise to your "boss" for me will you, and I promise I won't tell a soul.'

The men left, locking the door behind them. There was a bulb in the light above her, but it must have been the smallest wattage ever made, and it spread a very dim light. So, she had an hour to calm down and think. She decided that it was time to leave the police to this, and anyway Dan would be back soon. She suddenly remembered that Paula's party was to have been when Dan had returned from the oil rig and wondered whether Paula still wanted that party. Maybe it was best to postpone or cancel it since Paula already had her presents. That horrible dream kept coming back to her though, it had been the sort of dream that a child dreams. Surely it didn't mean anything, but it was so vivid, so stupid. Why would Jez be pleading to be killed by Erica, just so that Erica could kill Marjorie? It didn't make sense.

Marjorie had been so rapt in her own thoughts, thinking about how really strange the last two weeks had been, that the hour passed surprisingly quickly. She sat stock still when she heard the "boys" returning to let her out, but George had been nowhere in sight as she was blindfolded, and her ears were plugged. It hadn't been long before she was waiting for the front door to be unlocked, and for the blindfold and ear plugs to be removed.

'Remember this day,' said one of the men as the door was opened to the freshest air she had ever smelt.

It was 11.35 am. 'Damn,' she thought. 'I've missed my coaching session.' As she went to find a phone box a lie came quickly into her head. 'I must get that flat tyre repaired.' It had never occurred to her that she was remarkably unscathed after her ordeal, and that if she continued her investigating this way, she might not be so lucky next time. 'I might as well go and see Erica after I make the phone call,' was the next thing to enter her head.

Chapter 20. Paula's dad.

That afternoon, Paula returned home to find her dad sitting in their living room. 'DAD!' she shouted, 'I have missed you so much.' She gave him a hug.

'It's lovely to be home', said Dan. 'I'm sorry that I wasn't here for your birthday, but Joe needed time with his wife, so I swapped with him. How was your birthday?' Paula's birthday had been wonderful, but she wasn't ready to tell her dad about her relationship with Jez.

'It was fine,' she replied. 'Mum bought me the usual stuff and we had a cake. Jemma bought me some lovely stuff too, but I really missed having you here dad.'

'Are you getting on any better with your mum?' asked Dan

'I suppose that I am really,' she replied. 'We don't argue as much as we used to, but dad, she still thinks I'm a child. I'm 16 now.'

'To your mum you will always be a child love,' said her dad. 'It's how it can be with mothers. It was a long time before my mother realised that I had grown into a man. My first girlfriend almost left me because my mum always wanted to know where I was going, and once actually followed us to make sure that I wasn't lying!'

'How old were you then dad?'

'Now Paula, why would you want to know that? Anything you want to tell me about?' He had a twinkle in his eye as he asked that.

'No. I just wondered how it was with girlfriends and boyfriends back in the dark ages!' Her dad laughed.

'You're talking about sex aren't you.' Paula blushed, which was unusual for her.

'Yes, I know it's not the sort of thing you would talk to your old dad about, but I don't think you'd ask your mother either would you? I know that she can be a dragon at times.' This comment had whisked Paula back to the first time she had spoken to Jez. Her heart stopped momentarily.

'Look love, you are 16 now, and in many ways your life is now your own, so I don't want to know about your encounters with boys unless you want to tell me. I will tell you though that boys of your age were *just the same back when I was your age*. I can assure you that everything in my day was pretty much as free as it is now. So don't worry love, I have no idea what your mother was up to at 16, and for God's sake don't ask her, but remember that we grew up in the 1950s, and that was the decade when sex, drugs and rock and roll were invented!'

Paula laughed. She loved her dad, nothing seemed to upset him, and she realised how much better she felt now that he was back. She would tell him about Jez, but not yet. She expected her mother to tell him about his death and her potty attempts to find his killer, but she would tell her dad the rest herself.

'Have you got me a present then?' she asked her dad.

'I did, I will go and get it. I hid it in your mother's wardrobe in case you came home early and found it. I knew that you wouldn't look in there. I'll just get it.' He wasn't gone long and came back downstairs with a really large box. 'Winter's coming.' Paula unwrapped, then opened the box. Inside was a thick coat and, surprisingly, was one of those that she had seen Princess Diana wearing during one of her visits to Scotland. It was the height of fashion and, once she had tried it on, she was surprised to find that it fitted her very well.

'Dad it's ace,' she said. 'How did you know that I wanted one and how did you know my size?'

'Dads aren't as thick as people believe you know.'

'I notice that your mother has added a new racquet to her collection. Where did she get that from?'

'I don't know,' said Paula. She hasn't mentioned it to me. How do you know she's got a new one dad?'

'When I hid your coat in your mother's wardrobe, I noticed that the rack she keeps them in had moved from the left side of the wardrobe to the right, so I had a closer look. She has them all arranged like records in a rack, and I noticed that there was now only one space left in that rack. She must have thirteen now, but I'm sure she only had twelve when I left for the oil rig.'

'She must have got it from one of her students then because we haven't been anywhere since you went away. Should we ask her about it?'

'No! There will be hell to pay if you do, first because I have been in her wardrobe without her permission, and second because her collection is none of our business, or so she will say. I only know how many there had been before I left because I do an annual valuation of household goods for the insurance company, and I needed to know what was in her wardrobe. She has always boasted about that collection, and she reckons that it's worth thousands. I wonder what the new one is worth?'

'The only way to find out is to have a look at it but she'll be home soon. I wonder what's for tea?'

'Probably pizza,' said her dad. 'Tell you what, why don't I go and get fish and chips. I haven't had them for ages, and it'll be my treat. If your mother brings pizza home, it can go into the freezer.'

'Lovely idea dad. Bainbridge's chip shop opens at 5, so if you go now mum will be home when you get back.'

'Right, I'll be off then.' Dan left in his car and within minutes Marjorie had returned.

'Hello love,' she said to Paula as she entered the living room. 'I thought your dad might be home.'

'He is, he's gone for fish and chips as a treat, he shouldn't be long.'

'OK. I've brought pizza from that new pizza place that's just opened but they aren't cooked so I can put them in the freezer. What's that?' Marjorie pointed to Paula's present.

'It's my birthday present from Dad.' She and Paula both tried the coat on and there had followed a discussion about how even men can sometimes make the right decision about clothing. They then heard the front door, but Dan had returned wearing a quizzical look.

'The chip shop was closed today. There was a notice on the door about how it was closed today because one of their staff had gone missing, a bloke called Mark. What was that about do you think?' Paula and her mother looked at each other. He knew something was up. 'What's going on?'

After they had finished their explanation of everything that had happened while Dan was away, and after they had eaten their pizza and washed up, Marjorie announced that she was taking the car to fill it with diesel. She said that she had an early start tomorrow and wouldn't have time to fill it then. Once she had left, Dan turned to Paula and asked her how well she had known Jez.

'I knew him a bit, he was in the year above me at school, and then when mum started to coach him, I saw a lot more of him.'

'Are you sure that's all there was to it? I saw your face while your mum was telling me about Jez and there was real hurt there. It wasn't just a reaction to the horror of somebody that you knew being found dead, was it? Though that is shocking you looked desperately anxious to me too. Then there were your questions about teenage sex, but you haven't told me you have a boyfriend. So, I think that you and Jez were close, weren't you?'

'Oh Dad,' sobbed Paula. 'Please don't tell mum. We were going to tell you and mum at the party that we should have had today. I thought that she wouldn't be able to be angry with lots of people here. Yes, I loved him, and he loved me.'

'Why would your mother be angry love?'

'She didn't like Jez. She didn't have a good word to say about him, but I think she would be like that about any boy I met. Remember when I brought home Patrick when I was

14? She made him so uncomfortable here that we had to go out, and so that didn't last long. Jez was lovely, trouble was he didn't know that. He blushed all the time, but he was ace dad, and you'd have liked him.'

'Aw love I'm so sorry. I know how you must be feeling, and I won't say those things like "you'll meet somebody else" because, though it's true it's unhelpful now. I don't suppose you have a photo of him?'

'No, we didn't get around to all that photo booth stuff. We were only together for about 3 weeks all in.'

'I'll make you a drink Paula, you look like you could do with something!'

'Not yet,' said Paula. 'I want to tell you everything.'

'That you had sex with him. Don't worry, I worked that one out. It's fine love, except that it makes losing him harder.'

'The thing is dad; we couldn't meet here so we used to snog in the woods on the way home. We did wait till we were both 16 before we, you know, got our kit off,' at which Dan smiled, 'but the place where we did it is the place where they found his body. I was supposed to be with him that night, but mum made me wait in for the carpet fitter, a man that didn't come till she got back anyway. Dad, if I was with him that night this might not have happened!'

'Look love, we can't change things in life. What's to say that if you *had* been with him, you might not be dead too?' At this they both sat silent for a while. Suddenly Dan said, 'Did anybody see you in the woods when you were, you know, without your kit on, as you put it?'

'I don't know, I wouldn't have thought so. Why do you

ask?'

'Just a thought love. Seems odd that his body was found near where you had your liaisons. I wonder whether there's a link?'

'Maybe dad, but leave it to the police, and *promise* me that you won't tell mum any of this.'

'I promise, as long as you don't tell your mum about the rock and roll days before I met her.'

'Deal,' said Paula, who was surprised just how much better she felt now she had told her dad. She was sure that telling her mum would have had the opposite effect.

'By the way dad,' added Paula after they had sat quietly for a while, 'I don't think that mum has gone out for diesel. She fancies herself as an amateur detective and she has been "interviewing" people that she thinks are connected with Jez's murder. She got Jez's mum to sit near to the path where Jez was found and make a list of all the people that walked there at about teatime. Poor Valerie, that's Jez's mum by the way dad, sat all morning on Monday with a flask of tea and spoke to lots of people. She ended up with a list of 5 names of people that walk along there when the school empties out. She gave that to mum. Mum has actually been to talk to some of them. She even got your friend Joe to go with her one day.'

'Has she indeed? And roped Joe in too. She'd better be careful. I think I'll ask her about it when she comes home and get her to stop. So, you think she's round at the chip shop, do you?'

'Please dad, don't mention to mum that you know. Let her tell you. She thinks she's some woman called Jane

Marple from an old book. Leave her to it.'

'OK love. I might go to see Joe tomorrow anyway. He'll be off to the rig tomorrow night. How is Jez's mum coping with the loss of her son? Is she OK?'

'We have only seen her a few times and she's really cut up. She was happy to help mum to start with, but once everything sank in, she was so upset that the police told her to go away from her house for a few days. She's gone to stay with her sister I think.'

'Does she know about you and Jez?'

'I don't think so. Should I tell her?'

'I think it will help her to know, to know that he had been happy with a girlfriend. Maybe not tell her yet though love.'

'I'm tired dad, I think I will go to bed. We have a late start tomorrow by the way. There's a staff meeting or something, so I don't need to be at school till 11. I will see you in the morning.'

'Goodnight love.'

Instead of filling the car, Marjorie had been to the police station to see Inspector Roberts. Unfortunately, he hadn't been available so the officer on the desk had made her an appointment for Friday at 10am. She hadn't any coaching booked for then, so she was quite happy with that. She couldn't wait to tell him about the visits she had made, and the conclusions she had drawn. The police would be so pleased with her! She wouldn't mention Joe though. He wasn't to get any of the glory. She had to try to see Freda before that meeting; she would go there first thing in the morning, but just to make sure that Dan was correct she had driven past the chip shop on her way to the police station. The shop had indeed been closed, but she did notice that there was light coming through from the basement window.

Chapter 21. Discoveries.

The wake-up alarm played radio 2 in Marjorie's bedroom at 7.00am the following morning (Friday 11th) and Dan got up first, at about 7.10am, to make breakfast. He had missed this task when on the oil rig because he loved his morning routine. He enjoyed seeing the sun rise as he made the coffee, cereal and toast. On the rig he had just lined up with everybody else to get pre-packed slop of some sort which was served with instant coffee.

Marjorie joined him about 10 minutes later – she could never resist the smell of coffee in the mornings! 'What are your plans for the morning love?' asked Dan as they munched on toast and locally made marmalade.

'I have coaching all day with my first slot at 9am,' she lied. In fact, her first appointment wasn't until 10am and she was going to make sure that it finished in good time for her appointment with the inspector. She had also fully intended to see Freda at 9am and then maybe call in to see Joe.

'What are you up to then Dan?'

'I am going to see Joe to bring him up to date with some developments that he ought to know about before he goes out to do his engineering inspections. I don't think he will be very pleased with some of the modifications they made while I was there. He's senior to me so he might get something done.'

Marjorie was rather disappointed with this because she had hoped to discuss "the case" with Joe that morning. She would have to catch him later. Of course, she didn't mention any of this to Dan and instead replied with 'Why is Joe senior to you when he is so much younger?'

'He has that degree Marjorie. It really propels you up the ladder having one of those. Remember I just have "A" levels, and not very good grades at that. I am lucky to have done as well as I have.'

'It's not luck Dan, it's talent and hard work.' Dan looked astonished because complements from Marjorie were rare! 'I'll just go and wake Paula. That girl gets later than ever!'

'No need to love,' said Dan. School doesn't start today until 11am so you can let her lie in a bit. She's a woman now by the way, not a girl. I know she's our little girl, but we need to acknowledge that she isn't a child anymore.'

'Has she been complaining then?'

'No love. It's just that being away sometimes means I see the changes in her that you might miss through seeing her every day. Have a proper look next time you see her, you'll see what I mean.'

'Hmph,' said Marjorie. 'I'll just get ready then and be off,' and with a peck on his cheek she was gone.

A little later Dan left the house and arrived at Joe's at about 9.30am. He was surprised to see both Joe's and Trish's cars in the drive and after knocking quite a few times Joe let him in while wearing a slightly sheepish grin.

'Were you busy when I knocked?' asked Dan.

'Yes, we were rather.'

'Oh, sorry,' said Dan and smiled a knowing smile.

'No, not that,' replied Joe. 'We are actually busy packing. Remember that promotion I told you I had applied for? Well, it has come through and we are leaving tonight.'

'Excellent!' replied Dan as he shook Joe warmly by the hand. 'Bit short notice though isn't it?'

'It's been on the cards for a while, and Trish gave in her notice a while ago. She's been continuing to work with her company as a temp so that we could move immediately.'

'Oh,' said Dan. 'What about the house, won't it take a long time to sell it?'

'No, it's rented. We are paid up until Christmas and we'll lose that payment, but it's worth it. The furniture is being picked up later this afternoon and it's going into storage. We'll pick it up when we have a house to put it into.'

'So, what's happening in the meantime, where will you stay?'

'We have a place booked for a few weeks. We'll find somewhere when we've been there a little while.'

'And where is it you are going; you will keep in touch won't you?'

'Afraid not old mate. The new job isn't something I can talk about – it's hush hush government stuff and nobody must know where we are. To everybody we know it's promotion and a new start, but we haven't told anybody that we are leaving today. If you hadn't called in this morning you wouldn't know either. We don't like doing this to our friends, but we have no choice. I must swear you to secrecy and if you can't promise to say nothing, I'll have to shoot you.'

'Gosh,' is all that Dan could think of to say.

'Help me with this will you Joe?' came Trish's voice from upstairs. 'Oh, Hi Dan', she said when she saw him. 'It's hello and goodbye I'm afraid.' Dan went upstairs to help her with a suitcase that was very full.

'Do you need any help with anything?'

'No thanks,' they sang out in unison. All three laughed.

'It's very exciting leaving like this,' said Trish. 'Very cloak and dagger, but I am so pleased Joe got this job. We are looking forward to being out in the wilds of...'

'Trish!!!' said Joe, and she stopped just in time.

'Sorry Joe, I will have to get used to that. It's a good thing my friends are all away or at work because I couldn't have kept our secret from them.'

'You can tell them all about it when we are finished the job,' said Joe.

'We?' said Dan. 'Are you both taking part in this business then?'

'Yes,' again in unison. 'We'll be carrying out the same work, but Trish will concentrate on the bits she does well but that I am rubbish at, and vice versa.'

After a little more chat it had become obvious to Dan that he had better leave them to it because they clearly had a lot still to do. He wished them both well, expressed sadness that he wouldn't see them again, and said goodbye. He drove away feeling rather sad and more than a little envious.

In fact, packing wasn't quite the last thing that Joe had to do before leaving the area for good. After telling Trish that he needed some documents that were still at work, he went back into the office, arriving at 10.45am, knowing that most staff would be having morning coffee at that time, and was pleased to find that his floor was almost deserted when he got there. He went to his "special locked cupboard" and withdrew a carefully wrapped Betamax video tape. He dropped it into the specially prepared box he had brought with him, which he had pre-labelled with "Urgent, for the attention of the officer in charge of finding Jeremy Carter's killer", and the full address of the police station. Inside that box there was a covering letter detailing everything that had transpired between him and George Dickinson on that Thursday afternoon. He added that he would not be available to confirm the details in person but hoped that the contents of the tape would provide enough evidence for the Inspector to gain a warrant to search George's house. He also added that, unfortunately, the tape cleared George of any involvement in the death of Jeremy Carter. He went on to mention that Marjorie Jones, Jeremy Carter's coach, had been to see George to try to get him to confess to that murder. He wished the inspector luck in his search for the boy's killer and that he hoped that George and his "boys" would spend a long time behind bars. He had finally added that the inspector would likely find George and his Boys "at home" during the mornings. Though he had added his full name, Joe had given no address.

Before returning home, Joe took his parcel down to the company courier's office and placed it in the "two-hour delivery" box. He hoped that the inspector would have his parcel by lunchtime.

That was the last that anybody in Basingrove saw of Joe and Trish. Trish had no idea that their new incognito existence was not necessary from a company point of view, but it had been at Joe's insistence and, though they had no idea why he needed such anonymity, the company had agreed to give him his secret identity. In consequence, it had turned out that working in that way had made Joe very good at his job and Trish had found herself excelling too, doing rather better than Joe in fact. Working "incognito" as they were had helped their company to make some very high profits, and Trish and Joe were able to retire at age 55 with a really healthy bank balance. They never did tell anybody where they had gone and neither had missed their old life. They had both retained their first names and continued to be known as Trish and Joe and, curiously, just as in Basingrove, nobody ever asked for their surnames!

Chapter 22. Showdown.

(Still Friday)

Earlier that morning, Mark was still just outside his prison door, where he had slept soundly, and he opened his eyes just after 5am. His first thought had been that he had to formulate a plan to explain his disappearance, but he was hungry, so he ate and drank, bread and fizzy pop again. The bread was quite stale by now, but he didn't care. He was finally going home.

As an employee of the chip shop Mark had been given a set of keys to the front door so he was able to let himself out, and he locked up behind him "to maintain the integrity of the evidence". He had heard that on "Miami Vice" on TV and it had sounded good to him today. Once outside, and in fresh air, he headed for home, and he arrived there at 6.30am. He was soon knocking loudly on the door. After quite a while, and several attempts at knocking, he heard his mother shout 'Who is it?'

'It's me mum.' The door then opened very quickly, and his mum dragged him in to many hugs and tears. Later she had made him sit down and said she would make him some breakfast.

'Breakfast,' thought Mark. 'Has a 16-year-old ever been so pleased to be offered breakfast by his mother?'

Over coffee and cereal, (he really didn't want any toast because he had had enough bread for now), he told his mother everything. He had left everything in, even telling her that he and Harriet had been found naked. He told her how Freda had tricked him into being in the stock room by getting him to tidy it up and his mum was particularly annoyed that Freda had got him to work before she locked him in.

'And you have been there since Tuesday night?'

'Yes mum. I thought that she was going to let me out on Wednesday night, but she didn't even open the shop. I was really narked when I saw the notice on the door as I left this morning, telling everybody how upset she was, when it was, she who was hiding me all the time. I didn't starve though, plenty to eat, but I was a bit panicky at times.'

'I'm sure that you were love, I know how you get in confined spaces. I had better call the police to tell them that you are safe.'

'Not yet please mum,' and he went on to describe a sketchy plan to her.

'Alright,' she said, 'But whether or not we are finished sorting out this mess, we must go to see the police no later than just after lunch. They *are* still looking for you.'

'Agreed. I hope you don't mind about me and Harriet sleeping together. It was quite hard telling you to be honest, but I made my mind up because it's important you know everything.'

'Whether or not I mind is something that isn't important at the moment. I'll talk to you about that later. What's important now is that you go and get a bath or a shower.

You really do smell terrible and it's not just from being in the fish shop!'

'Yes mum.'

At 8am Mrs Buckingham telephoned Harriet. It was Freda who answered the phone so Mrs. Buckingham had pretended that she had got into a bit of a state about Mark's disappearance, fearing now that he might be dead, but about how she hoped he was alive and well and that he would be found in due course. Eventually, bored with the "pleasantries" with Mark's mum, Freda had gone to fetch Harriet. Harriet had picked up the telephone receiver anxiously because she was worried that it might be bad news about Mark.

'Hi.'

'Good morning, Harriet, this is Mark's mum. Would you come to see me about Mark, as quick as you can please? I am in a bit of a state, and I need somebody to talk to.'

'Oh my God he's not dead, is he?' asked Harriet as she sat down with a thud.

'Not as far as I know but I do need to talk to you.'

'Have they found him?'

'Just come and see me, PLEASE Harriet.'

'OK. I'll set off now.'

'What's up?' asked Freda suspiciously.

'I don't know mum, but Mrs Buckingham's in bad way. She's got a bee in her bonnet about something, and she wants me to go and see her. I'd better go now. I hope it's not bad news.'

'What about breakfast?'

'I'll expect Mark's mum to give me something after she's got me to trail all the way over there.'

'OK, but don't be too long.'

A few minutes later she heard the front door bang and, knowing exactly where Mark was, Freda was able to happily get on with her morning routine without worrying about whether or not he had really been dead.

Freda had actually formulated a plan herself to get around the fact that it was she who had deliberately imprisoned him. She had decided that Mark had accidentally locked himself in the stock cupboard because she thought he had already gone home when she had bolted the storeroom door. She had unwittingly made this go on for longer than was necessary because she had shut the shop on Wednesday as a mark of respect for her missing employee. Then, when he hadn't been found quickly, she was so devastated that the shop could stay closed until the weekend, so she hadn't been there to let him out the young fool, (laugh laugh laugh!). She would threaten Mark with all sorts of things if he didn't comply with these tales. She had seen him naked of course, so lots of accusations had come into her nasty mind, which she would share with Mark and threaten to use herself if he refused to go along with her story. She had it all sewn up and now the plan was ready she would let him out this afternoon, the little sod. At that time of course, she had no idea that Mark had actually freed himself.

Ten minutes later Harriet was knocking on Mrs.

Buckingham's door and very quickly the door was opened, and Harriet was ushered in. There were a few quick pleasantries, Mrs Buckingham did indeed offer Harriet breakfast, and she left her alone while she went to make tea and toast for her guest. Harriet had been sitting wondering what was going on when the door opened and in walked the now bathrobe clad Mark.

'Morning Harriet,' is all he said.

'Mark!' Harriet ran towards him and gave him a big hug. 'You haven't been here all the time have you rotten sod,' she cried as she beat him gently on his chest. 'I will murder you myself if you have been, just to make us all worry.'

Mark sat her down and began to tell her the tale of what had really happened from the moment Freda had found them together to the moment she had locked him in the stock room while he was busy tidying up. 'But you are terrible with enclosed spaces, you won't even get in a lift so how did you manage in there?'

'I nearly didn't,' he replied. 'I had to curl up with the light off to imagine that I was outside, otherwise I think I would have had a heart attack. But I got through it and here I am. I told you that penknife would come in handy one day.'

'Tell me you are not making this up to get at my mother.'

'I'm not. The padlock is still in the bolt, and I couldn't put that on myself if it was outside the door. It will have your mother's fingerprints on it and if you want, we can go back there now and I can show you my makeshift toilet arrangements, you will certainly smell them if you go in now.' At that point Mrs Buckingham brought the tea and toast.

'I want to kill my mother,' said Harriet.

'There'll be none of that talk,' said Mrs Buckingham. 'There's been enough nasty business, and don't forget that it must have been a shock to go into that room, expecting to see bread rolls and drinks and stuff and seeing you two with no clothes on, especially him,' and she pointed at Mark who looked more than slightly embarrassed.

'Thanks mum!' At this point they laughed, a very uncontrolled laugh which had been more relief than anything else.

'I'm glad you are home, especially after it turns out that the other missing boy is dead.'

'Really?' said Mark, who had missed the release of this news because he was entombed at the time it had been made public. 'How terrible. Was he murdered?'

'Yes, and we were worried that you had been the second victim of a serial killer.' added Harriet.

'Wow,' is all that Mark could come up with. After they had eaten and drunk, but with no more food for Mark, it was Harriet's turn to speak.

'We'd better go to the police and mum will have to pay for what she has done. I wonder what the punishment for enforced imprisonment of somebody is?'

'I don't know,' said Mark, 'but I have come up with a plan that will keep your mother out of prison and hopefully get us back together, and my jobs back.' He outlined his plan to Harriet and his mother, and they both agreed that it was worth a try. Harriet said that Mark was being far too kind to her mother, but she agreed to call Freda and ask her to come to see Mrs Buckingham.

After taking a while to compose herself, Harriet telephoned her mother about ten minutes later. She told her that they both needed some support and that she was to come over immediately. After some complaining, Freda Bainbridge set off for Mrs Buckingham's little house.

Once there she knocked on the door and was surprised by how quickly it had been opened. 'Harriet must have been looking out for me,' she thought to herself.

It was indeed Harriet that had opened the door to her mum, and she asked Freda to join her and Mrs Buckingham in the living room. On entering, Freda was invited to sit down, and Mark's mother left to make some refreshment, coffee this time. Harriet chatted to her mum for a while but suddenly Mark popped into the living room and said 'Hi Mrs. Bainbridge,' as casually as he could.

'You!'

'Yes, you weren't expecting to see me, were you? I escaped you see, and we thought that we should let you know that I am now free, so you don't need to come and let me out of your stock room.'

'But!' is all that Freda could manage and at that point the coffee arrived. There was silence as Mrs. Buckingham passed around the cups.

'Mum, Mark has told us what you did, that you made him tidy up the stock room and that you then locked him in. He told us that you said it was for a night, but it went on longer didn't it mum.'

'I did intend one night, but when he was reported missing, I thought I had better leave him longer, to soften him up a bit, just in case he ran to the police when I let him out.'

'Mum, do you know how evil that sounds, and for how long you will be in prison? Mark is claustrophobic and he could have died from the stress!'

'I knew he would be alright the little toad.' Mark had been told to stay silent while Harriet spoke and he was managing to do that, but only just.

'Mum, *we* don't want you to go to prison, so Mark has thought of a way to tell the police what happened and make it sound like an accident. But we expect you to give Mark his job back and write to Tesco and tell them his absence from work was a mistake on your part, because he might lose his job there too.'

'Go on.'

'Mark will tell the police that you had asked him to get rid of a huge spider in the stock room, which he did, but that he then tidied up the mess he had made while catching it. You didn't realise he was doing that, so you assumed that he had gone home for the night when you locked the stock room door, and then also left for the night yourself. Then you left the shop closed on Wednesday as a mark of respect because Mark had disappeared. You were too upset to open on Thursday and it wasn't until he had escaped that you realised what had happened.'

'I won't give him his job back. He defiled you in my stock room and I won't have him back!'

'Mother, he hasn't defiled anybody, not to my knowledge at least. I know that he hasn't defiled me.' Mark was becoming fidgety, but Harriet gave him a look that meant be quiet.

'He's not coming back to work for me, and I don't care about his job with Tesco.'

'In that case mother we will bring in the police and they will find your fingerprints on the lock that you fitted to the stockroom door bolt. They will also find all the other evidence, including Mark's makeshift toilet. This will put you away for years. Do you really want that?'

'It won't come to that. You forget that I have seen Mark naked, and I have spotted some little details that mean that if you go to the police, I can say that he sexually attacked me. So, if you do go to the police, I will say that I locked him in because he had stripped off and was attempting to have his way with me, and that I just managed to escape with my life.'

Mark's mum had sat in silence while this exchange was taking place but now, she had had enough. 'STOP!' she shouted, and, to everybody's surprise, there was instant silence. Then, very calmly, she began to speak. 'Freda, you have, in front of witnesses, declared that you are prepared to tell lies about my son if he tells the truth, and that you are prepared to use the fact you have seen him naked to invent tales of a threat against you. That means you are going to lie to the police and accuse him of unwanted sexual advances against you. How dare you? Are you honestly prepared to invent a tale of attempted rape or sexual attack just because my son loves your daughter? You stand there, pretending to be so saintly and proper, and yet it is you that is evil, and you have a thoroughly perverted outlook at that. You have expressed disgust about finding Mark with Harriet, yet you have clearly kept an image of my son's naked body in your mind to further your attempt to hide the fact that you locked him up, a young man that you know suffers from claustrophobia, just because you disapprove of his affair with Harriet. Let me just tell you now Freda Bainbridge, that if you try to tell these lies, I will make sure that it's you that is seen naked, not in your stock room but in the showers of a women' prison. Your daughter and my son have given you an opportunity to hide the fact that you are guilty of enforced imprisonment, or even attempted manslaughter because of his severe claustrophobia. Now either take the option you have been given or I will call the police now and get them to examine your shop, where they will find enough evidence of your rotten deeds to lock you up for years!'

There was silence for a while. Mark stood in shock after hearing Freda's intentions so clearly spelled out. Not only had Freda locked him up but now he might end up in real prison and on terrible charges.

Harriet was absolutely aghast. She couldn't believe that her mother could be such an evil cow, or that Mark's mum could be so eloquent! Freda just stood open mouthed for a while and then sat down, with a bump. She knew that she was beaten.

'You're right,' is all she said. 'Mark, thank you for agreeing to bend the truth a little. I am sorry I locked you up, I don't know what came over me. If you report to the police as you suggested I will back you up, and I will write to Tesco to apologise for your absence, explain that it was my silly fault and ask them not to sack you. I will even tell them that, since you were just trying to protect me from a spider in a tiny stock room, your heroism as a severe claustrophobe should be applauded, and hope that they might extend your hours a little. Of course you can come back to work for me.'

There followed a long pause as everybody calmed down. 'I will leave you and your daughter to chat while I clear away these tea and coffee things,' said Mark's mum, 'Give me a hand Mark please?' and they left Freda and Harriet alone. Whilst in the kitchen she spoke to Mark. 'Are you OK Mark?'

'Yes mum. I'll be better in a few days when things get back to normal.'

'Will you be OK working for Freda after all this?'

'I think so, but I will only work while Harriet is there.'

'Are your feelings still the same for Harriet, are you still sure that you love her?'

'I think so, but we will have to see how it goes. I'll get my life back first, I think. Play some football and stuff like that.' His mum smiled and said, 'It's good to have you home Mark.'

'Mum, how could you have done this to Mark?' Harriet said calmly.

'I don't know Harriet. Perhaps I just didn't want you to grow up and leave. It's not Mark, I suppose that he's a good lad really. I would have done the same to anybody. I am sorry.

'I am sorry too.' Then Harriet had a little test for Freda. 'Mrs Buckingham has said that I can come to live here so that I can be near to Mark. So, I will be moving out. Now you have apologised shall I tell her I have changed my mind?'

'No Harriet. If that's what you want to do, then it's your life. You aren't 18 yet so I could say no, but I've done enough damage already.'

'There's only two bedrooms here mum so I will have to sleep with Mark.' Freda sighed.

'If you really are sure then that is what you must do, I won't stand in your way.'

'Thanks mum. Actually, I think Mark should have his own room and his old life back for a while. Perhaps I won't move in just yet!' For the first time in ages, they smiled at each other.

A week after these exchanges had taken place, Mark received a letter from Tesco offering him a new thirty-five-hour contract with them. This meant that he no longer needed to work for Freda and, since it had seemed to everybody that this was a good offer, he decided to accept it and his employment at the chip shop came to an end. This had caused great relief in the Buckingham family home.

Chapter 23. Things begin to resolve.

(Still Friday)

While Dan was talking to Joe that Friday morning, detective inspector Roberts had been at his desk rubbing his temples. He had no idea what do next because he had a dead boy, a missing boy, and now a missing officer on his hands. He had no motives for any of the disappearances, no murder weapon for the dead boy, and absolutely no new leads to follow. His officers had combed the area and spoken to many people, but nothing had emerged to help.

Tom (PC Hollingsworth) had first been missed on the Thursday morning when he hadn't turned in for his shift. Sergeant Bulmer had telephoned to his landlady at 10.30am because he was due to start work at 9am, and it wasn't like him to be late.

'Could I please speak to Tom Hollingsworth?' he asked her.

'He should have left for work by now, but I will try his door for you if you like?'

'Yes please.' After the sound of footsteps wandering off and then returning, her reply was slightly anxious.

'He's not answering when I knock, so I'm anxious as to why you are ringing? Has he not turned up for work? He's such a good lad usually, but I'm a bit worried because it's bin day, and he always puts his little bin out for me to empty on a Thursday. It's not there sergeant.'

'Do you have a key to his room?'

'Yes. Do you want me to go in?'

'Yes please, just tell me what you find, see whether he has emptied his wardrobe or something like that.'

'What if I find him dead, or if he's not decent when I go in?'

'I'm sure that won't be the case,' said the sergeant, though he wasn't actually sure of that himself. After a pause of about 3 minutes Tom's landlady had returned.

'He's not in his room sergeant. He has an en suite bathroom and everything in there's dry, and his kettle's cold. There's a very dried up mug and cereal bowl too so I don't think he came home last night at all. What do you think has happened to him?'

'He'll be about somewhere so don't worry. Probably been out all night in a secret stake out that nobody's told me about. We'll sort him out and scold him for worrying you.'

'I just hope that he's OK, especially after that other boy's gone missing too.'

'Don't you worry madam. He'll be back soon. Goodbye for now.'

'Goodbye,' said a very worried old lady.

Following that call, the sergeant had tried to find out where Tom had been the previous day and noticed that they had heard nothing from his radio since just after lunch time on Wednesday. That radio was now either turned off or faulty, because he couldn't be contacted that way and, after asking around, he found that nobody really knew where he had gone that day, though Sergeant Windsor *did* have some useful information.

'I saw Tom at a computer terminal yesterday and maybe he found something on there that he decided to go and investigate. Perhaps he's got himself into some sort of bother.' Sergeant Windsor was slightly worried about Tom because she had a soft spot for him. He was twelve years her junior, and she felt very protective towards him, and she did love to tease him, but then he was a rather serious young man and so he was easy to tease.

It was well known that it was he that had found Jez's body, so sergeant Bulmer decided that perhaps Tom had been following up on a lead about that. Unfortunately, he knew nothing about computers, and he didn't know that his search data would be recorded in the County's main database, so a search via the computer system wasn't done immediately. Other concerns meant that Tom's absence had to be left as a mystery, for the present.

* * *

Paula had eventually got out of bed just as her dad was leaving to see Joe. She wasn't due to be at school until 11am, and she had been disappointed not to see her dad before he left because time with him, and without her mum, was precious to her. She had also been very thoughtful and a bit anxious because she didn't know what to do now that her dad had found that racquet. Usually there was such a great song and dance about a new racquet, everybody would be shown it, they would be told where her mother had bought it, whether it was new, antique or vintage, who had played with it and whether it was signed by somebody famous. She was always particularly keen to tell them if the racquet had been a present from an adoring student, just to emphasise how good she was! Paula felt that she had to do something.

She rarely went into her mother's room; it was forbidden territory so it was a bit odd being in there, but she knew where the key to the wardrobe was, and where the racquets would be. They were kept to the left of her mother's fancy wardrobe but, as her dad had said, she had moved them. Paula had seen the collection before, and when she counted them there was indeed an extra one. She took them out, one at a time, and looked at them. Some were shiny, some were old, and some were signed but, right in the middle as though her mother had tried to hide it in plain sight, she picked up a racquet that she recognised.

This racquet was a really nice one: it looked quite old, and it had some signatures of current players on it. Paula had seen it a few times, Jez had shown it to her and told her all about it, how it had been his dad's racquet and that this was the reason he was so keen to play badminton!

'This is certainly Jez's, but what do I do about it? Dad knows something's up because mum has kept this one a secret. What if he goes to the police?'

She looked at the racquet for a while, thinking back to the last time she saw Jez play with it. Carefully, after wiping them to remove any fingerprints, she returned the racquets to their slots. She didn't wipe Jez's racquet though because she thought the police might need to get fingerprints from it.

She left everything as she had found it and closed and locked the door. She was shaking.

'Now what?' she thought. 'Do I tell mum that dad has found the racquet, or do I tell the police and leave it to them to decide what to do? Do I ask dad what to do?' She had no idea what should happen next so she decided that she would do nothing for now. Maybe dad would ask her mother where it came from anyway, although he would need to justify finding it so he probably wouldn't.

She got to school in good time for the start of the day, but her mind wasn't on her work. If only there was somebody she could confide in. Then she remembered that Mr. Johnson had said to see him if anything came to light, so she decided to try to speak to him before her second lesson of the day.

* * *

Mrs. Jones' appointment with the inspector was due at 11am, and she arrived on the dot. The inspector was ready for her, and he hoped that whatever she had come to tell him was important.

'Good morning, Mrs Jones, please sit down. Would you like coffee?' Expecting it to be dreadful she declined.

'Please, call me Marjorie.'

'Now Marjorie, what can I do for you?'

'I hope that I can help *you*,' she replied, and went on to tell him everything that she had been up to, but he interrupted her at a point part way through her "report".

'Can I just point out here that impersonating a police officer is a very serious offence, so I hope that isn't what you were trying to do. Apart from the potentially criminal element I can't use any information you give me if that was the case.'

'Of course I wasn't impersonating a police officer,' she said with a bit of a snap. 'When I last saw Jez, I didn't expect to be talking about his death, so I wanted to do something to help. Valerie had collected the names of some people that often walk along that path where (sob) Jez was found, and I told her that I would ask whether they had seen anything, just to help you. If anybody asked, I always said that I was helping gather information *for* the police.' The inspector apologised and asked her to go on.

'This is a list of the people that I went to see, and what a funny bunch they all turned out to be.' She handed the inspector a piece of paper on which was written the following:

Old Erica Briggs and her dog Eric.
Geoffrey Smithson and his dog Fred.
Maureen Davidson who walks home that way after work.
George Dickinson, a local villain according to rumour.
Freda Bainbridge and her dog Pickles, the chip shop owner.

'Don't you see inspector, the lad that's just gone missing worked for Freda, and I never got around to speaking to her. She might be involved and maybe her employee Mark had found out. Perhaps she has killed him to shut him up.' At that point there was a knock at the door and Sergeant Bulmer came in.

'Package for you sir marked "Urgent, for the attention of

the officer in charge of finding Jeremy Carter's killer".' He placed the package on the inspector's desk.

'Thanks sergeant.' Marjorie looked at the package and wondered what it contained. The address had been done with a typewriter and she couldn't see any post mark.

'Well, well, I wonder what he's put in there?' she thought. Once the sergeant had left the room the inspector continued.

'How did you compile this list?' Marjorie described how she and Jez's mother had found out who regularly walks along that path at school closing time.

'So, which of these people have you spoken to?' he asked.

'All except Freda Bainbridge. Both Erica and Geoffrey are as mad as a basket of frogs, so I'm sure that they had nothing to do with this, and Maureen was too gentle to have done anything, especially with her husband being as he is.' Marjorie recounted her "interviews" with those three and she then gave the inspector a very abridged version of her first encounter with George Dickinson, but she didn't mention Joe.

'George has been very cheery with me, and I find his broad Glaswegian accent very attractive. There are two strong looking blokes that seem to follow him about and he's obviously gay or bisexual, based on the posters adorning his walls. If I *were* a police officer officer, he would be my chief suspect'.

'Why do you consider him to be your chief suspect Marjorie?'

'Perhaps he has been targeting teenage young men and perhaps he had taken a fancy to Jez, but when he tried to have his way Jez had resisted, and he ended up dead.'

'And have you managed to uncover any evidence to back up your suspicions?'

'No inspector, but he had a cagy manner, and that suggested that he was lying to me about where he had been while I was coaching Jez on the day that Jez died.'

'Well thank-you very much for your help, Marjorie. Is there anything else that you yourself have remembered that might help us?'

'No inspector. You already have everything that I remember.'

'Well goodbye Marjorie, and thank-you for coming in. You have made my day, we now have at least one extra person to interview, and we may speak to the others again in due course, especially Freda Bainbridge. I must ask you not to try to go back to see George Dickinson. He *is known to us,* and we believe that he may be very dangerous. If you do go to see him, it may also hamper any investigation we might begin. Thanks again and I will get my sergeant to show you out.'

'By the way inspector, I passed Freda Bainbridge's shop last night and I couldn't help but notice that, though it was closed, there was a light on in what must be a basement. I saw light coming through the window in the pavement.'

'Now that's interesting,' said the inspector. 'Thanks for that, and I will get somebody to look into it.' He laughed at his own humour. 'Goodbye for now then Marjorie.'

'You will keep me in the loop, won't you?' said Marjorie as she left.

'Of course,' said the inspector, though he would only do that if he thought she could help further. His officers had spoken to all those on Marjorie's list anyway, except for George, who had always seemed to be out when anybody had called to see him.

'Goodbye then Mrs. Jones, and remember what I have told you. Leave this to us now.'

She left and he turned his attention back to his unexpected mail delivery. He was just about to open his package when a call came through from the desk sergeant.

'Inspector, I have Mr Johnson on the line for you, from the school that Jeremy Carter attended.'

'Put him through please.'

'Roberts here, how can I help you?'

'Good morning inspector. I have Paula Jones with me, daughter of Marjorie Jones. She has found out something this morning which might be related to the death of Jeremy Carter, and this has caused her some distress. She would like to speak to you and wondered whether we could both come to see you later today.'

Intrigued, the inspector thought for a moment. 'Things are piling up now, but perhaps I will see these two, but only after I have opened that parcel.' It was now approaching 11.20am.

'Could you both come in at 12am?' he asked. He heard Mr. Johnson speak to Paula.

'Yes, that would be absolutely fine. We will arrive then and presumably head for the reception desk?'

'Ask for me directly,' the inspector said as he rang off. 'Now that's interesting, but it can wait because I want to know what's in here.' He began to undo the wrapping on the mysterious package but, unfortunately, he didn't get far with that because sergeant Bulmer arrived and told him that there was a group of people that wanted to see him.

'Can it wait a while because I want to open this?'

'I think you ought to see these people right now sir, really I do.' Bulmer had been with inspector Roberts a long time and he knew when it was wise to heed his sergeant's advice.

'Send them in then Bert.' Sergeant Bulmer returned a few minutes later and introduced his "guests" as though he were announcing at a dinner party.

'Sir, please welcome Mrs. Freda Bainbridge, Harriet Bainbridge, Mrs Buckingham *and the previously missing Mark Buckingham!*' In they all trooped, and the sight of that missing lad caused the inspector to sit down with a bump.

'Well, am I glad to see you,' he said, as he was shaking Mark by the hand. 'Perhaps you should tell me all about this, so who's going to be spokesman?' It was Harriet that obliged and the whole, slightly altered, tale of Mark's "accidental" imprisonment came out, with some occasional sobs from Freda.

'Mark, exactly when were you able to get out of that basement and have you been back to the Fish and Chip shop since you escaped from your confinement?'

'I got out earlier this morning sir, so I headed straight home to tell mum that I was OK, and to have a shower. I got home at about half past six. No inspector, I haven't been back to the chip shop at all today. As Harriet said, she and her mum joined me and my mum immediately after I had showered and tidied myself up a bit, so they won't have been back there either.' The Bainbridges nodded their agreement.

'After my shower we spent some time getting back together, and I really needed some proper food after living on bread rolls and fizzy pop. As far as I know, the locked bolt and my makeshift toilet are still there.'

'Hmm,' said the inspector. 'Mrs Bainbridge, may we enter the premises to do some forensic investigations, just to confirm that what you have all told me is true?'

'Of course,' said Freda, and she handed over her shop keys.

'The fish and chip shop must now be regarded as a potential crime scene, so I must ask you all to stay away from even the front door until our investigations are complete. Delighted and relieved as I am that this is cleared up, I must also ask you to leave now as I have another appointment, but Sergeant Bulmer here will take statements from all four of you before you leave.'

Thanks were expressed all round and the inspector heaved a sigh of relief. The inspector knew that he didn't need to tell the sergeant to take all of the statements separately, but he had a slight feeling that what he had heard was not entirely the truth. He wanted to make sure that their accounts tallied perfectly, so he was pleased that he could rely on Bert. All he had to do now was to find Tom and solve Jez's murder! He rang through to the front desk.

'Have Mr, Johnson and Paula arrived yet?'

'Yes sir.'

'Apologise to them for my being late and ask them to come up. Oh, and send out for some coffee and a ham sandwich for me please, and bring it straight in when it arrives, I'm starving!'

Mr. Johnson and Paula had walked into the inspector's office with some trepidation, but the inspector smiled at them, and they were able to relax a little. 'Good afternoon,' began the inspector. 'I do apologise to both of you for being a little late. Would either of you like refreshments?'

'No thank you.'

'What can I do for you Paula?' asked the inspector, addressing her directly.

'Go on Paula,' said Mr. Johnson. Paula told the inspector how her dad had found a new racquet in her mother's wardrobe, and that when she had gone to look at it herself, she realised that it had belonged to Jez. She went on to explain how she knew that it had belonged to Jez and, in some detail, explained that her mother never kept a new racquet a secret.

'You are absolutely sure that the racquet you found in your mother's wardrobe is the one that had belonged to Jeremy Carter?'

'Yes.'

'And I assume that you haven't asked your mother about it?'

'No! She'd be furious to know that even dad had been in her wardrobe.'

'You seem to have been very familiar with the racquet and clearly knew it really well, so I am forced to ask whether you two were an item?' said the inspector.

'Yes, we were,' replied Paula, her eyes filling with tears.

'I'm sorry that I had to ask you that, but it will really help my investigation to know everything. Had you known each other long?'

'No,' she replied, and she went on to tell the inspector just enough about their brief and fairly rapid courtship.

'Now, this is important. Does your mother know that you were in a relationship with Jeremy?'

'No inspector. I was going to tell her at my 16th birthday party, and that had to be two weeks after my actual birthday because dad was away. I didn't want to tell her because she wouldn't have approved. I would have felt safer telling her at my party because others would be around, and she wouldn't make a scene. Once Jez had been found dead, I couldn't see any point in telling her, but I have told my dad now that he's back.'

'Where has your dad been?'

'Dad works on an oil rig sometimes and he had swapped shifts with Joe, his friend, because Joe and his wife Trish needed some time together. This meant he would have missed my birthday party if it was held on my real birthday. Me and Jez didn't get, you know, together, until I was actually 16.'

'Hmm,' said the inspector and he asked her for Joe's address so that he could speak with him if necessary. Unfortunately, Paula didn't know where Joe lived, or what his surname was. Everybody had just called him Joe, though she *could* tell the inspector that he was married to a Trish.

'Have you any idea how your mother could have acquired Jez's racquet?'

'No, that's the problem because I really can't think how she could have got it. That's why I asked Mr. Johnson what to do and he told me to speak to you. I'm sure that she didn't

Page 236

murder Jez so perhaps his killer gave it to mum and told her to keep quiet.'

'Paula, there are many ways that your mother could have got hold of that racquet. It's quite likely that she saw the racquet for sale in one of her haunts and bought it without questioning the seller. She possibly doesn't know that it belonged to Jeremy, or she might know but didn't tell you because she realised that it would upset you if she had shown it to you. It's probably best that you don't mention to your mother that you have found the racquet, or to anybody else for that matter. Ask your dad to keep it to himself too. We knew that his racquet was missing but we don't want that widely known yet. So, neither of you must mention this outside of this room. Tell me again, *exactly,* why did your dad swap shifts with Joe? Surely, he wouldn't have wanted to miss your birthday?'

'I think that Joe had said that he needed time with his wife or something.'

There was some further general chat, but the inspector ended their interview by asking Paula to get her dad to bring something personal from her mother, the contents of a hairbrush or a used glass for example. He asked her to tell him to bring it to him in person because he wanted to talk to him anyway, and this would avoid another visit to the Jones house. He explained that these items could be used to remove her mother from their enquiries. The inspector then thanked them both for coming in, and he wished them well.

The inspector had begun to formulate a theory as to what had happened to Jez, and about who had murdered him, and these snippets of information fitted nicely with his theory, as did the reappearance of Mark Buckingham.

After eating his sandwich, the inspector got back to the parcel and extracted a video tape and a letter. The letter was signed by Joe, which the inspector assumed to be the same Joe that Paula had just mentioned.

'Interesting coincidence,' he thought, but his head was beginning to spin so he decided that it was time to have a break. To help clear his head he left the building and went for a walk. He thought that he would get to work on the letter and video later that afternoon.

After thirty minutes or so of walking, the inspector had become impatient and he was soon back at his desk, the letter now open and in his hand. It read as follows:

Dear Inspector Roberts,

My name is Joe, and I am a close friend of Dan Jones, the husband of Marjorie Jones. Actually, I know Marjorie quite well too, as I will detail later. I am writing this letter to accompany the video I have sent to you because, by the time you read this, my wife and I will have left this area to take up a promotion within my company, and my employers have agreed that my whereabouts from this point on will remain a closely guarded secret. Please don't look for me, I am sure that, with the resources available to you, I can easily be found, but once you have seen the video you will understand why nobody must know my whereabouts. My wife will be working with me and, though she knows nothing of my past with George, or this video, she has taken similar precautions and all of our friends will have no idea where we have gone. You will not be able to contact me by phone but, just in case there is anything that I have forgotten to tell you, I will ring the police station at exactly 10am next Monday, 14th October. This will be from a phone box and will be from nowhere near where we will end up; we are doing a road trip around the country before ending up at our final destination, which may, or may not, be in this country. Please have somebody available to take that call.

You need to be aware that I am the son of wealthy parents and, as seemed common at universities at the time, I got into wild parties in my university days, and many of those were well supplied with drugs. I had the money to buy them, and I ended up so drug dependent that I would do anything to get them, even as far as sleeping with the dealer, regardless of their sex. Fortunately, my parents had the money to get me into rehab and, after taking a year out of university, I am now clean. Despite this, I have had some lapses along the way and, when first married, I bought some cannabis from a tall, blonde dealer called Jean-Paul, and when he died his "round" was taken over by a man called George Dickinson, a Glaswegian now living in Basingrove. I imagine that your paths will have crossed before now. George has now reached my name in his little book of dependents, and he has come after me a few times to try to sell me drugs. Unfortunately, he has photographs of me buying drugs from Jean-Paul and he has threatened to use them against me. George is bisexual and he knows that I partook of such things whilst "off my head" at university, so I was able to persuade him that a night with me and a "small purchase" would be sufficient payment keep him off my back (so to speak) for a while. Fortunately, I was able to video that encounter, including chat about the drugs he was offering, the *price he was charging, and a small purchase that I had to make from him. I even got him to admit that all the necessary equipment was at his home. I am sending you this very long video in the hope that it will allow you to get a warrant to search his house, where you will find facilities to process and divide a range of substances intended to cause harm.*

Marjorie Jones (the badminton coach) may have told you that she suspects George Dickinson of the murder of a boy called Jeremy Carter, one of the young men that she has coached. Unfortunately, my liaison with George took place on the afternoon of 3rd October, so this video recording gives him an alibi for that murder because you will hear the radio playing in the background, and it's time and date checks confirm that George was nowhere near the lane where the body was found or where the missing lad was last seen, on that date.

Marjorie may even have mentioned that she had persuaded me to go with her on one occasion to act as her "muscle" while interviewing George. She wasn't aware that the only reason that he let us both into his home is that he was gathering evidence to further blackmail me, and he thought he could use my apparent relationship with Marjorie to get me into buying even more from him. In fact, Marjorie and I had once slept together after a very drunken party, so George possibly knew about that.

You need to be aware that Marjorie still seems to have "the hots" for me and she has tried to get me back into bed, including on the night of Carter's death. Please also be aware that I have resisted these approaches, and I was relieved when she couldn't "take me to her king-sized bed" as she had wanted to do that night.

Though she did ask me to continue to accompany her while "interviewing" George, I took no further part in Marjorie's amateur sleuthing, so I don't think that I can help you further on that score.

Best regards

Joe

'Well,' thought the inspector. 'What a lot to take in. This morning I had one dead sixteen-year-old, another missing and a missing constable. Now that count has fallen by one and his reason for disappearing is known, subject to confirmation from scene of crime officers. That leaves my missing officer and the perpetrator of Carter's death to find. Then there's my amateur sleuth associate Marjorie Jones and her suspicions, but there's also the mystery as to where she found that badminton racquet. I suspect that if we deduce where that racquet was found, or from whom it was bought, then we will be much nearer to solving this murder. In the meantime, I must find a way to watch this video.'

Chapter 24. Video evidence and tying up.

It had been towards the end of his shift on Friday 11th, and while the inspector was preparing to go home, that Sergeant Bulmer had come to see him again.

'The tech boys have finally got back to me, and they tell me that we don't have a Betamax player in the station, we only have a VHS one, and they also tell me that your tape is a 6 hour one so he must have used a Betamax machine to get the whole evening's events onto one tape. Looks like you'll have to watch all 6 hours I'm afraid sir, I hope it's not too sordid!'

The inspector had allowed the sergeant to read Joe's letter and there were some rather choice expressions to describe the "pleasure" that would be derived from watching such events on screen. But once he had heard the necessary radio, time and date checks the inspector would be able to speed through it and watch at eight times speed, according to the techies. Provided that he didn't doze off he could whizz along and note the times of any important events that he would need to get his warrant. This video recording would exclude George from further investigation into his part in Jeremy Carter's death, but the drugs handover, and Joe's letter, would hopefully allow officers the right to search

George's home. That might be more important for the town because the inspector had already interviewed George on drugs allegations, but there hadn't been enough evidence to proceed. He now hoped that he could conclude that prosecution.

'The techies tell me we can have a machine over here by Sunday morning if you want to come in, and perhaps more importantly they will have searched the computer database by tomorrow morning. That means that tomorrow we might know where Tom went on Wednesday.'

'Excellent stuff there Bert. Are you in here tomorrow?'

'I am sir, all day as it happens now that we are short staffed.'

'Will you ring me when there's news of Tom? He's been gone two days already and I'm worried about him. He's still young and goodness knows what he might have let himself in for! He will have gone after somebody that has turned out to be too much for him, I expect, and I don't want to find that he is dead too. So, tell you what Bert, arrange for a few constables to wander by George's house. Not too often because I don't want him to notice them, but I want an idea of the comings and goings of his gang. Get the constables to stroll along the rear of the house particularly and give them permission to remove their helmets and tunic tops before they go up there.'

'Will do sir. How often should they go along there? We are short of staff, and I really don't want to send our WPCs. They will likely attract too much attention.'

'Actually, I think WPC Bradley might be a good choice for this task because she is very keen to solve Jeremy's murder so you might do well to use her. There does seem to be something connecting all these crimes and I want to know what George has to do with them. Get her to go along there but make her promise not to engage anybody in conversation and not to take any risks. Try to have somebody stroll along there every hour or so and make sure they don't gape at or stare into his house.'

'Will do sir. Did you get anything from Mrs. Jones?'

'Yes sergeant. She has a list of names of people that she has "interviewed" as an amateur sleuth. George Dickinson is one of them and I am interested to know what she said to these people. She was clearly hiding something when she told me what George Dickinson had said to her and I can't believe that he let her into his house because he refused entry to me when I last tried to speak to him. We had to arrest him and bring him here. It's a shame he wriggled out of those drugs charges, so I want to get him this time!'

'Thanks sir, and I will get on with those tasks you gave me.'

After the sergeant had retreated the inspector went home. It had been an early departure for him, but he would have to break the news to his wife and children that more overtime was needed that weekend. They wouldn't be pleased.

Back at George Dickinson's house, Tom had begun to get used to his enforced surroundings. Unlike Mark he had suffered no symptoms of claustrophobia and he had settled himself to do some reading. He had been fed and watered and his bucket was emptied daily so things could have been a lot worse. He had also been calmed by the statement from George's "boys" that he would be released when George moved on, and that it wouldn't be too long before that happened.

Valerie Carter returned to her own home at about lunch time the next day, which was a Saturday, exactly a week after Jez's new trousers had arrived from the catalogue. She had told her daughter about Jez on Thursday night, exactly one week after his death. She couldn't tell her about it over the phone, so she had endured three tedious bus journeys to get to Emma's flat, where a very difficult exchange had taken place. In response, Emma had told her mother about her apparent illness that Thursday evening. They considered whether it had been a reaction to Jez's death, and were helped by assuming that it was, and they had agreed to meet up at home on Saturday to sort through Jez's belongings. After thinking things through, Valerie had decided that nothing in the universe would bring Jez back, so they would carry out the difficult job of sorting out his things to dispose of them. Some to charity shops, some to bin, and a very very few to keep. Valerie had felt that Jez's things would not help her to remember her son, those memories she had of him would be stored alongside those of her late husband, in her mind.

Emma arrived at about 2pm on Saturday afternoon.

'Hello love,' said Valerie and they hugged for a moment.

'Hi Mum. How are you coping? Are things getting any easier?'

'To be honest love, this seems to be a way of life now. Your father went and I sorted things out and had to move on, now I have to do this for Jeremy. I can't think very clearly at the moment, and I miss him terribly, but there's no point dwelling on what can't be changed. Your dad told me that a few days before he died and he asked me to keep him in my heart, not in his belongings. He had already given the only physical thing he cared about to Jez. I would like to now pass that racquet on to you but it's missing. The police don't seem to know where it is, but I do have his haversack. He got that to start secondary school five years ago and he has used it ever since. While his pals all started using those sport bags, the ones that look to me like shopping bags, he kept using this,' and she had showed the haversack to Emma before adding: 'Look, I remember watching him paint that flap. He would have been only about 11 but he did it with great care and it took him ages. His dad had bought him David Bowie's album "Scary Monsters (and Super creeps)" as a present and it was never off the record player, so he painted the name "Bowie" on his haversack flap. He tried to make it look like Bowie's signature on the album sleeve, but it didn't quite come off. I watched that haversack going down to the start of that lane every school day, watching Jeremy get bigger and the haversack seem to get smaller and smaller. Then I would see it with his racquet sticking out of the corner. I didn't get to see him leave for school after my shifts changed, but the vision is still in my head, and at work I would look at the clock and imagine it, going off into the distance, and bouncing as he walked. I will keep that haversack in the corner over there. That's all I want to see of Jez in this room.'

'OK mum. If you're absolutely sure?'

'I am.' They had begun their task by stripping the bed and

putting the sheets in the washing machine, but when they opened his wardrobe and his bedside drawers, they had been amazed by how little Jez actually owned. Valerie hadn't known about his plans for weekend shopping sprees with Paula, and by how much he had planned for his wardrobe to grow. He had always thrown away his clothes as soon as he grew out of them, or wore them out, and he only had his school clothes, 2 pairs of jeans and 3 polo tops otherwise. They binned all of these, realising that they weren't really good enough for a charity shop. The new trousers that had arrived on the Saturday after his death had gone into the charity shop bag along with any of his records (there weren't many) that Emma hadn't wanted, but the Bowie album went into Valerie's collection. There were a few odd toys and his old Scalextric set but that was about it. These last few items had gone onto the charity shop pile and then they were done. Emma volunteered to put the charity shop stuff into her car and to take it up there before the shops closed for the day, leaving Valerie on her own.

'I don't know what to think now, there's just me and Emma left. Should I move into a smaller house? Should I take a lodger? But then perhaps I shouldn't let all this get me down like this. I suppose there's no point in that, just like there's no point in weeping.'

She sat and tried to remember her husband and Jez in a better frame of mind, but it wasn't working, and when she heard the washing machine do its final spin, she went downstairs to get the sheets pegged out on the line. Emma returned about 20 minutes after Valerie had finished that job.

'Hi mum. I was thinking about Jez's badminton racquet, and I can't remember where you said that it was.'

'It was missing from his things when the police found them and if they find it, I want it back. I have changed my mind about passing it on to you Emma. I won't give it to you because it's last two owners died at too young an age. I don't want to pass that bad luck on to you.'

Emma felt that that was very sad but was content with her mother's decision.

After a pleasant dinner Emma left her mum quite late that night to return to her flat, but only after Valerie had assured her that she would be fine. She hadn't got as far as the end of the road before she turned the car around and was back at her mum's before Valerie had even gone back in. Emma had forgotten to ask about the funeral.

'I will let you know when the funeral is after I have made the arrangements. I expect you to be there!' is all that her mother said.

On Sunday morning, Inspector Roberts had been told' by his wife and children, that he was expected back home no later than 1.30pm, because that's when Sunday lunch would be ready, and they were all going to the park together afterwards because a local band were playing there. The inspector was happy with that, but he had decided that he had better start work early to make sure that he could get everything done, and at 8am he had already arrived at his desk. In front of him was a note from Sergeant Bulmer and a set of instructions detailing how to use the Betamax player. These included how to freeze frame, advance or rewind, but there had been no means of capturing a still image from any part of the tape.

The inspector made himself some coffee before inserting the tape and settling down to watch. Joe must have started the tape at about 3.50pm on that day because it wasn't long before the first-time confirmation was heard.

'That was "Music all the way", our regular music slot for lovers of gentle music everywhere. We now go to the news which will be followed by "The David Hamilton show". This is radio 2 and it's just coming up to 4pm.'

The inspector listened to the news that followed that announcement and stayed for the "David Hamilton show":

'Good afternoon listeners, it's Thursday the third of October and here's Fleetwood Mac to open our show today.'

'That's a good start,' thought the inspector. 'The techies can get the BBC to confirm that the news is correct for October 3rd,' and he made a note of the position at which the news had appeared (those machines had a tape counter but no actual time display). He then sat through some general chit chat between Joe and George which, though a fan was running, could be heard clearly enough. Joe didn't say very much. His main topic of conversation was what he got up to as a student, being careful not to say which university he had attended. George could be seen very clearly, and his broad Scottish accent was really clear so there was no doubt as to his identity, but Joe never once looked at the camera so identifying him would be more difficult. George had talked non-stop about really mundane things, politics, the cost of petrol, why couldn't he buy sweets at night etc. He was all for Sunday opening, relaxing betting laws, legalising cannabis and making fox hunting illegal. 'Poor wee things have no chance.'

Eventually though it was time to get down to business and George had offered Joe some cocaine. Joe had refused saying that he would never take that stuff again.

'You said you need to be off your head Joe. Sounds like you fancy me after all, but maybe just some cannabis then Joe?'

'No, but I'll have some more whisky.' Joe already sounded quite drunk, but the evening progressed physically and by about 6.30pm George declared that their evening of entertainment together was at an end, and that it was time for Joe to make his purchase.

'You remember our deal, Joe? Enjoyable as tonight has been I still need to make a living don't I Joe, so what will you be requiring? I can offer you cannabis, cocaine or some special mixes that I make myself. What will it be Joe?'

Joe bought the minimum amount of cannabis that he could and then told George that he was done. The inspector watched until George and his boys had left, and he turned off the machine. He had been taking notes and he jotted down where each important event could be found on the tape should it be needed later.

It was now just after midday and the inspector was trying to resist having a snack. Lunch was at 1.30pm sharp and he loved his wife's cooking, so he had settled for more coffee before beginning the task of requesting the warrant, which was a long-winded business. He had to carefully note all of his evidence and justify the need for the warrant to be issued urgently, the inspector hoping that he might get it tomorrow. While filling in all the forms, which were still paper forms in 1985, he remembered the note from Sergeant Bulmer. On opening that he realised that he had now received another reason for getting the warrant urgently. He read with interest that the last two people that his missing officer had looked up online were Angus Thompson and George Dickinson.

'That can't be a coincidence surely,' he thought and added this information to his warrant request. A missing officer whose last known whereabouts is likely to have been the home of George Dickinson would surely guarantee his warrant would come quickly. His charge sheet for George would likely contain charges of possessing and mixing recreational drugs with intent to sell them for profit, coercing an individual to have unwanted sex and, hopefully, the imprisonment of an officer. He was anxious about the latter statement because he feared that Tom's fate may have been rather worse than imprisonment.

Though he expected to get that warrant tomorrow he still hadn't made any further progress in the mystery of Jeremy's death. He decided against interviewing Marjorie Jones again because he wanted to talk to other people first. He was still hopeful that somebody had seen who walked along that path with Jez that night, and he would try to find out who had sold Marjorie that racquet. He would get sergeant Bulmer to arrange interviews with the known likely retailers of such things, and with Angus Thompson. It was now almost 1pm so he headed off for home and his lunch. The roast beef was superb, and the Yorkshire puddings had risen so much that they had almost taken over the oven. While eating his dinner, the inspector's *work* was absent from his mind, but the fate of Tom Hollingsworth had remained very much in his thoughts. He had been aware that nothing would be possible until he got that warrant so he had tried to put Tom out of his mind but had failed miserably. The lunch had been excellent but, unfortunately, the same couldn't be said for the local band that had played in the park.

The inspector had rather enjoyed his Sunday afternoon with his family, and he pledged to do it more often. Perhaps he needed more staff to help him or maybe more sergeants, like Bert, who always knew what was best. As he was winding down before bed, he thought about the days that were to come. He and his team would be expected to raid the home of a drug dealer, hopefully rescue Tom and probably have to evade bullets or other killing systems. Then he still had to catch the killer of Jeremy Carter and he knew that George couldn't have done that. But then he remembered that he was at home, and that these thoughts would have to wait until tomorrow, so he managed to relax, and sleep arrived eventually.

Chapter 25. Time for arrests (hopefully).

Monday 14th (Day 11)

Inspector Roberts was in his office at 9am by which time the Court clerk had arranged for a judge to look at his warrant application. It was expected that the inspector would have the judge's decision, and hopefully the necessary paperwork, by 2pm this afternoon. On opening his diary, he was reminded that Joe had said he would ring the station at exactly 10 am today so he sent for the desk sergeant. Sergeant Bulmer wasn't on shift that day, so it had been sergeant Ailsworth that entered the inspector's office.

'Yes Sir?' he enquired.

'Yes Ailsworth. Firstly, has Sergeant Bulmer left any reports with you that are intended for me?'

'Yes sir, there are two. Should I get them for you?'

'Yes please, but when you are back at your desk would you check to see whether any other messages have been left for me?' The sergeant disappeared and was back exactly four minutes later.

'These two reports are for you sir and no, there have been no messages for you since you were in yesterday.' He handed the reports over to the inspector.

'It is most important that a phone line is kept clear at 10am today. Would you make sure that everybody knows that and hang up on any callers that don't ask for me directly.'

'Certainly sir.' With preparations for the morning now set up he opened the two notes from Bert. The first note advised the inspector that the warrant application had been hand delivered to the court clerk at home, and that the clerk had gone straight into work to get the proceedings under way. The second note was a summary of the reports given by those officers that had patrolled around George's house. It seemed that George had received a large number of visitors while they patrolled, but that only four of them were seen frequently. George himself wasn't seen entering or leaving at all. From this the officers had deduced that George had at least four people that worked for him and that the others might have been to see him on "business".

The inspector considered this and decided that he needed a minimum of six officers to carry out the search, each equipped with stab and bullet proof vests. Since George had so many visitors it would be necessary for officers to arrive on foot, leaving their cars some distance away from George's house. George mustn't have any advance warning that the search was imminent.

After having some coffee, he wrote down his plan of action. He had hoped that he would be able to carry it out late tonight or very very early on Tuesday, early Tuesday being his preferred option. He glanced at his watch and put down his pen. It was 9.55am so he now had to sit and wait.

The phone rang at exactly 10am.

'Call for you sir,' said the sergeant.

'Put him through.' The inspector waited for Joe to speak,

and, after an infuriatingly long pause, a voice appeared.

'Hello inspector, lovely to speak to you. Lovely sunny morning in fact inspector. I bet you weren't expecting to hear from me were you inspector. It's a long time since I was in your office, so perhaps you have missed me. I have certainly missed you, so I thought we should catch up, so to speak.'

'Who is this?' asked the inspector, butting in during that short pause.

'Why it's your old friend George or should that be adversary inspector. I know our paths have crossed in the past but it's lovely to hear your voice again.' The inspector now recognised that the broad Glaswegian was indeed George Dickinson.

'Look, I need this line clear so unless this is important, please hang up.'

'Ah. My friend Joe. I had heard that Joe might be ringing, and I thought it might be today. How is Joe? I cannae find him at home or work and nobody seems to know where he is, but I thought that since he seems to have information for you then you might point me in his direction, if you catch my drift.'

'Damn, damn damn.' thought the inspector. He decided to try to bluff things out.

'George, I have no idea what you are talking about. I don't know a Joe and nobody of that name has approached me or this station, either personally or by phone, so I can't help you. Please get off the line.' All of these points had been factually correct, so the inspector hadn't told any actual lies.

'Well, you'll understand if I don't believe you inspector,

but I suppose I must trust an officer of the law, so if Joe does call will you tell him that I was asking after him? He's an old friend you ken, and I miss his company, so will you tell him that inspector?'

'*You* will understand that I cannot do anything of the kind,' said the inspector and was relieved that George had just hung up after that. 'What the hell?' thought the inspector. 'How could George have known about this? I was the only one to read that letter, though I did show it to Bert. Nobody could know, unless George had inside information. I'm sure that Bert wouldn't tell anybody, unless...' He sent for the desk sergeant.

'Yes sir?'

'Is there any indication of the number that just rang me?'

'No sir, nothing came up on our systems.'

'Has anybody else called, somebody that might have left a name?'

'No sir. I kept all the lines clear, but once your call had come through, I opened the others up.'

'Go please sergeant.'

'Damn,' he thought again. 'What does this mean? Does George have access to this building? Has somebody tipped him off? Has he found Joe and is Joe now dead? Who has been in this office since that parcel arrived?' Stuck for answers to that he set about his preparations for the search of George's house, but at exactly 11am the phone rang again.

'Inspector, would you take a call from somebody called Joe?'

'Immediately please!'

'Hi inspector, Joe here. How are you?'

'More to the point how are you? I had George Dickinson on the line at 10 am and I was worried that he had found, and maybe imprisoned, you, or even worse.'

'I'm fine inspector. I had a feeling that George might somehow learn of my intention to call so I never intended to call at 10am. I'm here now though so was there anything you wanted to ask me?' The inspector was very careful not to give anything else away over the phone in case there was indeed an information leak at the station.

'Have you thought of anything else since you sent that document?'

'No, but I was wondering whether a coach has been to see you recently?'

'A coach? Yes, we have had a coach through here, a very driven, slightly brusque one.'

'OK. Be wary of that coach, the driver is indeed very driven, if that makes sense. The driver is inclined to take short cuts that sometimes lead to crashes, and then to unfortunate leaks.'

'Thanks. That explains a lot because I have been concerned about the coach that arrived. I will use it with caution in future. I will perhaps further investigate this shortcut taking driver.'

'Very wise inspector. Anything else?'

'Yes, just one thing. Paula Jones told me that you and her dad had swapped shifts on the oil rig, so they had had to postpone her 16th birthday party. She said that it was you that had asked for that swap. Is that true?'

'Yes, I had asked Dan Jones to swap with me, but only because Marjorie Jones had asked me to. She never told me *exactly* why she had wanted that swap but, as I mentioned in my note, she did later tell me that it would be worth it because she had an empty king-sized bed at home. She is still after my body perhaps. She threatened to tell Dan Jones about our night of passion if I didn't agree to the swap.'

'Well, you never know do you? Thanks for that.'

'Anything else inspector?'

'No but be aware that I am happy with the clarity of your report and action is being taken. I haven't been able to share that report with anybody because the content was too delicate.'

'Delicate is a good description of my report! Goodbye inspector.'

'Goodbye.' The line went dead.

It was now just after eleven and the inspector sat down to think for a while. He had arranged a meeting of a selection of officers for 3pm, and he had hoped that the warrant would arrive by then.

The meeting began on time and there was a total of ten officers present. 'In case any of you haven't yet heard, *one of our own* is missing. Tom Hollingsworth hasn't been seen since last Wednesday morning and nobody has been able to shed any light on his whereabouts. Thanks to our technical team, and those new computer terminals, I now believe that the last person he went to see was a man called George Dickinson.' There came a rumble of recognition from many of the team.

'I assume that George has had something to do with our

PC's disappearance and I hope that Tom hasn't met the same fate as Jeremy Carter.' Many of the team now stiffened and the mood became more sombre.

'As it turns out, George has an alibi for the night of Jeremy's death, but that same alibi has given us enough evidence to apply for a warrant to search for drugs and related equipment at his place. That warrant hasn't come through yet, but I hope that it will be here soon.' The staff remained silent as the inspector continued.

'Some of you have already come across George, and you will know that he is a very slippery customer. We've had him in here before with some pretty good evidence, but he's managed to get out of it. We also know that he has a team of "minders", beefy but intelligent men that look after his back. So, searching his place will have to be thorough, exactly according to the book, and it will have to be a surprise. I am aware that knowledge of our suspicions seems to be reaching George so DO NOT repeat anything said here to anybody else, and be warned, we will be watching every one of you very carefully, and any hint of attachment to George will be extremely seriously dealt with. All of you remember that police officers have a rough time in prison!' Much shuffling of feet now took place, but nobody said a word.

'So be vigilant. You must all regard each other as a potential evidence leak.' During the chatter that the inspector's last comment had caused there came a knock at the door.

'Shh! Come in.' The desk sergeant entered the room.

'This has arrived for you sir. I thought that you ought to get it immediately.'

'Thanks sergeant.' He waited for the sergeant to leave and then opened and read the contents of the package.

'The warrant has arrived so here are the arrangements. Please assume that you won't see your families for the next 24 hours because, though I will assign each of you a specific task today, I won't tell you the time of the search until the last minute, more or less.'

At precisely 5.30 am on Tuesday 15th, six officers in full uniform received a message on their radios that it was time to begin. There was a mix of constables and sergeants in the group and all of them had been offered a full role in the search. Though he had the highest regard for his female officers, the inspector had decided that *these* six should all be male because he had expected a lot of resistance when the search began. The four female officers though had a potentially more dangerous task in store.

By 6am, those six male officers had left the two police vehicles that had parked some distance from George's farmhouse and walked up to preplanned positions around the property, ready to go. Sergeant Bulmer crept carefully and silently up to the house and positioned himself by the front door. A signal was then given by another officer indicating that the only constable with an active radio should request the car with the battering ram. Once Sergeant Bulmer had received "the nod" that the car was on its way, he knocked loudly on the front door. There came no response, so he knocked again. No lights had come on inside the building so after giving a full three minutes for the occupants to open the door he signalled for the battering ram to be brought. It arrived promptly but the officers with the battering ram tried the door before battering it and were surprised to find it unlocked.

'Damn,' thought the sergeant. He was sufficiently experienced to know what must have happened. He radioed to the female officers, who had positioned themselves on the outer edge of the property, and asked them to search for anybody leaving, and to apprehend them. He had realised that George had flown the nest and all of this planning and overtime had perhaps been for nothing!

Chapter 26. Tom gets embarrassed.

Armed with the warrant, Sergeant Bulmer and two of his officers entered the property by the front door, while three others entered by the only other entrance, which was at the rear. Lights were switched on and the officers began their search. In the living room they found furniture (a table, those settees on which the "boys" had sat, and an elderly TV) but nothing else. The posters had gone, and all other traces of habitation had gone too. Very carefully they moved into an inner access hall and tried a door each, all of which were unlocked. Disappointingly they found nothing in any of those rooms. There had been no signs of any previous activity, each room being remarkably clean. Having then ventured up the staircase that led from one of those rooms, they had found nothing but another empty room.

At the rear of the house the other three officers found only 2 doors; neither of them leads into the rest of the house which they thought odd. It was as if this was two separate houses built to look like only one. PC Thompson had almost fallen as he had opened one of the doors because it opened towards, and onto, a *downward* staircase. He had inadvertently stepped out into empty space but managed to grab a handrail to steady himself. He shouted for PC

Danvers who then accompanied him down the stairs. There was only one door at the bottom of this staircase, and it was locked. They had tried kicking the door open but it opened *towards* them so they couldn't budge it. Danvers then had to run back for the battering ram, which had delayed them somewhat, but they had suspected that the drugs equipment they wanted to find was in there, so it was important that they gained access to it. Between them they managed to batter a hole in the door that was big enough for them to crawl through, but they had to stand back a while because the smell had been overpowering. Danvers entered first and he was hit by a very unpleasant, musty smell of urine and mould and he had to retreat for a moment. After a while he went back in and found the light switch.

'Thompson,' he shouted, 'In here quick!' PC Thompson crawled in to see PC Danvers leaning over a body that lay on a tatty bed.

'Is he alive?'

'I think so. Radio for an ambulance.' Once that had been done, they decided to get the body into fresher air, and they managed to get him out through the hole and up the stairs. They laid him down on the landing and looked at him. What they had found was a young man wearing just shirt and underpants and breathing very very gently. PC Thompson went to find sergeant Bulmer who arrived swiftly and immediately recognised the man as Tom Hollingsworth.

The ambulance arrived while Bulmer was reporting the discovery to inspector Roberts back at the station. The ambulance crew had calmed everybody by confirming that Tom's vital signs were not too bad before taking him to the nearest hospital.

The search continued but nothing had been found either in the rear house or the entirety of the front part, including upstairs. Swabs were taken from the walls of each room in case traces of drugs had been left behind but there was extreme disappointment amongst all concerned. When they left, they closed the doors behind them and reconvened in the staff canteen back at the station. They were offered a free full breakfast, and most accepted that offer, but sergeant Bulmer took his up to the inspector's office where he could talk and eat at the same time. The inspector spoke first.

'Well, here we go again. George Dickinson seems to have a charmed life and he still manages to be one step of us. What do you think Bert, had the house been empty a while or do you think they cleared out yesterday?'

'It seems to me sir that they must have started their move out a few days ago because all traces of occupancy had gone. The house still smelled of people though, so at least some of them must have been there as recently as yesterday.'

'I have arranged for an all ports warning to be sent out just in case he tries to flee the country. Border force officers will stop him.'

'Good idea sir.'

'And what of Tom? What was the room like that you found him in?'

'It was like an old prison cell sir. It smelled terrible and that was partly because Tom had been given an uncovered bucket to use as a toilet, and that hadn't been emptied for a few days. There were cups and plates on a little table in there, so they did at least feed him. There was a bookcase full of books and there was one by the bed, so Tom must have read to keep himself busy. The light was off when Danvers went in, so I think it likely that Tom had turned it off before going to sleep. The ambulance staff said that his vital signs were reasonable, so I imagine that George's bunch had drugged him before they left.'

'I want a police guard on him around the clock Bert.'

'I have sent WPC Windsor to sit with him sir. I'll arrange a change every four hours to stop boredom setting in too heavily.'

'Thanks Bert. Finish your breakfast then have a break. I will need to think for a while.'

'OK.' Bert left the inspector at about 9.30am but at 10.30 he was back.

'Tom's awake sir and he wants to see you immediately!'

'Right. I will go there now, and I don't want to be disturbed unless it's really urgent.'

The inspector found Tom sitting up in bed when he arrived at the hospital. He gave a weak smile when he saw the inspector.

'How are Tom?'

'Not great sir. I stink to high heaven; I have a thumping headache and I feel quite sick. The medics think that I have been drugged and they have given me a flush or something like that to try to get rid of it. I have to drink that jug full of water and then they will bring me more. They've sent off some of my blood for analysis, and they took loads of it too.

'Sorry about that Tom. Do they think you will pull through?'

'They reckon that if I was going to die, I would be gone by now. The drug must have been in my food so it must have been last night when they gave it to me.' He smiled and added 'They are going to give me a bed bath later because they want rid of the smell, but they want my blood pressure and stuff to stabilise before I can even get out of bed. I hope they send a nice young nurse to do that because I need cheering up!'

'Well after that comment you sound OK to me! Why did you ask to see me anyway?'

'Did you collect those books that were in my prison cell?'

'Yes, I believe so. Why?'

'Because one of my prison warders was a very well-educated man who called himself Karl. When he brought my food last night, he was looking through them and found "Hard Times" by Dickens. He asked whether I had read it. When I said that I hadn't he wrote a message inside the front cover and then said *"read this tomorrow"* in a voice suggesting that it really was in my interests to do that. I must admit that I was really tired last night, so I put out the light after eating, and that was the last I remember. It must have the drugs that they put in my food.' Just then a very tall, muscular man wearing a white coat and sandals came into the room. He was wearing blue gloves and spoke to Tom.

'Hi. I'm Gregor. You're due a bed bath to try to make you a bit less smelly, so now your pal here will have to go.' The inspector laughed heartily but Tom looked really disappointed, the image of a very attractive nurse washing him down had vanished. Could Tom's Day have got any worse?

'Bye inspector.'

'I'll call back tonight,' said the inspector as he was leaving, but on the way out he had instructed WPC Windsor to go back in and watch the blanket bath to make sure that the bather wasn't on George's payroll.

'Certainly sir, I will make sure that I miss nothing,' she said with a smile.

Gregor had clearly not understood the concept of modesty and Tom's embarrassment, especially in the presence of his superior officer, had been enormous. The top sheet was gone in seconds, thrown deftly into Gregor's linen bag. Tom had only been wearing one of those backless surgical gowns and that was off with another of Gregor's very precise, professional manoeuvres. Tom had then been rolled onto his side and the bottom sheet was partly removed. He was then rolled the other way and that sheet had also been despatched to his linen bag. Tom was then instructed to raise his arms above his head so that Gregor could get into all the necessary places. The bed bath had been done on just the plastic mattress protector so that plenty of water could be used. Only when all of that water had been dried off, and a new sheet had been applied was Tom given his new clean gown.

As instructed, WPC Windsor had missed nothing and, after Gregor had gone, and all of his bedding and clothing had been removed, and Tom had been left smelling pleasantly of disinfectant, all that he could think of to say to sergeant Windsor was 'I'm going to sleep now,' which he promptly did.

When Tom awoke it was no longer Sergeant Windsor but WPC Bradley who was sitting next to him and he felt mightily relieved. He would find it difficult to look Sergeant Windsor in the eye for quite a while.

Chapter twenty-seven.

After grabbing a pub lunch, the inspector was back at his desk at 1pm. He needed to think, and he needed to do that away from the hustle and bustle of the station. He picked up his phone and rang the desk sergeant.

'Is Sergeant Bulmer around at the moment?'

'No sir, he's out with a new constable showing her the area.'

'Ah. Would you know whether the items taken from the search this morning are still here?'

'I believe that they are down in the dungeon sir,' by which he meant that they had been put into storage. 'Would you like me get somebody to fetch some items up for you sir?'

'No thanks, not at present.' The inspector rang off and ventured down to the dungeon himself. Once there he had been met by "The dungeon keeper" who asked whether he needed anything in particular.

'No thanks Paul, if you could just let me in to look at the haul from this morning that will be fine.' The inspector was led into a room that was some way away from the dungeon's entrance and Paul left him there alone. There wasn't a lot to see as it turned out, Tom's urine bucket had been sealed and brought along, as had the books from his prison. Since there was nothing else of use in the house, this had been the total extraction. He looked at the books and, like Tom had done while in his prison, he marvelled at the highbrow nature of the books. The inspector decided that it was likely that they had already been in the house when George had moved in. Investigations had shown that George had begun renting the farmhouse about 8 months ago and that he had always paid the rent on time, every month. His landlord was satisfied with him as a tenant but, since he would only do an inspection once a year, he had no idea of the state of the place. He had done an initial inspection one week after George had moved in, but everything had seemed absolutely fine then, it was all surprisingly clean in fact.

The books had been stacked on a high shelf and the inspector had to stand on a lower shelf to reach them, but there, second row up was "Hard Times". Once he had retrieved it the inspector sat down to look at it. He had read the book while at school, but it was only the inside of the front cover that he was interested in today. There he found some very small block capitals and it was lucky that he had his magnifying glass with him. It read:

_EOR_E _OIN_ BACK TO LASOW. TEM_OR_ S_AY AT NY15 _DD 17DZ.

That was the entire message. This wasn't a difficult code to decipher but the inspector realised that the intention was just to make it disappear into the page, in the way that a child's doodle might, rather than make it too complex to read easily. It was clearly "George going back to Glasgow. Temporary stay at NY15 add 17DZ."

Adding NY15 to 17DZ gives the UK postcode NY15 17DZ. The inspector assumed that the message meant that George had set off for that postcode as a temporary stopover on his way back to Scotland and that "Karl" had wanted him to be apprehended. The inspector sincerely hoped that George and his gang were still there. Having memorised the postcode, he returned the book and returned to his office, having made it clear to Paul as he left that he had removed nothing.

Once back at the office he was able to use his new computer terminal to identify the location of NY15 17DZ, which the police database had assured him was in North Yorkshire. The screen gave him a map reference and that turned out to be a small garage about a mile from Richmond. He picked up the phone and asked whether Bert was back yet, which he was.

'Send him up please.'

'What can I do for you inspector?'

'Bert, I am going home because something has come up. I have to go away for a few days but there's nobody to cover for me, so I will ring in every day in case you need anything. Please don't broadcast this in case my visit ends badly, but if you could sort things out while I am away, I would be very grateful.'

'I will do that. It's not a medical problem is it sir?'

'No Bert, but I am actually leaving quite soon so I hope

that you will be OK left in charge.'

'Leave things to me sir. I'll be fine and I hope things go well at your end.' The inspector arrived at home only minutes later and, once there, he picked up the phone and made a call to the head of CID, North Yorkshire division. Once the call was connected, he asked the division head to arrange a scrambled call between Richmond CID and the inspector at his home address. That call had come later in the afternoon, just before his family returned from school.

At about the same time, back at the station, sergeant Bulmer had received a call from the desk sergeant. 'Mrs Jones to see you sir.' Bulmer groaned; this wasn't what he needed while the inspector was away.

'Send her in will you. I had better get this over with.' Marjorie was shown into the inspector's office, but she was disappointed to see the sergeant, rather than the inspector. Sergeant Bulmer noticed her change of expression.

'The inspector is away on family business for a few days, and he has left me to take care of things for a while, but I *will* pass on everything you say to him. May I audio record this meeting to help with that?'

'No sergeant, just in case the recording gets into the wrong hands.'

'Then perhaps you will be patient with me because I write rather slowly,' he said with a smile. 'What can we do for you?'

'It's about Jeremy Carter's badminton racquet.'

'Go on.'

'I have it at home.' The sergeant looked at her, surprised.

'Let me get this absolutely straight, you have Jeremy Carter's missing badminton racquet, and it's at your house?'

'Yes, and I thought it important to tell you where I bought it!'

'That would indeed be very useful.'

'I have a "friend" who manages to source badminton stuff for me. I have a collection of badminton related stuff, he knows what I like, and he alerted me to this one. It's signed so he knew I would want it.'

'Just a moment. OK so who is this "friend"?'

'I can't tell you sergeant. He likes to stay in the shadows, and he would be very annoyed if I told you who he is.'

'I would rather that we were told Mrs. Jones.'

'If I have to tell you that then I will leave and I will take this information away with me.'

'OK, but I must warn you that we might not be able to use this person's version of events in court unless we can verify your account of events with him. In addition, if you have the racquet at home, we really should have it in here to check for fingerprints etc. It might be evidence by itself.'

'I don't think you'll need to do any of that sergeant. The important information is the name of the man who initially sold the racquet to my friend.'

'Do you think that your friend knew that this racquet had belonged to a dead boy?' Marjorie grimaced.

'I very much doubt that sergeant Bulmer. To my friend it will have just been a racquet with some signatures on it that he knew I would like. So do you actually want the name of the man who sold it to my friend sergeant?'

'Just let me finish writing this down first.' Marjorie rolled her eyes.

'OK Mrs. Jones, fire away.'

'I have met this man twice and I know he is a villain because of the way he treated me and my friend when we paid him a visit. It was George Dickinson sergeant. I told the inspector that he had something to do with Jez's murder, but I don't think he took me seriously.'

'Oh, I'm sure that the inspector takes what you say very seriously, so don't worry on that score, and he will certainly be pleased to have this information so thanks for bringing it in.' There was another pause as the sergeant finished writing down what she had said.

'Is there anything else I can do for you?'

'Can you tell me whether you have any new leads in this case?'

'I am sure you will understand that I can't say anything about that, but I can assure you that investigations are ongoing.'

'Is the inspector away because he is following up on a lead?'

'As I said, the inspector went home to his family early yesterday, and he said that he would likely be away for a few days. Thank-you for your help and we will be in touch if we need to speak further.'

When she was gone, Bulmer read through his notes to make sure that they were correct and added them to the growing pile of things he would need to tell the inspector when he rang in tomorrow.

* * *

The head of Richmondshire CID liked to be called Enrique. Nobody knew why, in fact few at his place of work knew his real name, but everything addressed to "Enrique" always ended up on his desk without any problems. He was a very large man in every way and, when he had been a beat constable, few would consider tangling with him during a disturbance.

Enrique and Roberts spoke for only about 10 minutes. It was agreed that Roberts would go to North Yorkshire and stay in a normal bed and breakfast establishment in Thirsk, which is a few miles away from Richmond, so that his proximity to the garage wouldn't be noticed. He would drive up there in a rented car and Wendy, Inspector Roberts' wife, would phone the B&B and book him in under the name Davidson, to arrive at about midnight tonight. Davidson would be a salesman who sold wooden products. This was because Inspector Roberts actually knew something about joinery, so he could bluff his way along if needed.

Wendy Roberts telephoned the B&B shortly after she got home at 4.20 pm and the inspector departed at 6.30pm, after a superb dinner. Wendy had looked worried as he left, but he assured her that any dangerous stuff was being handled by Richmondshire CID this time. His children were told that he was attending a university reunion party, so they had no worries. They were more interested in the mischief that they could get up to in his absence and in what goodies he might bring back for them.

"Davidson" arrived in Thirsk at about 11pm; the owner of

the B&B was pleased that he didn't have to wait up until midnight, so it was a good start with her. Breakfast was at 7.30 sharp, and Davidson was expected to vacate his room by 9am and not return before 4pm. That was fine with the inspector.

Chapter 28. Davidson and Enrique.

(Day 13)

"Davidson" woke early that Wednesday morning after a restless night. Being away from Wendy didn't suit him and he was anxious about meeting Enrique. He enjoyed a hearty breakfast though and then drove to a parking bay in a nearby industrial estate where he sat, apparently waiting, in his car. At precisely 9.30am a man walked up to him and demanded to know why he was parked there. The inspector replied that he was a salesman on business, that he was called Davidson, and that the factory he was intending to visit appeared closed. He said that he was waiting in the hope that it might soon open. He went on to ask the man whether he knew anything about the company and whether any other companies on the estate might be interested in timber products.

'Yes, that firm is closed for the next two weeks but there's another similar one about 4 blocks away. I'll show you the way if you like?'

'Thanks, get in.' Once driving, and with the windows shut, the inspector had asked Enrique what the plans would be.

'The postcode that you gave us only applies to one building, and that turns out to be a disused garage on the

A6108 about a mile and a half west of Richmond. It's surrounded by woodland and steep hills, and it's been boarded up for years. One of my officers drove by it last night and there was no sign of occupancy, but he thought he could just see a chink of light coming out from around one of the boards. There were plenty of places to the rear of the property where cars could be hidden so it's a perfect hiding place. I have already applied for a search warrant and that will likely be here this afternoon.'

'Excellent Enrique. Am I allowed to know your plans?'

'Certainly. We will carry out a search exactly as you did on Monday. You won't need to be involved but you will be expected at Richmond police station once men have been apprehended, and we will radio to tell you when that has been accomplished. You can identify Dickinson and then carry out interviews with whoever you want and whenever you want. Though we will do exactly as you did on Tuesday, we have the benefit of a very winding and remote road which is the only access to the garage. Officers will position themselves to block both sides of that road as soon as they hear that men are present in the house. That way nobody can escape by car and only those that know the area would survive leaving any other way.'

'That sounds perfect,' said Davidson. 'What shall I do during the rest of today?'

'You had better sell some timber,' laughed Enrique, 'and then why not take in some of our sights. It's going to be a sunny day so enjoy your time away from your normal routine. Somebody will call you on your radio when you need to come into the station, so the day is your own. It will be very late by the time you are needed.'

After just a few more minutes of driving, Davidson had pulled over, Enrique had got out of the car and had strolled off. It suddenly occurred to the inspector that he had no idea how Enrique would get back to his place of work but, in truth, he wasn't really all that curious anyway because he had some sightseeing to do. He hadn't previously been to North Yorkshire, and he wanted to make the best of his day.

Davidson had a very pleasant day exploring Richmond and its local attractions, and he returned to his B&B for dinner before spending a while in his room. Whilst there he unwrapped his gun and shoulder holster and put them on, just in case they were going to be needed. He then drove to a spot near to Richmond and parked up. He decided that it was a nice night for a stroll, and he left the car in a car park and set off to explore the area on foot.

It had been about 10pm when he had got out of his car and he walked for a while and, though he had thought the area to be quite nice, he hadn't been prepared for the extreme darkness that can envelope rural areas at that time of night. After about another 30 minutes he headed back to his car and at just after 11.30pm his radio vibrated in its holder.

'Davidson.'

'You are needed sir!' That's what the inspector had wanted to hear and, feeling relieved, he set off for the station, but only after he had consulted his road map!

It turned out that the search had gone perfectly, and the

occupants of the garage had clearly not been expecting anybody to know their whereabouts. The Richmondshire officers had apprehended 5 men, lots of equipment and a number of substances that would be sent off for analysis. The gang had appeared to be ready to eat but no meal had been found. The garage occupants had drunk significant amounts of alcohol, which had made arrests much easier to carry out, and three vehicles were in the process of being towed into the station lock-up. George Dickinson (recognised because he seemed to be doing a very good impression of Billy Connelly) and two of his boys were taken to Richmond police station where they had the pleasure of a cell each. The other two were taken further away to a police station in Darlington.

Once at Richmond police station, inspector Roberts had asked to see Dickinson immediately, and it was at 11.55pm that he sat down in front of him. 'Detective inspector Roberts, how lovely to see you. I have missed being bothered by you, but I am glad to see you now and to enjoy the satisfaction of looking at you, knowing that you wasted all that time raiding my empty house! I imagine that you weren't very pleased to find me gone.'

Roberts said nothing in reply to that but the tape recorder had already been switched on so the interview could begin. The usual official requisites had been carried out, but George had declined the invitation to have a solicitor present and the inspector announced that he and Sergeant Aggarwal were in the room with George.

'You have been apprehended today after a search, which was fully authorised by warrant, was carried out at a garage where you have taken up temporary residence. Do you have anything to say before I go on?'

'No inspector, you carry on.'

'Before I get into the issues around the equipment and materials that we have found today, I want to talk to you about the murder of Jeremy Carter.'

'Not that damned thing again! I am tired of you and that bloody woman going on about it. I had nothing to do with that boy so don't try to pin that on me again.'

'We know that you didn't kill him.'

'Then what the fuck are you on about?'

'The racquet!'

'What racquet?'

'You had a racquet that belonged to Jeremy Carter.'

'Like hell I did. Why in God's name would I want a tennis racquet? I can't bear the sport.'

'A racquet which you then sold to a dealer who sold it to Marjorie Jones.'

'That lying cow?' George was clearly annoyed now. 'Do you know that she came to "interview" me more than once? She claimed that she was helping you lot, the lying bitch, but after the second visit I realised she was doing no such thing. She was trying to get me to confess to that boy's murder so that she could be some sort of hero, but I wasn't going to do any such thing because I had nothing to do with it. She kept coming back though. She claimed to have a different piece of evidence each time and that she would use it if I didn't confess,' he paused a while.

'How did you know it wasn't me, and anyway why are you talking to me about it now if you know it wasn't me?'

'You were seen that afternoon on the other side of town, so we know that it wasn't you, but I still want to know how you got that racquet?'

'Will you listen to me? Ah keep telling you I never saw any bloody racquet. Why the hell would I want to buy a tennis racquet unless it was worth millions. Is it worth millions?'

'No, it isn't.'

'Then she's lying again, just like she was when she said my spit was all over the body. I don't want sex with with boys and I wouldn't be daft enough to leave any of my bodily fluids on anybody if I had killed them now would I? Seriously, you don't want to believe anything she says, she's as mad as a drunk in the Clyde. I reckon I'm in shit anyway so I would just tell you if I had got him to screw me and then I murdered him, but I didn't. And somebody is walking about out there that did!'

At this point the inspector had decided to stop his interrogation and announced to the recording machine that he was going outside for a few moments. There he made a few notes in his notebook and after a while he returned.

'PC Tom Hollingsworth?'

'Aye, I know, bless him. New isn't he and so keen. It broke my heart when I had to lock him up. He was well looked after though, and I did release him before we left that house.'

'Now it's you who is telling me lies! We found him locked up in a basement room at your farmhouse.'

'No, I'm not telling porkies. I told mah boys to drug him and leave him outside where he would be found. I just needed to be clear of the place before he woke up in case we were followed. If he did remember anything we'd be long gone so, he wasn't given much of the stuff. I was expecting him to be left in the garden at the back, but he was left in the basement you said?'

'Yes.'

'That's not what I ordered mah boys to do. He was a bonny lad, too young for me though or I might have kept him. Is he still alive?'

'When I last saw him, he was very poorly but he was still alive.'

'Genuinely, I'm glad he's OK.'

'OK, but if anything does happen to Tom it will be a murder charge.'

'OK, fair enough.'

'Moving on to Joe.'

'Joe?' asked George.

'Yes, Joe. That man you telephoned me about on Monday. Do you remember that conversation George?'

'Aye, I do.'

'Why did you ring me then George?'

'We had just got clear of the house, and I thought I would wind you all up a bit.'

'But why mention Joe in particular? There were plenty of other red herrings that you could have sent us.'

'Because of that bloody woman again.'

'What?'

'The Jones woman. She comes to see me yet again on Sunday night. We were just settling down to watch Songs of Praise on TV and there she is again, knocking on my door and without the famous Joe in tow this time.'

'Go on.'

'OK. She tells me that her mate Joe has sent you a parcel. She's seen him leave the house with it on Friday morning and then it had turned up on your desk while she was talking to you. She said it probably had something to do with Jez's murder, that Joe must have found out something because she and he were working together, and that I had better tell her everything or she would go to the police.'

'And what did you tell her?'

'Nothing. I gave her 10 seconds to get out of my face or she'd never see the light of day again. This time she legged it, stupid cow.'

'So do you know what was in that package George?'

'Honestly inspector, I have absolutely no idea. But I do know that Joe and the lovely Trish have buggered off somewhere so I reckoned your parcel must have had something to do with me. I thought that if you were given a hint that I'd been given inside information you'd waste time looking for an informant instead of chasing me.'

'So, you still deny having that badminton racquet?'

'Well, there y'are, I didn't even know it was a bloody badminton racquet, so I genuinely don't know what that lying bitch is on about.'

'OK, I think that's enough for now,' said the inspector.

'How did you lot find me anyway?'

'We have our ways,' said the inspector. 'But just confirm for me, you really had thought that Tom had been released?'

'Aye. I'm beginning to wonder whether I can trust anybody these days. Maybe mah boys forgot about him. I'll have words with them when I see them next.'

'It will be a while before you see any of your boys again. We have all four of them.' George was quiet for a while. 'Only four!' he thought to himself. He remembered that Karl had gone out for fish and chips. He also remembered Karl saying that it was "a bloody long way to go for fish and chips" but he didn't remember him coming back. Perhaps he had seen the police on his way back, realised what was going on, and escaped from the long arm of the law. 'Good for him.'

Karl had indeed set out for fish and chips on that Monday night but on his way there he had seen quite a few police cars along the road, and he had become suspicious. He had driven back towards the abandoned filling station but had been stopped by those very same police officers. They were erecting a roadblock and they had advised him that if he proceeded, he might not get back through until very late that night or early the next day. He had decided to turn around and he told the officer that his journey could wait until tomorrow.

In a strange twist of fate, Karl's real name turned out to be Jeremy Carter, and after having escaped George's clutches he drove North for about 50 miles and stayed in the car overnight. He went into a cafe for breakfast on Tuesday morning and heard about the arrests on their radio. He was delighted. He then drove to the nearest railway station and checked times to Edinburgh Waverley railway station. He found a deserted street in which to abandon the car and walked back to the station. Two hours later a very relieved

Jeremy Carter was back in Scotland and was saying hello to his wife and three-year-old son.

George Dickinson turned out to be a lot less important a villain than he had thought. Nobody turned up to break him out of jail and his "round" was soon being covered by somebody else. In court, the evidence had been overwhelming, and George had been given the maximum allowed sentence for drug trafficking, and he finally spent twenty years behind bars in a maximum-security wing of a prison in Wales. He didn't survive long once discharged. He just couldn't keep away from the game and, like Jean-Paul before him, he had ended up crossing the wrong people.

George's "boys" had fared rather better. They had all been recruited easily by George because they each owed him a debt, but, within five years, they had all been released and were able to return to their previous lives *relatively* unscathed.

Chapter 29. Conclusion.

After the events in Richmond had been concluded, inspector Roberts invited Marjorie to attend the station for interview because he "had some matters to discuss with her" and he was looking very serious as she entered the room. They exchanged pleasantries, the inspector invited her to sit down, and the interview began.

'Thank-you for coming in today, Marjorie. I need to advise you that this meeting is being recorded. Are you happy to proceed?'

'OK. I suppose I don't object, but it's odd to record what I might tell you, isn't it?'

'Tell me about Joe and George please Marjorie.'

'What about them?'

'You tell me.'

'There's nothing to tell.'

'Oh, but there is. And tell me about 10am on Monday 14th.'

'What are you talking about?' asked Marjorie, now looking very perplexed.

'Where is Joe?'

'I don't know. All I know is that he's gone away

somewhere.'

'And how do you know that?'

'My husband Dan told me.'

'So, your husband knows that Joe has moved away?'

'Yes. He went to see him and caught him just before he left. What has this got to do with anything?'

'Did Dan know that you had also been to see Joe on that Friday morning?'

'I have no idea. How did *you* know that I had been to see Joe?' The inspector ignored the question.

'I think that you went see Joe to persuade him to help you to put more pressure on George Dickinson, to make him confess to the murder of Jremy Carter, but when you got there you saw Dan leaving. You gave him time to get a distance away in case you were seen, and you were about to go and knock on the door when you saw Joe leave too, carrying a parcel. You stayed in your car, but you could see that parcel's distinctive label. You then saw it again when you were in my office, and you saw that it contained evidence about Jeremy Carter's death. You had no idea what it might contain so you visited George again that Friday night.'

'Disgusting man. He should be locked up.'

'Why *did* Dan tell you that Joe was leaving?'

'He had to, he had to explain why Joe wasn't swapping places with him on the rig.'

'Why would you need to know that Joe wasn't making the swap with Dan?'

'We are all friends, so why wouldn't I want to know? All

right, I admit that I did go back to see Joe again, it was on Friday night after I had finished coaching, but he wasn't there so I was curious, and I can always get secrets out of Dan.'

'Did you know that George had also left town, and that he telephoned me on Monday at 10am?'

'No, I really didn't know that, but I admit that I did find out that George had left his house.'

'Did you find out what had been in that parcel from Joe?'

'No. I couldn't get anything out of George. He just made me go away.'

'Now Marjorie, you have done your best to be helpful in this investigation, and we are making progress, but there are still loose ends. Is there anything, anything at all that might help us further?'

'No inspector.'

'Then please don't go anywhere, I might want to see you again.'

'Goodbye inspector.'

Marjorie was now furious. It was Tuesday afternoon, and she had no more coaching so, in a real temper, she decided to go back to see Erica and "that bloody dog". If it wasn't George that killed Jez, then perhaps it really was Erica. Ten minutes later she was outside Erica's house and, after a few moments knocking, Erica opened the door and Marjorie marched in. Remembering her dream she carried on really furiously at Erica.

'You bloody witch, it's you isn't it. You're a murderer and you've been having me on about your ex-lovers. You murdered Jez, I think you murdered all those men on your walls and your dog is terrified of you. You didn't jilt them, you screwed them then murdered them, every one of them. I will make sure you pay for those crimes you old hag. Come here.' Marjorie lunged at Erica and took her by the throat. She had hoped that that would make her confess, but, to Marjorie's horror, Erica just crumbled in Marjorie's hands, the life draining away from her. Eric had come to lick his owner, but Marjorie just froze.

'What the hell have I done? I've got so carried away with this, and now a woman's dead. What the hell do I do now?'

For the first time in her life, Marjorie was regretting her actions and she flew into a real panic. After a moment or two she recovered enough to run back to her car and drive to a phone box. She called an ambulance and then just sat there, waiting.

'Now what?'

After what had seemed like hours, she heard a siren and so she drove back to Erica's house, where she parked up a few doors away.

'Oh God, what will happen to me? Did anybody see me? Will I go to prison?' Just then she saw the ambulance arrive, a paramedic got out and very quickly ran into Erica's house. Though still in a panic she decided to get out of the car and stand and watch. She would pretend that she had just arrived if anybody had seen her. She had been standing, ringing her hands when a man approached her.

'What's going on?'

'What does it look like you pillock?'

'Charming!' Marjorie calmed down and apologised to the young man, who turned out to be called Gerald.

'Marjorie. Hi. I have just arrived to see Erica and I've seen this. I'm a bit worried now because Erica is elderly. I hope she's OK.' This was a stupid comment because she already knew that Erica was dead, but she and Gerald remained outside the house while the paramedic did her work, the driver remaining in the ambulance. Now calming down, Marjorie waited patiently, expecting to see the paramedic come out for a stretcher to ferry the body to the morgue but, after nearly fifteen minutes, the *driver* went *into* the house. 'This will be it,' thought Marjorie, but after a few minutes they both emerged, and Erica was following them. *She was waving them goodbye.*

'What the hell? She was dead, I killed her. She collapsed!' As the ambulance was leaving Erica spotted Marjorie and Gerald and waved them over.

'Hello. Are you two waiting to see me? Come in and have some coffee.' Marjorie just had to stand for a while. Gerald expressed his pleasure that Erica seemed absolutely fine and was soon on his way, but Marjorie was still frozen to the spot. 'What's up Marjorie? You look like you've seen a ghost!' Marjorie felt that she had just done that very thing and she thought back to her dream.

'What the hell? Is this woman immortal? She just died in my arms and now she is offering to make me coffee? That's it. I've finished with sleuthing. I'll leave all this stuff to the police, I've had enough.' Marjorie and Erica sat for about 30 minutes drinking coffee and chatting. Nobody mentioned the ambulance but then Erica spoke.

'Diabetes. You're wondering about the ambulance people, aren't you? Somebody must have called an ambulance, and it was very lucky they did because I had gone into a diabetic coma. If I find out who it was, I will thank them, because if it weren't for them, I would probably be dead by now.'

Erica hadn't been immortal after all; she was a diabetic and Marjorie had just saved her life. Marjorie had gone from expecting a prison sentence to being pleased with herself, and she wondered whether this week could get any more peculiar.

The week did indeed become much more more peculiar, on Wednesday in fact, because the inspector had called Marjorie and asked her to make an appointment to come in to see him again. She had been thrilled and didn't waste time, arriving for interview at 11am on Thursday, exactly three weeks after Jez had last been seen alive.

'Marjorie, please sit down while I turn on the recording machine. This is sergeant Windsor.' Marjorie sat. 'I have invited you here today because we think that we can make an arrest in the case of the death of Jeremy Carter.'

'Excellent,' said Marjorie. 'It's only been a few weeks since he died so well done. I have stopped trying to find evidence for you because it was making me ill, but was it one of my suspects that did it? Was it George after all? I never liked him. Something creepy about him. Or was it Erica?' She paused as she thought about Erica. 'And was my input helpful? Will I get a mention when you publish?'

'You will get a mention when we publish Marjorie because your help has been invaluable. Your interrogation of our main suspect George was particularly useful because it helped clear up some inconsistencies that we couldn't explain.' Marjorie beamed when the inspector began his summing up, assuming George to have been arrested as the perpetrator.

'This case has had us baffled right from the start. No motive, no murder weapon, and it has sometimes felt as though the killer had been interfering in the investigation. Do you agree with those arguments Marjorie?'

'What are you talking about?'

'Since Jez was left for dead, it's been as if the killer has seemed to be interfering in our enquiries, actually the first person whose house I visited after he was pronounced missing.'

'How can that be? Who was the first person you visited?'

'Think back Marjorie.'

'You were waiting to see me and Paula that Friday.'

'We were.'

'You can't think that Paula had anything to do with this surely.'

'Not Paula.'

'Me? You can't think.' Marjorie stumbled a bit but went on. 'I have been helping you find his killer. Jez was my badminton pupil and my daughter loved him. Why would I...' but the inspector interrupted before she could finish that sentence.

'So, you *did* know about him and Paula. Paula told me that you didn't know. *She* certainly didn't tell you.' Marjorie thought for a while.

'Yes. Alright I admit that I did know. But what's that got to do with anything? Why do you think it was me that killed Jez?'

'At this point I must ask you whether you want a solicitor present during this interview.'

'No. Just get on with it. You know damn well that it wasn't me.'

'All this time you have pretended that you didn't know about Paula and Jez. Paula had kept it a secret from you because she is just turned 16. She would have told you, after her delayed 16th birthday party, the party that you delayed because your husband was away. Why was he away Mrs. Jones?'

Marjorie noted the change to "Mrs Jones".

'You know why,' she said. 'He had to go away for a 3-week stint on an oil rig. You do know that he is a mechanical engineer?'

'And who arranged that stay on the oil rig Mrs. Jones?'

'He did.'

'He didn't. We have spoken to Dan, and it turns out that he had swapped with his mate Joe at Joe's request. Why had Joe requested that change Mrs. Jones?'

'God knows,' said Marjorie.

'Yes, He does, and so do we. We have talked to Joe, but then you know that don't you. He knows that you fancied him. You persuaded him that if he swapped with your husband you could sleep with him because Paula would be away too, and you would have the house to yourselves. The fun could last for days.'

'He is making that up. Paula had no plans to be away then.'

'No, but *you* had made plans with her to stay with her cousin. You arranged it so that Paula should spend a week

Page 294

with her, but Paula didn't want to go away, did she? This ruined your plans to take Joe to your king-sized bed. Maybe it wasn't Jez that you originally had in your sights that night. Maybe he was a substitute to make up for not seeing Joe.'

'What the hell?' The inspector interrupted her.

'Joe hadn't been persuaded to join you that night, so you felt frustrated. Jez was old enough, and you thought he would fall into your arms when the opportunity arose. You only had to present that opportunity.'

'Rubbish. You have no evidence.'

'On that night you told Paula to wait in for Nige who was fitting your new carpet. Paula was extremely annoyed about this, but you put it down to a teenage mood. You had no idea that she had other plans, did you?'

'So?'

'Nige was never coming at that time, was he? Paula waited in for two hours, but he didn't turn up. But you knew he wasn't coming because you would never have left Paula alone with *any* tradesman, would you? But you even made a phone call to Paula after coaching ended to make sure that she was still in the house. You didn't want your plan spoiling if she turned up at the club, did you?'

'So, I wanted a carpet fitting, but I wanted some peace that night. I put him off. So what?'

'But you didn't put him off. He arrived at about 6.30pm which was the time you had told him to arrive. We've spoken to him too. It meant that with Paula stuck at home you could follow Jez as he left the club. You knew that nobody would be about at that time in early October, but you weren't expecting his refusal of your advances, were you?'

'Put your brain away you pervert,' said Marjorie. 'Who the hell do you think you are?'

'Did you know that there was saliva residue on his chest and stomach?'

'No.'

'But you did know. We didn't tell you the contents of the forensic report, so only if you were Jez's killer would you have known about it, yet you mentioned that saliva to George Dickinson didn't you, *and* you used it to try to get him to confess to Jez's murder. Since George didn't commit this crime, and you knew it, how did you think that would work? Did you think that he would just cave in?' Marjorie didn't reply.

'There was certainly enough saliva for our forensic team to find, enough in fact to carry out a positive DNA test on it. Have you heard of DNA testing?'

'Yeah yeah,' said Marjorie. 'Won't you need some of my DNA to match it up?'

'We have some thanks, we have some hair follicles from your hairbrush, given to us willingly by your husband.' Marjorie looked increasingly angry.

'You still have no evidence.'

'We have spoken to Paula, Joe and your husband. Paula is the one who first alerted us to the possibility that you at least knew something about this because she recognised his racquet in your collection. You thought that nobody would look there, did you? Then the pathologist was able to identify saliva on his chest and lower abdomen. I'll bet the DNA matches yours. There was no semen by the way, so whatever sexual fantasy you had didn't work, did it?'

'George murdered Jez and he sold me his badminton racquet.'

'Funny idea that because George knew nothing about a racquet. He couldn't have taken it anyway because he was nowhere near the murder scene. He told us that it was you that told him about the saliva on Jeremy's chest. Only the killer and our pathologist knew about that.'

'George must have planted my saliva on Jez, and he has no alibi.'

'Now how would he achieve that, and actually he does have an alibi. On that night he was having sex with a man who owed him a debt, a man who had the foresight to video the whole evening in case George continued to blackmail him. There's also no way that George could have had, or planted, your saliva. It's time to come clean now Marjorie.'

Marjorie sighed and the events of that night came back to her as though it were a film script. She had tried her best to frame somebody else for the murder of Jez, but it was no good. Her memory of that night was very clear.

'Why won't Paula go to stay with her cousin for the few days I've arranged. Paula has often stayed over there, even during term time, but this time the little sod won't go. I was looking forward to meeting handsome, muscular Joe while Dan's away. I persuaded Joe to swap oil rig shifts with Dan so we could meet up in our very empty house, but now it's not empty. Where can we go instead?'

She could think of nowhere and she was equally disappointed that Joe didn't seem bothered when she told him that their evenings and nights of passion had been cancelled. That really annoyed her.

'But then there's that boy Jez. That floppy hair, narrow waist and cute, very innocent smile. Innocent! I can have a night of passion with Jez, help him lose that innocence. He must be a virgin surely. Paula says that he isn't very popular, and he doesn't talk about girls much. I will turn him into a real man, he won't be able to resist me.'

That evening Jez had seemed less happy than usual, and his game had suffered accordingly, but Marjorie decided not to be too harsh on him. He was clearly unhappy about something so she would be kind and give him an evening to remember. 'A night of sexual pleasure will really cheer him up and he will be really grateful. He might even want to do this regularly.'

After the coaching ended Jez had gathered his stuff together and put his racquet into his haversack as usual. 'Goodnight, Mrs. Jones.'

'Jez, wait a while, walk with me and we can have a chat.'

'OK.' Jez had seemed reluctant but agreed anyway.

'You seem a bit down tonight, Jez. We have never really talked you and I, have we. I know very little about you, about how you got into badminton and how you got that signed racquet. Can I walk and talk with you on your journey home tonight?'

'If you like,' replied Jez. They looked a very unlikely pair, Jez in his slightly oversized kit and Marjorie wearing her expensively professional outfit. Marjorie asked him about his mum and dad and any other family he had. He replied politely enough and told her that he only had his mum and sister really. He went on to tell her about the signed racquet his dad had given him, and how good his dad had been, including his performance at County level. She had seemed impressed.

'Do you always walk home this way?' she asked.

'Yes,' he replied.

'Is it always as quiet as this?'

'Yeah. It's even quieter if you walk through the wood.' He said with some bravado.

'Are you not afraid to go in there? It looks dark.'

'It's not so dark when you get in there, and it's true that I really never meet anybody anyway.'

'Is that the way into the woods?'

'Yes.'

'Let's go that way.' Jez wasn't keen and said so. 'You'll be safe with me,' said Marjorie. They entered the now fairly dark woodland, and they walked in silence for a while, but Jez's heart skipped a beat as they approached the grassy mound.

'Let's sit there for a while,' said Marjorie.

'No.' thought Jez. 'I can't do that because that's where me and Paula have sex. I can't sit there now, especially not with her mother!'

'I really should be getting back,' he replied. 'I would prefer to just go home now.'

'Just sit down here for a while. It looks cosy.'

'OK.' When they sat down, she put her arm round him.

'You really are a good-looking young man.'

'Thanks. That's nice of you to say.' Then quickly he added: 'Hang on, did John put you up to this? I bet he did.' He got up to leave.

'No. I don't know who John is. I really have thought you a very handsome young man since I first saw you. You have such a look of innocence about you, and I love your smile, and who could resist

Page 299

your hair.' Jez was starting to panic and realised with horror that John had been right about her. She did fancy him.

'I had better go.'

'Stay and show me how good you are at kissing.' Marjorie beckoned him back.

'No.'

'Just one or two. I bet you are very good.'

'No. I am going now.' He began to walk away.

'I will get you banned from the badminton club if you don't!'

'No don't, please don't.' He thought for a moment then said, 'I don't think it's right for us to kiss, but maybe just once.' Jez reluctantly went back to Marjorie. She pulled him close, and they kissed each other, twice.

'I'll go now then.'

'Not yet. Do you find me attractive? I have seen how you look at me sometimes. I think that there is a chemistry between us, and I would love to do more than just kiss you. Come here and sit down, we can have a few more kisses, then we can talk about helping you to lose your innocence tonight. Now in fact.'

'What the hell', thought Jez. 'Is she offering me sex? She's Paula's mother too! She must be mad.' The panic was severe now. He got up to leave. 'No thanks. I am going home now.'

'I really will get you banned.'

'Then I'll find somewhere else. I don't care about the club that much, not enough to have sex here and certainly not with my badminton coach. John was right about you. Leave me alone.'

'I really fancy you Jez, please come back, lose your virginity.'

'No. I don't want sex with you, and I am not a virgin anyway, so you couldn't actually do what you just said!' Marjorie was surprised.

'Who would go out with a wimp like you? Paula said nobody seemed interested in you in that way. Unless Paula was telling lies!' His reaction told her everything.

'You have been screwing Paula, haven't you?' Jez decided that it was time to leg it.

'I am leaving now.' Unfortunately, he was looking back toward Marjorie while he ran, and he didn't see the thick branch that he proceeded to trip over, and he caught his chin on another branch as he fell. He hit the ground hard, and he felt dizzy when he got up. He didn't feel at all well and he couldn't see properly, but Marjorie was on him like a shot, and she dragged him back to the mound. He told her that he now felt very weak and faint, but she didn't care and continued to drag him along. He wasn't able to stop her, and she pulled him to the back of the mound and began to take revenge for everything that hadn't happened that night, and for the realisation that he was having a secret affair with Paula.

'Let's see what she is getting then you little pervert.' She laid him down and pulled off his tee shirt. He was now beginning to recover a little and he started to get up, but Marjorie had him in a vice like grip. She pulled both his arms behind him and pulled him down onto his back. She then leant over him just using one arm to keep his arms beneath him. She leant on his chest which, because of his weakened state, kept his arms beneath him so he couldn't move.

He began to try to scream so she adjusted her position to place her left hand over his mouth and her right leg across his knees, effectively pinning him down and shutting him up. Being athletic was really working for Marjorie now.

'He might start going to the gym after this!' she thought. She *leant forward and began studying his torso.*

'You have a very fit body Jez. Who'd have thought it?' and she began to work her way down his chest, then rather further down, with her mouth and tongue, kissing him as she went. When it became clear that nothing was happening, and he wasn't even remotely aroused by this, she shouted 'are you gay or what?' But he didn't respond. She got up and realised that, though he was moving a little and definitely breathing, he was almost unconscious.

'Shit.' She quickly put his kit back on him. He was now moaning softly so she reckoned that he would come round soon. She left him to it and was walking away when she realised that when he came to, he could go to the police.

'They'd never believe him. Or would they? I'll just go back and wake him and let him know what will happen if he blabs.' When she reached him though she realised that his condition was possibly serious. She took his badminton racquet from his haversack and pushed him almost into the bushes. She walked away again. 'Somebody will find him, and they'll think he's been mugged. I'll go and see him in hospital and make enough threats to stop him talking about the assault. He might forget anyway, or even have amnesia. I expect somebody's found him by now. I will see him in hospital when I can.'

Marjorie left her daydream and realised that it was time to confess her actions, and to try to persuade the inspector that nothing had been intentional.

'Is that tape still running inspector?'

'Yes.'

'Alright.' With some minor alterations she recounted all of those memories for the tape. She then added: 'I did put my hand over his mouth, but only to shut him up, I wasn't trying to smother him. I had watched him fall but didn't realise how badly hurt he was. I had started leaving but he wasn't moving, so I went back to help him, but he was so still. I pulled him to the side and tidied him up. I took his racquet because I didn't want it to be stolen. I really did think somebody would find him at some time and that he would be OK. My main worry at the time was that he might remember that I tried to force him into sex. I didn't hit him or anything, so I didn't kill him. I am not a murderer, and I am so very sorry that he is dead.'

'Marjorie, nobody *did* walk along that path to find him, and Jez lay there where you left him until my officers found him. Nobody would make a detour through woodland in the dark, not unless they had a particular reason. Even the lads that drank in there didn't bother that night. Jez actually died from a bleed on the brain made worse by the lack of oxygen caused by the killer partially restricting his mouth. Had you not covered his mouth he may have recovered enough to stagger out of the woodland area. As it was, he lay unconscious for over 24 hours, and he died just minutes before he was found.'

'I'm sorry inspector. I really am.'

'The official cause of death was ischaemia and inflammation of the brain caused by a brain haemorrhage, and aggravated by partial asphyxiation. The pathologist also noted that, with immediate treatment, he would likely have made a full recovery, and the probability was that it was unlikely that he would remember the events surrounding the assault. Had an ambulance been called it was likely that none of these later events would have happened, which means that the manslaughter charge that you are now facing was completely avoidable.'

Marjorie just looked away, so the inspector decided that it was time to give the formal caution: 'Marjorie Jones, I am arresting you for the sexual assault and the manslaughter of Jeremy Carter, contrary to section 1 of the ways and means act of 1953. You are not obliged to say anything, but anything you do say may be taken down and given in evidence. Do you understand the charge?'

'Yes,' said Marjorie.

'Sergeant Windsor, please take Mrs. Jones down to the cells.'

'I'll just adjust my boot first, something's sticking into my leg.' There was indeed something pressing against Marjorie's leg, but she withdrew it quickly and, before either the sergeant or the inspector realised what was going on, she had a *Raven MP-25* pointing at both of them.

Dan had bought Marjorie that gun when he was working in the USA. It had been difficult to get it back to Britain but eventually it had arrived on their doormat, via a courier. Dan arranged for it to be fully licenced; he had bought it for her after there had been reports of women being attacked late at night. He thought that it might help protect Marjorie after late night coaching sessions, and she had taken lessons in how to fire it. She had become very competent, but now she had decided that it was her only chance for freedom. 'Marjorie don't....' began the inspector.

'Shut up. This is loaded. Both of you, over to the door, now.'

'You won't.'

'Yeah, I know, you won't get away with this, blah blah. Just watch me. Open that door and then march out of here. I will follow you with this in my pocket so don't say a word. Clear?'

'Where to?'

'Just out. Aim for the car park and my car.'

'OK.' They did as Marjorie had instructed and they reached a sort of "airlock" that separated the front door from the rest of the station. The hatch that was in there had been unmanned for days.

'Freedom,' thought Marjorie as they entered that lobby, but then she heard a shout.

'Mum.' Paula and Dan were sitting in that little room, having been invited to attend the station by the inspector.

'Hi Marjorie,' said Dan. 'What are you....... ah.' The gun was now clearly visible in Marjorie's hand.

'Don't stop me now.'

'Mum, what the hell are you doing?'

'Go outside and go home. Keep out of this.'

'No,' said Dan.

'Paula and Dan. Do as she says,' shouted the inspector. 'She says it's loaded.'

'No. This has gone far enough.'

'Mum, what the hell is going on?' All of Paula's fears about what would happen if her mother was arrested focussed in her mind, and she realised that that arrest had just been made. Dan was having similar thoughts and he felt his blood run cold.

'Marjorie, for God's sake put that down.' Paula was now thinking hard.

'Mum, why not go ahead and get it all over with. You want your freedom from us? Then get on with killing us both and have it.'

'Paula, go home, NOW,' shouted Marjorie.

'No. I want to talk to the police first.' By that time Dan had moved to stand in front of Paula.

'If you want to leave this station alone you will have to shoot all four of us,' said Dan.

'Have you ever been shot love?' asked Marjorie.

'You know damned well that I haven't.'

'Then this is when you find out what it's like,' and, raising the gun, she aimed, using both hands as she had been taught in training.

'Think you're a hero, do you? See how you enjoy this!'

'Mum, No!' The gun fired and then there was silence.

Chapter 30. The follow up.

The bullet had landed in the wall, just to the left of the inspector's head. Marjorie had been so engrossed in her little speech that she hadn't noticed that sergeant Windsor was no longer by the inspector's side. Then, as soon as things had looked serious, the sergeant made a world beating attempt at a rugby tackle. This hadn't gone entirely to plan, but the effect had been all that had been required to bring Marjorie to the ground. It was Dan that had picked up the gun and handed it to the inspector. Within seconds of that, the sergeant had picked Marjorie up from the floor, and she had been handcuffed by the sergeant. A little later they were all, except Marjorie, back in the inspector's office. While they sipped coffee, which was surprisingly good, the inspector gave Paula and Dan an abridged version of what Marjorie had said she had done on the night of Jeremy's murder, and he emphasised to Paula that she hadn't ever had any intention to kill Jez.

'I knew that she had a thing for Joe. I had no idea that it had got this serious and if Joe were still here, I would slap him.'

'Joe hadn't followed up on Marjorie's passes at him Dan. I have a letter from him that makes it quite clear that he was happily married and didn't want an affair with anybody, certainly not with Marjorie.'

'What now then?' Dan asked, after his temper had cooled a little.

'Are you sure that you want to hear this Paula?' asked the inspector.

'Despite what mother thinks I am a grown woman. Yes, I do want to hear it.'

'Your mother has already been charged with the sexual assault, and the manslaughter, of Jeremy Carter. She will now have to face further charges of resisting arrest and threatening behaviour, depending upon how we feel it best to phrase those charges.

'I want to go home,' is all that Paula said after hearing that.

'Why *did* you invite us here today anyway inspector?' asked Dan before they rose to leave.

'I wanted to confirm a few things with you and to ask what you wanted us to do with Jeremy's racquet. It does, of course, need to go back to Valerie Carter, but it occurred to me that one of you might want to return it to her.'

'Could I return it please?' asked Paula.

'Of course, Paula. I will leave the arrangements for that to you.'

Inspector Roberts had asked the family liaison officer to pay another visit to Valerie the following day because he wanted her to hear the full story of Marjorie's alleged deeds on that Thursday night, to reassure Valerie that Jez hadn't been actually murdered. The officer had explained the whole series of events to her, as explained by Marjorie, minus the more sordid bits, but Valerie had sat frowning.

'She did murder him then.'

'We don't believe that there was any intention to kill that night, so the charge will be of manslaughter.'

'But she persuaded him to walk along that path so that she could have sex with him, and during the ordeal he suffered he became unconscious, and she left him there because he wouldn't let her have her way with him? She then did nothing to help him, and didn't even ring for an ambulance for him?'

'Yes, if the allegations are true then that that would appear to be correct.'

'And if she hadn't lured him into those woods, he would not have died that night?'

'I can't answer that, Valerie.'

'I can. Jez is dead because she lured him into a position that caused his death. To me that's murder. Will she plead guilty or is there a chance that she might get off without going to jail?'

'I can't answer that fully, but it's almost certain that Marjorie will go to jail for her threatening behaviour when she was arrested' Using a quieter tone, the officer added that the body would be released soon, and that Valerie could arrange the funeral at her own convenience. After asking whether she needed any more help or counselling, which Valerie declined, and after further pleasantries and more commiserations, the officer left, assuring Valerie that she was still available to her if needed.

Valerie didn't know what to think. She wanted to murder Marjorie herself. After about half an hour of this thinking, and much daydreaming, there came a knock at the door. She answered it to find Paula standing there. Paula was carrying a parcel.

'Paula, isn't it? Marjorie's daughter.'

'Yes Mrs Carter. I wasn't sure that I would be welcome after what my mother has done but I wanted to bring you this,' and she held up a parcel.

'Of course, you are welcome, you aren't responsible for your mother's actions so come in.' They entered Valerie's small living room and Paula handed her the parcel which she unwrapped, realising quite quickly what it was.

'Jeremy's racquet! Did your mother keep it?'

'Yes,' said Paula. 'She couldn't resist it. She has quite a collection and dad noticed it in her wardrobe when he got back from the oil rig. I knew it belonged to Jez as soon as I saw it and I told inspector Roberts about it. That's what gave her away.'

'Oh Paula. Come with me will you please?' She led Paula to Jez's room, which now contained just a well-made bed and Jez's haversack. Valerie opened the haversack and put the racquet inside exactly as Jez would have done. She fastened the flap and then replaced the haversack in the corner of the room.

'There,' she said. 'Back where it belongs and where it will stay.'

'I like this room,' said Paula. 'There's a nice atmosphere in here, very calming.'

'Yes,' said Valerie, 'Just like Jez himself. I believe that he is still here. Come down and have some tea.'

'Can we have it in here?' asked Paula.

'Of course we can.' She left Paula there while she went to make the tea and Paula was deep in thought when she returned with it on a tray but, as Valerie was ascending the stairs, she had been sure that she had heard Paula speaking to somebody.

Over tea, which they had drunk while sitting on what had been Jez's bed, Valerie and Paula chatted for quite a while about her schoolwork, her dad, and her plans for when she left school etc. Valerie soon realised that Paula knew just a bit too much about Jez.

'There's something I want to ask you,' said Valerie. 'We found a packet of condoms in Jeremy's pocket when we looked though his clothes. I have a feeling that you know why he had them.' Paula blushed heavily.

'I think that you were his girlfriend.'

Paula sighed. 'Yes. We had been seeing each other after badminton coaching, and when I turned sixteen it seemed natural to go further, which is why he had the condoms. We were supposed to be meeting up that night. On our first date, Jez was so nervous, because he was convinced that his friend John had put me up to going out with him, but I loved him Mrs. Carter, I really did. And he loved me I think.'

'I knew there was something making making him happy, and I assumed that it was a girl. Did your mother know?'

'Mother didn't know. We were going to tell you both at my party when dad got back. We were both 16 and sex seemed perfectly natural, and we took all the precautions.

Jez was really sweet and what is really awful is that we used to spend our time together near to where he was found. It's so sad that he died there. I hope you aren't angry that we were having sex Mrs Carter.'

'I am not angry Paula. Had he still been alive I would likely have had words with both of you, but now I am quite pleased.' She gave Paula a hug. 'Actually, his life seems to have been more complete than I had thought, and if only you had been there that night to use those condoms, he might still be alive today.'

(Day 25)

Jeremy Carter's funeral was attended by Valerie Carter and her sister Beverley, Jez's sister Emma Carter, Paula Jones, Dan Jones and Miss Hofmann, who was representing the school. Paula and Valerie were holding up well until they entered the church and saw the name "Jeremy Carter" printed above his photograph on the proceedings of ceremony sheets. The ceremony had been intended to be a celebration of Jeremy's life, rather than a sad affair, and the service had thankfully been brief. The mourners were soon out in the autumn sunlight.

After the service a cortège drove his body to the cemetery where he was to be buried, but what none of the mourners had been expecting was that a number of school students had lined up waiting for the hearse and the car containing the family. They had formed a sort of line of honour along the pavement outside, and leading into, the cemetery. The school had allowed time off for those attending, not expecting quite so many to want to go, but even some additional staff had gone along too.

John had decided not to go to the funeral because he felt that he had let his old friend down somehow. He had actually been in a decline since he heard about Jez's death, and he had become quiet and reserved. He now rarely met up with girls, especially those older than himself. He still had bad dreams that contained memories of his tormenting Jez, especially the condoms and his reaction to those stupid trousers. It wasn't until after he had left for university that he managed to regain some of his original get up and go. Actually, his three years at university had turned out to be surprisingly like those that Joe had enjoyed but, like Joe, he had eventually settled down to a happy married life, with a woman of his own age, but not in, or anywhere near, Basingrove.

Chapter 31. The trial.

Marjorie's trial had taken place 3 months after her arrest, by which time DNA matches had been confirmed between the saliva on Jez's body and the DNA extracted from the hair follicles that had been provided by Dan Jones. There had been no fingerprints found on Jez's racquet other than Marjorie's and Paula's, not including those left by Jez. Despite this, and though she had already pleaded guilty to the charges of "resisting arrest" and "threatening behaviour", she had still pleaded not guilty to the remaining charges and that had necessitated a full hearing with a judge and jury.

The trial, which had begun with Marjorie pleading not guilty to the charges of sexual assault and manslaughter, proceeded with the presentation of evidence to the court, given by inspector Roberts, and a member of the forensic team. Joe's letter had been shown to the judge and parts of it were read out to the jury, but the identity of the writer was not released to the jury or the general public. Paula and Dan weren't at the trial, but their evidence had been recorded and also presented to the court. Testimony from George Dickinson had also been presented, in his absence.

The hearing lasted for three days, with quite a bit of time taken up by legal arguments submitted by defence counsel, but the judge, in her summing up, had directed the jury to return a verdict of guilty on both charges.

It had taken the jury several days to reach a verdict on which they had all agreed. Two jurors argued that it was impossible for a female to sexually assault a male, arguing that no lasting damage could ever be caused by sex in that direction. One had felt that men would always accept an offer of sex anyway, no matter who was offering it, so she had agreed with the previous assertion. This had taken many hours to argue but it had been resolved when one juror pointed out that she had a 16 year old son, and the idea of him being forced into sex with an older woman, or anybody else for that matter, was abhorrent to her, and she suggested that the remaining jurors should consider how they might feel in the same situation. She had also argued that an unwanted sexual advance was an assault, regardless of the gender of both parties.

On the second charge, of manslaughter, there had been a similar discussion. Three jurors had felt that, because Marjorie hadn't actually struck a blow against Jez, she had nothing to do with his death. One had even said that "he should have been looking where he was going". Others argued that if he hadn't been running away from unwanted sex then he probably wouldn't have tripped because he had known the path well. This had taken a lot of arguing, but eventually there *had* been unanimous agreement. They all had to admit that, based on the evidence presented, Marjorie had intended to have unwanted sexual intercourse with Jeremy, and that it was in pursuit of this aim that she inadvertently caused his premature death. Once back in court, and the judge had asked the foreman of the jury for a verdict, she was able to announce a unanimous verdict of guilty on both charges.

Mrs Carter had looked relieved when the verdict was announced, and she left the court immediately. She hadn't wanted to wait for the sentencing. Marjorie gave no reaction; in fact, her face had remained cold and impassive throughout the trial and the judge had taken that lack of reaction into account while passing sentence.

In her summing up before sentence the judge described Marjorie as a cold heartless individual who had used her trusted position as a badminton coach [to a young man] in order to try to obtain sexual gratification. She said that Marjorie was aware that Jeremy Carter had loved badminton, and that she had realised that a threat to prevent him from playing might have been enough to allow her to have unwanted sexual intercourse with him. In trying to fend off Mrs Jones the young man had suffered injuries that lead to his death, a death that seems unlikely to have occurred if an ambulance had been called in time. Mrs Jones had not called that ambulance despite, by her own admission, being aware that his condition was potentially serious.

'I have taken Mrs Jones lack of remorse into account while

making my judgement,' she had said before addressing Marjorie directly. 'As a result of the serious nature of your crimes, the decision of this court is that you be taken to a closed women's prison, there to spend a minimum of five years for the offence of sexual assault. Additionally, for the offence of involuntary manslaughter, I sentence you to ten years. These sentences are not to run concurrently. Do you have anything to say?' Marjorie again made no comment.

After the trial, Marjory was asked by her solicitor why she hadn't wanted to say anything after the sentence had been handed down. She had replied that she didn't want to comment because she knew that she would be going to prison anyway. She had erroneously expected that the charges would run concurrently, and she felt that she might have a relatively pleasant time in jail; she could teach racquet sports to inmates, so she didn't care how long she was there. In the event, her stay in prison was anything but pleasant, many of the inmates having had sons of around Jez's age and so they rarely spoke to Marjorie, except to arrange free coaching.

Her family had only visited her on her birthday and at Christmas time but, exactly ten years after she had been imprisoned, she was allowed out for a visit. *She had been given permission to visit Paula.*

Paula had left school at sixteen despite having achieved excellent "O" levels. She started work at Debenhams in the sportswear department, where she would serve customers but also model the sportswear during their bimonthly sports fashion parades. These were held to promote new lines, but it had been at one of these that Paula had been "spotted" by a modelling agency. By October 1987 she had turned professional, and the next two years had been something of a whirlwind for her. She had travelled the length and breadth of the UK and modelled everything from bikinis to ball gowns.

By 1988 she had decided to permanently leave Basingrove and to live in and travel around the country in a camper van; she loved her mobile life, and her career was going really well.

In May 1989 things cooled down in her whirlwind life when she met a young man called Ranjit. Two years her junior he was a simple soul, very caring and rather inexperienced with women. He was a thin man with dark floppy hair and an innocent smile, but their affair had broken up after just six weeks because he had gone away, without telling Paula, or anyone else, where he was going.

This, it seems, had made her go off men because it wasn't until 1995 that she met Paulo, an Italian design student. Narrow at the waist and with long, dark floppy hair and an innocent smile, she hadn't been able to resist him. After 2 months of courtship, it was Paula who announced that Paulo was going away, but this time *she* hadn't got away with anything.

Back in 1989, Ranjit's body had been discovered some months after his disappearance, but it was so decomposed that no pathology could be gleaned from it. He had been found tangled up in bushes in some local woods, and the death had been put down to "misadventure".

In 1995 though, Paulo, though also left for dead, had been

found by a passer-by and he was rushed to hospital. Unlike Jez and Ranjit, he had recovered fully and was able to give a full account of the attack on him.

Paula, it seems, had had an ability to hypnotise any man that she fancied, and none of her three "victims" had been able to resist her. It was this ability that had caused Jez's absolute obsession with Paula and explained his change from a boy unable to speak to girls to a confident macho boyfriend. It transpired that, for Paulo, Paula had arranged their usual night of passion, as always outside and in the shelter of some woodland, and all had begun as usual, but just as things were hotting up, he had felt a blow to the back of his head. Paula had used a small cudgel that she had been given as a present when she was fourteen, and that she often carried with her. It was a sort of mini club which she could use for self-defence if she was ever attacked, and she used it on that night to hit her lover hard enough to just knock him out. She had then set about removing what few clothes he had left on, sexually molested him while he was barely conscious and used a glove to shut him up if he made any sound. She had then given him another bash, this time on his chin (she knew just where to hit him for maximum disruption). This knocked him out fully and was intended to do some permanent damage. She then dumped his body and left, after replacing some of his clothes.

Like Jez and Ranjit, Paulo had suffered a bleed on the brain but, having been taken swiftly to hospital, surgeons had managed to save him. He remembered the attack very clearly and had given a very full statement to the police. The remains of saliva on his body were sufficient for a DNA match with Paula *and* there had been CCTV footage of the pair of them entering the woods, but only Paula exiting.

On cross examination by the local police, Paula had confessed to all *three* killings. It seems that, despite having loved all three men, she had quickly got bored with them, and hadn't the heart to say goodbye, so she had "despatched them all to a much happier place", where she said she felt sure that they would really be much better off than with her.

She had also made it known to police that, back in 1985, Marjorie had found Jez's racquet in Paula's room just days after his death, and she had confronted Paula with it. Paula had confessed the whole event to her mother and Marjorie, after exploding in anger, had said that she would fix everything. She had tried, and failed, to pin the blame on George Dickinson so, with Paula's help, she had learned a very full and very theatrical confession in case she was arrested by the police. Marjorie had learned it so accurately that she almost felt as though it were true, and the story had had to be so thoroughly learned that it had taken over her life. It had been living with that script that had led to her nightmare back in 1985 and which had prompted her attempt to frame Erica for Jez's murder.

DNA testing wasn't very precise in 1985, and there had been a sufficiently high familial match between Paula and Marjorie for the test to suggest that the DNA found on Jez's body had indeed been Marjorie's. It had never occurred to anybody to try to match it to Paula. The rest of Marjorie's confession had been true of course, she had tried, and failed, to get Joe to her home that night, but she hadn't even considered sex with Jez, nor had she thought that Paula would leave the house after she had phoned her.

The reality of that October night back in 1985 was that Marjorie and Jez had parted as they always did after a coaching session but, while Marjorie had been trying one final time to seduce Joe at his work, then enjoying a cup of tea in the shopping centre cafe, Paula had set off to meet Jez for one last time.

Jez had been surprised and delighted to see her walking along his beloved path that day, but within minutes of meeting and embracing Paula, his fate had been sealed.

Marjorie had been sure that she wouldn't have to go to jail though, partly because she thought that she would be acquitted, (women can't sexually molest a man), but mainly, in her invented story, she didn't actually hit Jez, he had tripped over a tree root, (just as he had done on the day that his association with the Jones family had first begun), and anyway, she had the gun that Dan had bought her. It would stay in her boot until she needed it and, if necessary, she had departure plans in hand for if she had to escape from Police custody. Unfortunately, she had panicked after being sentenced and Sergeant Windsor had foiled that escape plan.

After the trial Paula had been placed in the care of a psychiatrist for 3 weeks, after which she had been admitted to a secure mental facility. It was to visit that secure facility that Marjorie had been given permission on her day release.

Shortly after that visit, Marjorie was released rather earlier than originally planned and she moved house to be near to Paula. Her coaching days though were well and truly over.

Printed in Great Britain
by Amazon

28362523R00178